How Firm a Foundation!

Where your Bible came from

How you got it

Why you should trust it

■

KENT RAMLER & RANDY LEEDY

Teacher's Edition

Bob Jones University Press, Greenville, South Carolina 29614

To the Teacher

"But how do you *know* that's true?" As every junior high and high school teacher knows, something quite unsettling happens to the human brain between the ages of twelve and eighteen. Though we may like to attribute all the bothersome questioning to sinful insubordination, we must admit that this mental development is not entirely evil. The ability to analyze and evaluate an argument is an essential skill that God Himself expects believers to possess. Paul reasoned with his audiences when he preached in synagogues (Acts 17:1-2) and when he wrote under inspiration (Rom. 3:19-31). The development of critical thinking skills in our Christian young people is as necessary as their physical development. However, just as the adolescent must be taught how to control and use his changing body for God's glory, so he must be challenged to use his developing mind for God's purposes.

How Firm a Foundation! seeks to shape the critical thinking skills of Christian high school students by renewing confidence in the Bible as the Word of God. Most Christian high school students have heard and believed that the Bible is the Word of God since they were little children. Now, however, many have begun to doubt this important truth because they have become aware of certain factors that complicate that claim. In this course the authors desire to address these doubts and the complicating factors that raise them. Through the student text and the in-class discussions, the course deals with these problems, demonstrating that the Bible the students hold in their hands can be trusted because it is indeed the Word of God.

Increased effectiveness in evangelism is another goal of this course. Once the student is reassured that his Bible is the Word of God and becomes more skilled in answering skeptics, he gains greater confidence in proclaiming that book to others.

This textbook was written by members of the faculty and staff of Bob Jones University. Standing for the "old-time religion" and the absolute authority of the Bible since 1927, Bob Jones University is the world's leading Fundamentalist Christian university. The staff of the University is devoted to educating Christian men and women to be servants of Jesus Christ in all walks of life.

Providing unparalleled academic excellence, Bob Jones University prepares its students through its offering of over one hundred majors, while its fervent spiritual emphasis prepares their minds and hearts for service and devotion to the Lord Jesus Christ.

If you would like more information about the spiritual and academic opportunities available at Bob Jones University, please call **1-800-BJ-AND-ME** (1-800-252-6363). www.bju.edu

NOTE:
The fact that materials produced by other publishers may be referred to in this volume does not constitute an endorsement by Bob Jones University Press of the content or theological position of materials produced by such publishers. The position of Bob Jones University Press, and the University itself, is well known. Any references and ancillary materials are listed as an aid to the student or the teacher and in an attempt to maintain the accepted academic standards of the publishing industry.

How Firm a Foundation! Teacher's Edition

Kent Ramler, M.A. and Randy Leedy, Ph.D.
with Bryan Smith, M.A.

Editor: Stephen St. John
Cover: Ellyson Kalagayan
Composition: Rebecca G. Zollinger

©1995, 1999 Bob Jones University Press
Greenville, South Carolina 29614

Printed in the United States of America
All rights reserved

ISBN 1-57924-264-2

15 14 13 12 11 10 9 8 7 6 5 4 3 2

Overview

In systematic theology the study of issues related to the reliability of the Bible is called *Bibliology. How Firm a Foundation!* covers key aspects of Bibliology in five chapters.

Chapter 1
Focus: inspiration

Development: After demonstrating that the Scripture claims to be inspired, the chapter offers a detailed definition of the term *inspiration* and defends that definition biblically.

Goal: The student should be able to demonstrate that the Bible claims to be inspired. He should be able to explain what that claim means biblically and be able to identify and refute incorrect definitions of inspiration.

Chapter 2
Focus: canonicity

Development: This chapter identifies which books deserve to be called "Scripture." After an introduction dealing with the key issue—the Holy Spirit's testimony in the believer's heart—the authors outline the history of this issue, demonstrating the Spirit's unified witness concerning canonicity.

Goal: The student should know the key test of canonicity and be able to defend it. He also should be able to list biblical and historical observations confirming that the sixty-six books of the Old and New Testaments (and only those) are God's Word.

Chapters 3 and 4
Focus: preservation

Development: These chapters discuss the ongoing availability of those sixty-six books. First, the chapters present certain facts that seem to indicate that these inspired works are not fully available today. Second, by discussing the nature of the Hebrew and Greek manuscript evidence and the

CONTENTS

nature of translation, the chapters argue that believers do possess the Word of God today.

Goal: The student should be aware of the challenges to believing that the Bible is preserved today. He should also be able to demonstrate, by properly accounting for those challenges, that God's Word is preserved.

Chapter 5
Focus: **apologetics**

Development: In this final chapter the authors go outside the Scripture, amassing external evidence for trusting the Bible as the Word of God. First,

this section demonstrates that a person must be regenerated before he can correctly assess the evidence relating to the Bible's reliability. Second, the chapter discusses evidence for believing the Bible. This evidence is presented under four headings: science, archeology, fulfilled prophecy, and personal testimony.

Goal: The student should be able to explain the reason that compelling evidence for trusting the Bible often does not seem compelling to an unsaved person. He also should be able to argue for the Bible's reliability by using these four categories of evidence.

Suggested Approach

How Firm a Foundation! is one book in a series of Bible modular units dealing with issues especially pertinent to Christian high school students. As the name of the series suggests, these courses are designed to be stand-alone, versatile texts. The teacher may use these books to supplement his existing curriculum for just one day a week (or for a few minutes each day) over an extended period of time. He may, however, wish to use a modular course to replace his existing curriculum for four to six weeks. Since the latter seems to be the least complicated, this is the approach the authors assume the teacher will choose.

Since critical thinking develops best in an environment where interaction is encouraged, each Bible modular unit emphasizes learning through class discussion. However, the discussion method can be misused, resulting in highly stimulated but thoroughly confused students. Usually this happens because the teacher's ideas are not given sufficient consideration while the student's are given too much weight. Therefore, the teacher should carefully consider the following guidelines, which will help to establish him as the clear leader in the classroom.

First of all, as with any method, the teacher must always keep the students in order. Second, he should remain mentally ahead of the students by being thoroughly familiar with the information in the student text as well as the teacher's edition. Third, he must realize that not all student input is correct or even valuable. If a student suggests something that is biblically false, or simply illogical, it is the teacher's responsibility to correct that errant thinking and set the discussion in the right direction. Though kindly accepting every suggestion produces a more pleasant discussion, it also propagates error.

Fourth, since a discussion can be no better than its basis, the teacher must use the lecture method to lay the foundation for meaningful interaction. Having quizzed the students over their weekend reading assignment (see the section entitled "Review Questions"), the teacher should lecture through the chapter. As he lectures, he may take time to encourage class participation and discussion at several points: while going over the quiz, when mentioning a pertinent text box, when conducting a student activity, while going over the review questions, and any time a student asks an appropriate question.

The Bible Stands

The Bible stands like a rock undaunted
Mid the raging storms of time;
Its pages burn with the truth eternal,
And they glow with a light sublime.

The Bible stands though the hills may tumble,
It will firmly stand when the earth shall crumble;
I will plant my feet on its firm foundation,
For the Bible stands.

The Bible stands like a mountain tow'ring
Far above the works of men;
Its truth by none ever was refuted,
And destroy it they never can.

The Bible stands, and it will forever,
When the world has passed away;
By inspiration it has been given—
All its precepts I will obey.

Text boxes

Throughout the student book, text boxes appear. Though some simply serve the purpose of making the main text clearer (*Get the Big Picture!* and *Master the Terms!*), three of them offer additional information that the student should find interesting. The *Test Yourself!* boxes give some good suggestions for personal application. *Think About It!* boxes focus on the ramifications of statements made in the main text. The *Did You Know?* boxes mention special, related facets of the present study that the book cannot deal with at length. Thoughtful reading of the *Test Yourself! Think About It!* and *Did You Know?* boxes could produce meaningful in-class discussions.

Memory Verses

Memory passages are included at the beginning of a chapter. Chapter 4 has no verse because the topics covered there are simply a continuation of those introduced in Chapter 3. Therefore, the same verses apply for both chapters. Each verse has been carefully chosen and should be memorized if the student's education in this subject is to be complete. As the student works through the course, he should plan on being quizzed and tested over these verses.

Review Questions

Each chapter concludes with a review section. Each reading assignment should include answering these questions. To ensure careful reading and meaningful interaction with these questions, the teacher should plan to quiz the student over these questions the day a reading assignment comes due. Perhaps the best approach would be to assign a chapter over the weekend. Monday's class would begin with a quiz, and the rest of the week would be devoted to lecturing, discussing, and doing assignment activities related to that chapter.

Some questions focus on objective facts stated in the text, while others are more interpretive. Perhaps the most important questions are those requiring essay answers. Because of the difficulty of these questions, the teacher may be tempted to omit them from the assignments. However, he cannot do so without significantly lessening the impact of this course. If the student is to assimilate the material properly, he must consider these issues with thoughtful reflection and analysis. Furthermore, since this course has an evangelistic application, the student must be able to communicate what he is learning in paragraph form. Unbelievers will never ask the student to explain his view of the Bible's authority in a *true-false* format. He must learn to express these ideas in paragraphs.

Teacher Notes

The teacher's edition includes notes both in the margin as well as at the bottom of the page. The marginal notes focus on additional explanations of statements in the text and brief discussion ideas. These are designed to ensure that the teacher have a more thorough knowledge of the subject matter so that he can more effectively lecture and lead in discussions. The bottom notes offer ideas for discussion and class activities.

Appendices

There are four appendices in the teacher's edition. Appendix A contains masters to be photocopied as transparencies. These include memory verses, lecture outlines, and items to be used for class discussion. Appendix B offers reproducible pages for student activity exercises. Appendix C contains supplementary teacher notes. Since many activities are too involved to fit on the bottom of the page in the main text, many have been placed in this appendix. Appendix D reprints, with an accompanying paraphrase, the preface to the King James Version, "The Translators to the Reader."

How Can You Know the Bible Is True?

①

Memory Verses: II Timothy 3:16 / II Peter 1:20-21

What Would *You* Say?

I'll never forget one summer night several years ago; I was sitting in my aunt's living room when she turned to me and innocently asked a few simple questions. "Kent," she said, "aren't you a Christian?"

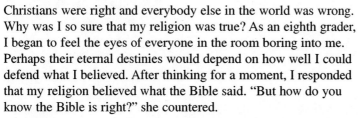

Several other unsaved relatives in the room stopped what they were doing and listened with interest. After I replied that I was, she asked me how I knew that Christians were right and everybody else in the world was wrong. Why was I so sure that my religion was true? As an eighth grader, I began to feel the eyes of everyone in the room boring into me. Perhaps their eternal destinies would depend on how well I could defend what I believed. After thinking for a moment, I responded that my religion believed what the Bible said. "But how do you know the Bible is right?" she countered.

Here was another basic question that for me was an extremely difficult one to answer. I mumbled a few things, and mercifully the questioning stopped. I don't remember what I mumbled, but I do remember feeling very stupid and wondering to myself whether the Bible could be completely trustworthy. Could I stake my present life and eternal destiny on a book that billions of people did not believe?

1

Personal Experiences

It would be helpful if you could contribute from your experiences. Were you ever confronted with this question? If so, what were the circumstances? Perhaps you even struggled with this question in the past yourself. Ask the students for illustrations from their own lives as well.

GET THE BIG PICTURE

- ❏ The Source of Scripture
- ❏ The Inspiration of Scripture
  - is something the Holy Spirit did.
  - involved human activity.
  - is essentially divine control.
  - guarantees its perfection.
- ❏ Some Questions Concerning Scripture

Years later I was traveling in the Chicago area with a youth evangelistic team. One night during the preaching, several teen guys slipped out the back and headed for the parking lot. Before they could reach their cars, I caught up to one guy named Bill (the name has been changed) and asked why he was leaving. He replied that his mom wanted him home before dark. It was 8:00 P.M., and the 17-year-old's appearance suggested that he was *not* the type to care about pleasing his parents. His excuse was lame to say the least. Bill proceeded to tell me that he did not believe the Bible but trusted in his own mind to determine his destiny. I asked him how he knew his opinion was true as opposed to the billions of other people who have opinions in the world. He shot back with, "How do you know that your opinion is true?" I told him that my opinion was based on the Bible and guaranteed to be true. If Bill had been inclined to continue the conversation, he would almost certainly have demanded how I could be so sure that *the Bible* is true.

Test Yourself!

Which challenge could you meet more quickly?
- "Give me two good reasons to trust the Bible."
- "Give me two good reasons you should have the car tonight."

What does your answer tell you about yourself and your priorities?

No Christian can avoid this question. Your decisions throughout life will reflect what you believe about the Bible, and your faith in the Bible's trustworthiness will be challenged constantly as you witness for Christ. The main thrust of this course will be to explore this question. As so often happens, we will find that trying to answer one question raises more questions, and we will deal with these related questions as well. Your search will not be fruitless; in the end you will have excellent reasons for accepting the Bible as God's Word and for proclaiming it as such to others.

What the Bible Says About Itself

Our question, you remember, is "How do we know that the Bible is true?" This is not a special question that applies only to the Bible. We are bombarded daily with information clamoring for our attention and acceptance, and a wise person evaluates information before believing it. These evaluations always start with the source of the information. The trustworthiness of the information is directly related to the trustworthiness of the source. I told Bill that the Bible is guaranteed to be true because it came from God, and He makes no mistakes.

But this claim leads to another question: "How do we know that the Bible came from God?" Think for a moment about how we know where ordinary books come from. If your literature teacher asked you who wrote *Romeo and Juliet,* you would answer, "Shakespeare." Suppose she asked you how you knew that. Perhaps you would say you knew it because his name is on the title page as the author. But suppose she pressed you further and asked how you could know for sure that Shakespeare didn't steal *Romeo and Juliet* (or for that matter all his other plays) from some other writer, publishing them under his own name. About the only reasonable answer you could offer is that Shakespeare claimed to be the author, the people of his day accepted his claim, and you have no reason for claiming otherwise. Indeed, most authors take credit for their writings, and the writings themselves often contain further information about their origin. The author expects the reader to take his word for these things, and the reader seldom has reason to doubt them.

> But soft, what light through yonder window breaks?
>
> You know, that just doesn't sound like Bill.

What about pseudonyms? Of course, there are exceptions to this general rule of accepting what the author says about his book's origin. Authors sometimes write under pseudonyms, and occasionally someone actually succeeds in deceiving the public about the authorship of his work. Such exceptions do not invalidate our reasoning at this point. We do not claim that what happens with ordinary books proves anything about the Bible; we simply maintain that the process of discovering the true source of a work must *begin* with the claims of the work itself. The reader is at liberty to discard those claims only when they do not check out against a source more reliable than the work itself. (For example, if legal records contain no evidence of a man named Mark Twain, we have good reason to suspect that Mark Twain is a pen name rather than the name of a real person.)

Any discussion about a book's origin, then, must begin with the author's own claims. Now, what happens when we bring this line of reasoning to the Bible? Does the Bible make any claims about its own origin? Obviously, the author's name is not printed on the cover. But the Bible asserts repeatedly that its ultimate author is God. In fact, more than thirty-eight hundred times the Old Testament uses language such as, "Thus saith the Lord" and "The word of the Lord came," claiming divine origin for what is written. If you set out to discover where the Bible came from, then you will soon find that the Book itself claims to have come from God. Your only reasonable choice is to accept this claim unless you can prove it false.

There have been many attempts to prove the Bible false, and we will eventually look at some of them. For now, though, we will confine ourselves to the question of what the Bible says about itself. Let's start with II Timothy 3:16: "All scripture is given by inspiration of God, and is profitable." This verse teaches clearly that the Bible came from God. But how did God "write" the Bible? With the exception of the Ten Commandments, no one has ever had God's Word in God's own handwriting! Instead, God prompted men to write His Word, and He helped them to write it accurately. This verse uses the word *inspiration* to describe God's activity in giving us His Word. What does the word mean? Furthermore, what really is *Scripture?* We say we believe that verse, but what does it mean?

The Meaning of Inspiration

For the remainder of this lesson, let's tackle the first of these questions, discussing what *inspiration* means and what the Bible says about the subject. What does it mean? In this verse the words "given by inspiration of God" come from one Greek word that

4

About the "Think About It!" Box
Try to engage your students in a discussion of the ideas in the "Think About It!" box. They would tend to distrust several of the sources because of the self-interest involved. The degree of distrust would depend on several factors. For example, if the mechanic were a close relative, you would trust him more than if he were someone unknown with whom you were dealing in an emergency. One of the reasons you tend to trust the in-struction manual is that it was written by the manufacturer. Similarly, God is like the writer of the instruction manual; the Devil is like the politician making false promises.

John Wesley on Biblical Inspiration
John Wesley has a simple and interesting line of logic proving that God wrote the Bible. You will find this quotation in Appendix C (p. 128).

Get Their Interest
Hold up a copy of the Book of Mormon and a Bible containing the Apocrypha. Ask the students separately if each is the Word of God. They might say that the Book of Mormon is not the Word of God because it does not say "Bible" on it. The other book will not be so easy to dismiss. It may even say "Holy Bible" on the cover. A quick reading through the contents will clearly show that certain books are unfamiliar. How do we know to limit our "Scriptures" to sixty-six books, no

literally means "God-breathed." Does this answer your question? Probably not. Here is a definition paraphrased from Louis Gaussen, a well-known scholar on the subject. Inspiration is the process by which the Holy Spirit guided the Scripture writers so that their words were the very words God wanted written, with nothing added, omitted, or mistaken.

Inspiration is something the Holy Spirit did.

Let's examine this definition to be sure you understand its most important points. From the outset, we must realize that inspiration is a work of God. More specifically, it is a work of the Holy Spirit.

How do we know this is true? Many New Testament passages clearly refer to the working of the Holy Spirit in the writing of the Old Testament passages that they quote (Mark 12:36; Heb. 3:7). Second Peter 1:21 states that the Old Testament writers were "moved by the Holy Ghost." Second Timothy implies this by saying that Scripture is "God-breathed."

Inspiration involves human activity.

Second, our definition of inspiration points out that men were involved in the process. Notice that II Peter 1:21 refers to both divine and human activity: "*men . . . spake as they were moved by the Holy Ghost*." The Bible did not just miraculously appear; God used *men* to do the actual writing. Thus Paul can call attention to his personal activity in writing the book of Galatians, saying in 6:11, "Ye see how large a letter I have written unto you with mine own hand."

Inspiration is essentially divine control.

It is easy enough to understand that both God and men were involved in the writing of the Bible. This third point of the definition is where matters become more difficult. How, exactly, did

"God-breathed." The two main components of the Greek word for inspiration are "God" and a root that means "spirit" or "wind" as well as "breath." Paul may be intending "God-breathed" to be a metaphor meaning "produced by the Spirit of God."

Another point of meaning this word seems to convey is the close connection between God and His Word. God's Word is not something external to Himself, detachable and optional. Rather, it is His very breath, an essential part of His existence. John's words come to mind: "the Word was God" (John 1:1). The human mind cannot fully comprehend the relationship between God and His Word—either the written Word or the living Word. But we can observe that the relationship is extremely close. The point of this observation that your students need to understand is that when they encounter God's Word, they are not far from encountering God Himself.

more and no less? Of course this question will be answered later but should arouse interest.

A special kind of *inspiration*. In talking about *inspiration* as it relates to literature, most people have in mind some effect that the literature has upon them. But as a theological term, the word signifies something God did to the Bible, not something the Bible does to the reader. Whether the reader gets "inspired" by the Bible is a subjective matter that depends upon the reader's disposition and character. God's inspiring the Bible is an objective fact, which in no way depends upon the reader's response.

God and men work together? Was it simply a joint venture between equal partners? What was happening between God and men in the writing of the Scripture? These questions lead us to consider what *inspiration* really means. You know what it means to sleep, to run, to think, and to laugh, for example, but can you explain what it means *to inspire* in the sense we're discussing?

Again II Peter 1:21 gives important information by saying that the Holy Spirit "moved" the human writers. We can understand the meaning of the word *moved* more clearly if we look to Acts 27:15 for an illustration. In that passage, Paul is traveling to Rome in a grain ship. A violent storm catches the ship, and the sailors can do nothing but surrender, letting the wind determine the ship's course. The Greek  word translated "let her drive" in Acts 27:15 is the same verb translated "moved" in II Peter 1:21. Just as the wind was totally in control of the ship's destination, the Holy Spirit controlled the whole process of writing Scripture. This is the basic meaning of *inspiration:* God's control over the human writing process.

6

Divine Control Does Not Necessitate Divine Dictation

The Bible itself contains evidence of divine dictation. The prophets, for example, often proclaim, "Thus saith the Lord," and the words that follow seem obviously to be dictated by God Himself. On the other hand, the various books reflect different writing styles, suggesting that the men who wrote them were free to express themselves as they chose, though what they wrote was still exactly what God wanted.

A good answer to the question in the "Did You Know?" box is the difference in the two men's backgrounds. Paul's academic skills and training in Jewish theology furnished him with writing skills different from those of John, a converted fisherman.

No one fully understands the exact nature of this control or the extent to which it reached. Some theologians believe that the human authors were like secretaries simply taking dictation. Others teach that God controlled the human authors' upbringing, education, and spiritual experience so that they could express God's truth through their own personalities. While this latter view accounts for differences in writing style from one writer to another, it does not deny the fact that the Holy Spirit ultimately controlled the writing process, keeping the human authors from making mistakes. When we learn the full truth in heaven, we probably will find that it is some combination of these views.

Inspiration guarantees perfection.

The fourth important point contained in our definition of *inspiration* is the fact that inspiration results in a Bible that contains no error. (The term used by theologians to refer to the absence of error in the Bible is *inerrancy*.) This belief in inerrancy is a subject of great debate in Christian circles today. Theological liberals (those who reject fundamental doctrines of the Bible such as Creation, the virgin birth of Christ, etc.) view the Bible as human literature that has, at best, slightly more of the truth of God in it than other literature. They think the writers were as prone to error as the writers of any other books. Liberals simply choose what they think is good in the Bible and ignore the rest.

On the conservative side of theology, there is widespread acceptance of the Bible as unique literature with God as its author in some sense. But even many of these people restrict the Bible's inerrancy to its teaching on moral issues, allowing for errors in matters of science, history, and geography. We will soon see, though, that this position is not acceptable. Traditional, orthodox Christianity over the centuries has maintained a firm belief in what theologians call *verbal inspiration*. This simply means that *every word* of Scripture is inspired and without error.

Let's look at some examples proving that Jesus and the apostles considered previously written Scripture as perfect. In Galatians 3:16 Paul builds his argument based on the singular "seed" (referring to the promise made to Abraham in Gen. 22:18)

Which Bible is perfect? Which copy, copies, translation, or translations of the Bible are without error is a question that will be treated later under the subject of preservation. Emphasize for now that the Bible is without error. A student may ask, "Which Bible?" Either give a concise answer or ask that he hold that question until the subject comes up later. You may wish to give an assurance such as, "You can trust the Bible you hold in your hands."

An explanation of *verbal* and *plenary*. *Verbal* in this context does not mean "spoken out loud." It is a technical term derived from the Latin word for *word*. *Verbal inspiration* means that the actual words of Scripture, not simply the thoughts lying behind them, are inspired (the contrasting term is *thought inspiration*).

You may also want to explain such terms as *plenary inspiration* (full or complete; as opposed to *partial inspiration*, which maintains that only parts of the Bible are inspired) and *infallibility*. The latter term really means "without mistake" but recently has been twisted by some to mean "without mistake in matters of faith and practice only." *Inerrant* is used by those who claim perfection for *all* of Scripture.

A *literal* Bible or an *inerrant* Bible? Some critics falsely charge that inerrantists take everything in the Bible literally. While inerrantists refuse to engage in unwarranted allegorization (e.g., in the early chapters of Genesis), they do recognize the existence of figurative language in the Bible (e.g., Ps. 98:7-9). To treat this issue fully would require more discussion than the limits of this course allow.

Inerrancy of the Originals

The traditional, orthodox view (the one we hold) is that inerrancy applies to the original Hebrew, Aramaic, and Greek autographs. Inspiration does not apply to the work of a translator. Translations are to be judged on the basis of their faithfulness to the original languages.

Sadly, many scholars do not believe that the Bible was inerrant in its autographs. Such men point to "discrepancies" in the text that they believe can be explained only as mistakes by the author. It is not our purpose to deal with alleged discrepancies of the Bible in this course. Lesson 11 in Level F of the BJU Bible curriculum handles several of these. For further study see *Alleged Discrepancies of the Bible,* by John W. Haley, and *Encyclopedia of Bible Difficulties,* by Gleason Archer.

Appendix C (p. 128) contains a case study on Clark Pinnock, illustrating the far-reaching effects that can result from giving way on the doctrine of inerrancy. You may wish to reproduce these pages for your class as a seatwork exercise, or you may simply tell the story and discuss it.

DID YOU KNOW? The fact that different writing styles are apparent throughout the Bible has been taken by some to prove that the human writers chose their own words under the Spirit's guidance. Others, however, maintain that the Holy Spirit chose the words for them, reflecting what He knew to be their personal style. Differences in style are an undeniable fact, but that fact ultimately proves nothing about the degree to which the writers' human personalities were active within the process of inspiration.

Can you think of any reasons that you would expect Paul, for instance, to write in a style different from John?

---

as opposed to the plural "seeds." Christ argues that the Old Testament teaches the doctrine of the resurrection (which some of His hearers did not believe) based on the present tense of the verb "I am" (Matt. 22:32; Exod. 3:6). Scripture clearly views inspiration as applying to words and verb tenses. God cannot make mistakes; therefore, His Word cannot have errors in it.

But, But, But . . .

But wait a minute. Doesn't Paul's reference to "all scripture" in II Timothy 3:16 mean specifically the Old Testament? And certainly II Peter 1:20-21 ("For the *prophecy* came not *in old time* by the will of man . . .) refers just to the Old Testament. Furthermore, those thirty-eight hundred instances where "Thus saith the Lord" is written are in the Old Testament. And when Jesus quoted and verified Scripture, the New Testament had not even been written. How then do we know that the New Testament is inspired on the same level as the Old?

The Teaching of the New Testament

These are good questions for which there are good answers. It is evident, for example, that Peter considered Paul's writings to be inspired. He implies in II Peter 3:15-16 that Paul's epistles were as authoritative as the Old Testament Scriptures. At the beginning of the same chapter, Peter equates the prophecy of the Old Testament with the commandments of the New Testament apostles. Furthermore, if you check the sources of Paul's quotations in I Timothy 5:18, you will discover that Paul put Luke's Gospel on a par with Deuteronomy. When we realize that the writings of the

Peter's opinion of Paul. In II Peter 3:16 Peter mentions that unlearned and unstable men were twisting Paul's writings as they had the *other* Scriptures. The important word here is "other." If Paul's epistles had not been Scripture, Peter would have written simply "as they do also the scriptures."

Luke on a par with Deuteronomy. In I Timothy 5:18, the first scriptural quotation comes from Deuteronomy 25:4, and the second quotation comes from Luke 10:7.

8

apostles (II Pet. 3:2), the epistles of Paul (II Pet. 3:16), and the Gospel of Luke (I Tim. 5:18) were all directly or indirectly pointed out as inspired, we can understand that claims of divine authorship apply to the New Testament as well as the Old.

The Aid of the Holy Spirit

We must deal with one more issue concerning the New Testament. These writings are based on three important foundations: the teachings of the Old Testament, the teachings and actions of Christ, and the truth of His death and resurrection. The second of these foundations required very accurate recall on the part of the apostles. How could men remember years later exactly what Christ had said and taught (the Gospel writers especially)? The first New Testament book was not written until fifteen years after Christ was gone. He died and rose again around A.D. 30. John did not write his Gospel until A.D. 85. That leaves more than fifty years between! Think back to a special speaker you heard perhaps as much as a year ago. Can you remember exactly, word for word, what he said? Of course not. Most people can't remember the sermon they heard last week.

The solution to this problem lies in some things Jesus said to the disciples in John 14 and 16. These chapters show the men in a state of discouragement because Jesus says He will be leaving them soon. To comfort them, He assures them that the Holy Spirit will be sent to bring all things to their remembrance (14:26). Later Jesus reassures them further by adding that the Holy Spirit will guide the disciples into all truth (John 16:12-13). Thus the Gospels are not exaggerated oral traditions passed down over the years until they were finally recorded. Neither are the Epistles a collection of "new truths" dreamed up by strange people with too

9

The Jesus Seminar

In 1985, seventy-seven liberal Bible scholars formed the Jesus Seminar, the goal of which is to reexamine the contents of Scripture. They put out a book entitled *The Five Gospels: What Did Jesus Really Say?* (the fifth gospel is the recently discovered Gospel of Thomas). Although it does not directly attack the deity or resurrection of Christ, the Seminar certainly undermines much of what Jesus said, claiming that 80 percent of Jesus' words in the Gospels were fabricated by His followers after His death. Examples of the rejected material include the Lord's Prayer, Jesus' words at the Last Supper, His messianic claims, and His teachings about the end of the world.

Chapter 2 contains further mention of the Jesus Seminar, and you should have little difficulty locating current material on what the group is doing or has done since the time of this book's writing, should you wish to discuss the group with your students.

much time on their hands. The Gospels are the actual words and events from Christ's life supernaturally brought to the writers' remembrance, and the Epistles contain the truth into which the Holy Spirit led the writers as they reflected on Christ's life, death, and resurrection.

Summary

We hope your understanding of inspiration is better now than it was when you began this lesson. Inspiration is a work of God through men controlled by the Holy Spirit, who insured that the writings are the very words that God intended, without error or omission.

Review Questions

1. When you evaluate the reliability of information you receive, the first thing you evaluate is the reliability of the

    source

2. An investigation into the origin of an ordinary book begins with

    the book's own claims

3. In II Timothy 3:16, the words "given by inspiration of God" are the translation of a single Greek word that literally means

    "God-breathed"

4. Which member of the Trinity was especially involved in the work of inspiration?

    the Holy Spirit

5. What verse teaches clearly that inspiration is essentially divine control?

    II Peter 1:21

6. The name of the doctrine that God inspired each word of the Bible is

    verbal inspiration

7. Which epistle writer quoted from Luke's Gospel and placed it on a par with Deuteronomy?

    Paul

8. Explain how the writers of the Gospels were able to recall the very words of Jesus with complete accuracy.

    ***The Holy Spirit brought these words
    back to their minds (John 14:26; 16:12-13).***

F 9. Jesus' teachings did not touch upon the doctrine of inerrancy.

F 10. Paul used the term *Scripture* to describe Peter's writings.

C 11. Which of the following statements is most precise?

    A. God wrote the Bible.
    B. Men wrote the Bible.
    C. Both A and B are true.
    D. The Bible is still in the process of being written.

B 12. Identify the theological danger in the statement "The Bible contains the Word of God."

    A. It does not explain the meaning of the Bible.
    B. It allows the possibility that some things in the Bible are not God's Word.
    C. It does not specifically describe the Holy Spirit's role in inspiration.
    D. It implies that only the Bible is God's Word.

A 13. Inspiration and inerrancy are foundational doctrines because

    A. the trustworthiness of all other doctrines depends upon them.
    B. Paul said they are the most important doctrines.
    C. they are the first things Jesus taught His disciples.
    D. they are accepted by all professing Christians, whether liberal or conservative.

The following statements are actual published definitions of the term *inspiration*. Match each definition with the description that fits it best. One description will be used twice.

A. good definition   B. weak on inerrancy   C. unacceptable

A 14. A work of the Holy Spirit, causing His energies to flow into the spontaneous exercises of the writers' faculties, elevating and directing where need be, and everywhere securing the errorless expression in language of the thought designed by God.

B 15. Inspiration is that influence of the Spirit of God upon the minds of the Scripture writers which made their writings the record of a progressive divine revelation, sufficient, when taken together and interpreted by the same Spirit who inspired them, to lead every honest inquirer to Christ and to salvation.

C 16. We call our Bible inspired, by which we mean that by reading and studying it we find our way to God, we find His will for us, and we find how we can conform ourselves to His will.

A 17. Inspiration is that inexplicable power which the Divine Spirit put forth of old on the authors of holy Scripture, in order to guide them even in the employment of the words they used, and to preserve them alike from all error and from all omission.

18. A publisher's blurb for *The Greatest Story Ever Told,* by Fulton Oursler, contains the following statement: "Originally written in 1949, the book has been acclaimed by the clergy of all faiths for its inspiration and authenticity!" Explain the difference between the meaning of inspiration in the advertisement and its meaning in this lesson. Did the publisher commit a sin by calling the book inspired? Why or why not?

[Key ideas: The publisher uses the word in a general sense while the lesson uses it as a specific theological term. The publisher did not sin, because the advertisement does not claim that God wrote the book; it simply uses the word inspiration in a very general sense. The aim of the question is to test the student's awareness that this lesson focuses on a very specialized meaning of the term.]

19. Evaluate the following definition in light of this lesson's teaching on the meaning of inspiration: "Inspiration is that influence of the Spirit of God upon the minds of the Scripture writers which made their writings the record of a progressive divine revelation, sufficient, when taken together and interpreted by the same Spirit who inspired them, to lead every honest inquirer to Christ and to salvation." (A. H. Strong)

[Key ideas: The definition satisfies the first two aspects of the meaning of inspiration: the involvement of the Holy Spirit and of the human authors. The definition is a bit weaker on the third point: influence is perhaps a weaker term than control, since influence is something that can be resisted. But the definition is still acceptable on this point. The definition fails, however, to assert inerrancy. Many noninerrantists want to restrict the Bible's absolute trustworthiness to matters of salvation, allowing for errors in matters of science, history, geography, etc.]

How to Write an Essay

Read
Carefully read the question.

Scattergram

On a separate piece of paper jot down the main ideas to be used in the answer. This activity will probably involve going back to the place in the chapter where the topic is discussed. Write down any statements or ideas that should be included. This somewhat jumbled list is often called a scattergram.

Outline
Look over the information included. What is most important? What is least important? Mark all points that seem to belong together logically. The result should be a rough outline.

Thesis
Write a thesis statement. The easiest way to do this is to turn the question into a sentence. However, this is often not possible. In such cases one should examine his outline and develop a sentence that well represents all the information in that outline.

Topic Sentence
Write a topic sentence that covers the first point of the outline and that ties in to the thesis.

Support
Write and support the topic sentence for each of the main points on the

20. Evaluate the following definition in light of this lesson's teaching on the meaning of inspiration: "We call our Bible inspired, by which we mean that by reading and studying it we find our way to God, we find his will for us, and we find how we can conform ourselves to his will." (Robert Horton)

[Key ideas: This is a very poor definition of inspiration. Not one of the four points developed in the lesson can be found in this definition.]

21. Evaluate the following definition in light of this lesson's teaching on the meaning of inspiration: "A work of the Holy Spirit, causing His energies to flow into the spontaneous exercises of the writers' faculties, elevating and directing where need be, and everywhere securing the errorless expression in language of the thought designed by God." (B. B. Warfield)

[Key ideas: The definition is good; it contains each of the four elements discussed in the lesson.]

outline. Give as much specific detail as time and space permit.

Proofread

Be sure to read over the finished essay to correct any errors and polish the flow of thought.

22. Explain how the description of a ship caught in a storm (Acts 27:15) contributes to our understanding of the meaning of inspiration.

[Key ideas: The same word used to describe the ship's being carried by the wind also describes the Scripture writers' being carried along by the Holy Spirit. The writers were under the Spirit's control, much as the ship was at the mercy of the wind.]

Which Books Belong in the Bible?

②

Memory Verses: Luke 24:44 / II Peter 3:2

A Tougher Question Yet

The previous lesson called attention to II Timothy 3:16, "All scripture is given by inspiration of God," and questioned the meaning of two terms: *inspiration* and *Scripture*. We have examined the meaning of the first term; now we must discuss the second. When we ask "What is *Scripture?*" what we are really asking is which ancient writings deserve to be recognized as the authoritative Word of God.

Did you know that the sixty-six books of our Bible are not the only books written by God-fearing people during that period of history? The Bible itself refers to other written works from its own time period, such as the books of the chronicles of the kings of Israel and of Judah. How do we know that our Bible contains all the right books? Obviously, someone had to collect these

GET THE BIG PICTURE

- ❏ Meaning of the term *canon*
- ❏ The key test of canonicity
- ❏ Identifying the Old Testament canon
  - • Two identical views
    - - Teaching of the Jews
    - - Teaching of Jesus
- ❏ Identifying the New Testament canon
  - • Three critical tests
    - - Apostolic origin
    - - Scriptural contents
    - - Widespread acceptance

17

books, choosing to include the ones we have in the Bible and to reject the ones we don't. How do we know that they made the right decisions?

Perhaps you have never even thought of this question before. Admittedly, an unbeliever is not as likely to ask you this question as he is to ask the question Kent was asked by his aunt. Most people do not know enough about ancient literature to be aware of these other books. But if you make a habit of talking to people about the gospel, you will eventually face this question, and it will come probably from someone who is intelligent and well educated. There are good answers to this question, though they are not simple. We hope you will take the trouble to think this question through so that you can have the answers ready when you need them.

You Can't Shoot the Canon

Considering which books belong in the Bible deals with the topic of the "canon." The word *canon* (pronounced just like *can-**non*) is the English spelling of a Greek word that means "straight rod," or "ruler," a device for measuring conformity to a standard. The canon of Scripture is the body of writings that measures up to the standard of divine inspiration and authority. A related word, *canonical* (accented on the second syllable), means "belonging to the canon." For example, the sixty-six books of the Bible are sometimes called the canonical books; other writings excluded from the canon are called noncanonical.

You should bear in mind that the noncanonical books are not entirely evil; indeed, you can benefit from reading them. But these books lack evidence of inspiration and therefore carry no binding authority.

Apocryphal Problems. Second Esdras, for example, claims to have been written by Ezra and frequently uses the language of the prophets ("Thus saith the Lord" and "The word of the Lord came to me"). But the book dates itself circa 556 B.C., one hundred years prior to the biblically well-established date of Ezra's return from Babylon to Jerusalem. It contains quite a number of other serious discrepancies as well. Most of the apocryphal books simply make no claim of divine origin, and at least one book specifically disclaims inspiration. Second Maccabees 15:38 reads, "If it has been well and pointedly written, that is what I wanted; but if it is poor, mediocre work, that was all I could do." See also the prologue to Ecclesiasticus and II Maccabees 2:27.

Do you remember what we said in the previous lesson about examining a book's own claims about its origin? If you approach the noncanonical books this way, you will find that most of them do not claim to have come from God. But what about those that do? Can we disprove that claim? We can; the noncanonical books that claim divine origin contain such obvious errors that everyone who studies them recognizes their imperfections. Rather than focus on the excluded books, though, the rest of this lesson will examine the reasons for accepting the sixty-six books of our Bible as we have them.

The Bottom Line Up Front

I remember reading with some interest a publisher's preface to Alexander Dumas's *Three Musketeers*. Encouraging me to read widely, the publisher reasoned, "A book becomes a classic only when enough people over an extended period of time decide they like the book." Then he exhorted me to be an avid reader and share with others the books that I find especially enjoyable. Thus I would become part of the very important process of making classics.

However, the publisher failed to realize that I no more make a book a classic than a child makes his dad his dad just by calling him "Dad." If a little girl lovingly exclaims "Daddy" when her father comes, she is simply recognizing a pre-existing reality. So also, when a reader discovers the inherent "classic quality" of a book, he does not make the book a classic; he only confirms what is already true.

19

That publisher's misconception is sadly common among students of the Bible. Many think that the sixty-six books of the Old and New Testaments became "the Bible" when the early church decided they should be. If that were so, the authority of these books would rest on man's opinion. In reality, the church simply recognized what was already true.

Christ told His contemporaries that His sheep have the ability to hear His voice and to avoid the voice of a "stranger" (John 10:2-5, 11, 27). For those early believers, as for us, the key test in determining canonicity was the testimony of the Holy Spirit in their hearts that the books were from God. Those that have a personal relationship with the author of Scripture hear the voice of God in the books He has written.

> *The key test of canonicity: the testimony of the Holy Spirit in heart of the believer that the books are from God.*

Some find this conclusion dissatisfying because it seems to make such an important decision entirely subjective. However, this God-chosen means of revealing which books are canonical is the ideal means. Think about it. If God had decided that *men* would identify which books are canonical by using their own system of tests, *men* would be standing in judgment over the text. However, neither God nor His Word will be judged by men. The Lord has initiated communication with man by producing a flawless text. Furthermore, He has commended that text to believers by placing in their hearts the same Spirit who wrote the Word. Thus the Word testifies to the Spirit in the believer's heart that it is from God. Not even when considering canonicity does man judge the text; rather, he is judged by it.

The rest of this lesson deals with various facts from history that demonstrate that the Holy Spirit has been confirming the divine origin of these sixty-six books in the hearts of His people for millenia. As you read through these observations, carefully consider how different these books are from all others.

The Old Testament

Since the Old and New Testaments represent different periods in the history of God's people, it is not surprising that the question of the canon involves somewhat different issues in each case. It will be easier, then, to discuss this question in two parts. Let's start with the Old Testament.

Which books belong in the Old Testament Scriptures? Traditionally, our Old Testament includes only thirty-nine books. Some groups (including the Roman Catholic Church) have insisted on including fourteen other books called the Apocrypha. Among the better known apocryphal books are I Maccabees, which contains fascinating accounts of the Jewish wars just before the time of Christ, and Bel and the Dragon, which adds information concerning the life of Daniel. None of the apocryphal books was written before 300 B.C., at least 100 years later than the last universally accepted book of the Old Testament. How should we view these books? Should we seriously consider them as Scripture?

The Jewish View of the Old Testament

Since before the time of Christ, the Jews have classified their scriptural books into three main divisions: the Law, the Prophets, and the Writings. The last of these divisions was sometimes called "the Psalms" because Psalms dominates that section. These divisions include the same thirty-nine books that we have in our Old Testament. The Jews, though, arranged them in a different order, beginning with Genesis and ending with II Chronicles. To us it

DID YOU KNOW?

One day Christopher Columbus picked up a book written by Pierre d'Ailly, a Catholic scholar. The author proposed that the earth was a sphere and that the distance from the western coast of Europe to the eastern coast of Asia could be sailed in only a few days. He based this estimate on a verse found in the Apocrypha of the Vulgate (the Catholic Bible in Latin). The verse states that God created the earth with six parts land and one part water (IV Esdras 6:42; non-Catholics call the book II Esdras).

This appeal to "the Bible" convinced Columbus. Although this misinformation led to the discovery of the Americas, it nearly cost Columbus his life.

21

More on the Law, the Prophets, and the Writings

We have very early evidence that the Jews held to a three-fold division of Scripture. The apocryphal book, Ecclesiasticus, was composed about 190 B.C. in Hebrew by Jesus ben Sirach. His grandson later translated the entire work into Greek about 130 B.C. and added a prologue. In the prologue the grandson mentions, "Whereas many and great things have been delivered to us by the Law and the Prophets and by others that have

followed their steps—my grandfather, Jesus, when he had much given himself to the reading of the Law and the Prophets and the other books of our fathers, and had gotten therein good judgment, was drawn on also himself to write something pertaining to learning and wisdom."

In Jewish thought, the Law (the Hebrew word is Torah) consists of the first five books of the Bible (the Pentateuch). The Prophets consisted of two sections: the Former Prophets

and the Latter Prophets. Joshua, Judges, Samuel, and Kings were called the Former Prophets. The major prophets (Isaiah, Jeremiah, and Ezekiel) and the minor prophets (Hosea through Malachi) were called the Latter Prophets. The Writings were made up of three sections: poetry and wisdom (Psalms, Proverbs, and Job), the rolls (Song of Solomon, Ruth, Lamentations, Ecclesiastes, and Esther), and history (Daniel, Ezra, Nehemiah, and Chronicles).

seems odd to put II Chronicles last, because it does not cover the last period of Old Testament history. However, the Jews focused on the date of *writing*, and they believe that Ezra wrote II Chronicles as the last scriptural book around 424 B.C.

The writings of a man named Josephus confirm that the Jews had this view of the Old Testament canon. Writing shortly after A.D. 70, he states that every Jew believed that no more books were added to the Old Testament after Artaxerxes, a Persian king who died in 424 B.C. They believed further that no material was added to the thirty-nine accepted books.

Jesus' View of the Old Testament

Let's zero in now on why our thirty-nine books and no others are recognized as canonical. In Luke 11:37-52, Christ condemns the Jewish leaders for their hypocrisy, pronouncing them guilty of the blood of all the prophets from Abel to Zechariah. Why did Christ single out these two martyrs? When we identify these men more carefully, the answer becomes plain. It gets a bit complicated, but stay with us; we're going somewhere worthwhile.

Abel, of course, is the son of Adam who was murdered by his brother Cain in Genesis 4. But who is Zechariah? Jesus says the man was slain between the altar and the temple. This probably is not the Zechariah who wrote a book of the Bible, for we have no indication that he died as a martyr. Instead, the proper identification is the Zechariah who was killed in the temple area, by order of King Joash, as recorded in II Chronicles 24:20-21.

Now we're ready to see how these words from Jesus confirm the limitation of the Old Testament canon to thirty-nine books. Recall that in the Jewish Scriptures, Genesis is the first book and II Chronicles is the last. Christ was saying that the Pharisees were guilty of the blood of all the prophets from the beginning of the first book to the end of the last book. Another way of thinking of it is that Christ was including all the murdered prophets "from A to Z." By making no mention of the Apocrypha, Jesus puts a clear stamp of approval upon the Jewish canon of thirty-nine books.

In the words of Josephus. The exact quotation comes from his *Contra Apionem* I:8. "From Artaxerxes until our time everything has been recorded, but has not been deemed worthy of like credit with what preceded, because the exact succession of the prophets ceased. But what faith we have placed in our own writings is evident by our conduct; for though so long a time has now passed, no one has dared to add anything to them, or to take anything from them, or to alter anything in them."

For a point of reference, Artaxerxes was the son of Xerxes. Xerxes was the husband of Esther.

More on Zechariah. The students might find it beneficial for you to review the details of the fascinating story of the near extinction of the royal line of David, of the coronation of young King Joash by the high priest Jehoiada, and of the ingratitude displayed in the slaying of Jehoiada's son Zechariah. See II Chronicles 22-24.

Not "A to Z" in Hebrew. In case the question arises, you should know that it is a coincidence of the English language that these names begin with the first and last letters of the alphabet. The name Abel begins with the fifth letter of the Hebrew alphabet and Zechariah begins with the seventh.

Two more facts about Jewish use of the Old Testament in the time of Christ may be helpful to you. First, the terms "the Law" and "the Law and the Prophets" were often used to refer to the whole Old Testament. Second, if you read elsewhere about the Old Testament canon, you may find the number of books stated as twenty-two or twenty-four rather than thirty-nine. This difference has to do with how the Jews combined several writings in one scroll; for example, the twelve minor prophets are a single book in the

Jewish scheme. For simplicity, this course uses the familiar number of thirty-nine canonical books, as found in English Bibles.

Is the Apocrypha Scripture?

The same line of reasoning we have applied here to a single statement of Jesus also applies to the New Testament as a whole. Most of the New Testament writers used the Septuagint (the Greek translation of the Old Testament made about 250 B.C.), which contained the Apocrypha.

Although those who accept the Apocrypha argue that this New Testament approval of the Septuagint includes those books, more careful thought reveals just the opposite.

The New Testament writers quote from nearly every book of the canonical Old Testament, but not once do they quote from an apocryphal work. Since the Apocrypha was readily available in the Bible the New Testament writers used daily, the absence of quotations from the

The Law

Genesis, Exodus, Leviticus, Numbers, Deuteronomy

The Prophets

Former Prophets
Joshua, Judges, I & II Samuel, I & II Kings

Latter Prophets
Isaiah, Jeremiah, Ezekiel, Hosea, Joel, Amos, Obadiah, Jonah, Micah, Nahum, Habakkuk, Zephaniah, Haggai, Zechariah, Malachi

The Writings

Psalms, Job, Proverbs, Ruth, Song of Solomon, Ecclesiastes, Lamentations, Esther, Daniel, Ezra, Nehemiah, I & II Chronicles

Another evidence for the rejection of the Apocrypha as Scripture is found in Luke 24:44. "And he [Jesus] said unto them, These are the words which I spake unto you, while I was yet with you, that all things must be fulfilled, which were written in the law of Moses, and in the prophets, and in the psalms, concerning me." Notice the threefold division recognized by the Jews. Again Jesus excludes the Apocrypha even though it had existed for hundreds of years by this time.

As we have already indicated, the Jews accepted only the thirty-nine books of the Old Testament as canonical. Jesus, Himself a Jew, grew up with this teaching and knew that His audiences believed this. When Jesus taught concerning the Scripture, if He had wanted to include the Apocrypha as inspired, He would have had to deal specifically with the issue in order to correct the faulty thinking of His friends and listeners. He never did so. He allowed them to continue believing that the thirty-nine books they accepted as inspired were the only ones that belonged in the Old Testament.

Apocrypha is significant evidence against the authority of those books in the minds of the apostles.

On the surface this argument may appear weak, being an argument from silence. Nevertheless, the contrast between this silence regarding the Apocrypha and the overwhelming chorus of acceptance of the canonical writings carries undeniable force.

The New Testament

Let's move on to the New Testament, which contains twenty-seven books of Scripture. Recently some unbelievers have renewed their efforts to omit certain books (such as Revelation) or portions (such as verses on hell) and to add books (such as the Gospel of Thomas). Such scattered challenges, however, should not disturb God's people, for the Holy Spirit continues to confirm the canonicity of these twenty-seven books alone. Nevertheless, in seeking a more detailed answer, we should consider the contributions of our spiritual forefathers. The early church, while facing challenges much greater than those just mentioned, developed several tests for recognizing which books belong in the New Testament. True believers since then have found these tests reassuring. they express concretely the "seal of approval" we all sense from God's Spirit.

Apostolic Origin

First, the early church concluded that each book had to be written by an apostle or by someone closely associated with an apostle. There is an important reason behind this test. Jesus made it clear that the apostles would be His representatives in founding the church and that their decisions would reflect God's truth and carry God's authority (John 14:26; Eph. 2:19-20; II Pet. 3:2). In a matter so crucial for the church as the writing of the New Testament, the apostles' role was vital. Furthermore, there is no biblical evidence that this divine sanction would carry on to succeeding generations of church leaders; the apostles were the *only* ones with such authority.

It was not necessary, though, for a book to have been actually *written* by an apostle. If a book originated in connection with an apostle's work, it could be assumed to carry the apostle's approval,

MASTER the TERMS
- **Canon:** the collection of books approved as meeting the standard of divine inspiration and authority
- **Scripture:** the sixty-six canonical books of the Old and New Testaments
- **Apocrypha:** Jewish and Christian works dated in or near biblical times but not accepted as canonical

24

The Gospel of Thomas

The Jesus Seminar, referred to in the previous lesson, has undertaken a full-scale effort to redefine the canon of the New Testament. Part of the impetus behind this effort is the recent discovery in Egypt (Nag Hammadi, to be exact) of a library of early gnostic literature containing some previously unknown works, such as the so-called Gospel of Thomas. The group also inclines toward eliminating at least the Book of Revelation, citing its misuse by extremist groups and cults. (The Seminar's lack of doctrinal integrity becomes apparent at this point; they dislike the use of Revelation by today's cults, but they are eager to embrace the work of the gnostic heretics of Nag Hammadi.) At the time of this book's writing, there is no way to gauge how widely accepted the Seminar's effort will be. The point to emphasize with your class is that the subject of the canon is not something confined to ivory-tower studies of history. It is a live issue at this very moment.

Martin Luther and Canonicity

If your students are surprised by Luther's comments on the canon, remind them that Luther grew up in the Roman Catholic Church, which accepted quite a spectrum of writings as infallible. In reforming his theology, Luther had to reconsider everything he had been taught and to eliminate any teaching that opposed the truth of justification by faith, a conclusion to which God had led him. Once your students understand Luther's background, it should not be hard for them

even if someone else wrote it. For example, James, the half-brother of Jesus Christ, wrote his epistle about A.D. 48 in Jerusalem. He was not an apostle himself, but he lived among the apostles, associating closely with them. If the apostles had not considered the book to be Scripture, it would be difficult to account for its wide acceptance by the early church.

We need to consider one more point concerning this test of canonicity. The test of apostolic origin puts a limit on how long the canon remained open to new writings. John outlived the other apostles, and he died around A.D. 100. It stands to reason, then, that nothing written after that date can be considered apostolic.

Scriptural Contents

The second test involved an examination of the contents of the book. Obviously, no book containing errors or contradicting other Scripture could be viewed as canonical.

Widespread Acceptance

The third test laid down the requirement that a book must have enjoyed wide acceptance and use by the early church. If Buwanna,

Think About It!

There is an important difference between Luther's questions about the canon and those of modern skeptics. Luther was committed (and submitted!) to the Bible as the Word of God; he labored over which books deserved that recognition. Today's skeptics accept nothing as divinely inspired. Their goal is merely to point out some books as having exercised sufficient influence on Christianity to deserve inclusion in that religion's body of sacred literature. Between these points of view lies a difference as great as the difference between life and death.

25

to see why he had trouble accepting, for example, the book of James, which speaks of salvation in terms that, on the surface, sound more like the theology of the popes than that of Paul (e.g., James 2:14-26).

Furthermore, it is worth noting that, while Luther was unsure of the canonicity of Hebrews, James, Jude, and Revelation, he viewed these books more highly than the Apocrypha. His translation of the Bible did include the Apocrypha, but he distinguished the apocryphal works from Scripture, saying that, while containing some profitable things, they carry no authority.

The New Testament Apocrypha and the Test of Apostolic Origin

This is the most objective of the tests and eliminates most of the books that were sometimes claimed to be part of the New Testament. Evidently, nearly everyone has found this test to be quite convincing. Unlike the Old Testament Apocrypha, the New Testament Apocrypha is presently not accepted as canonical by any major religious group. Following is a listing of some of the more important New Testament apocryphal works with the approximate dates when they were written.

a tribal chieftain in North Africa, had written a book, it probably would have been well received in his particular area, regardless of the value of its contents. After all, rejecting it would be hazardous to your health! But somebody in Rome or Ephesus who had never heard of this great tribal chieftain would pay it about as much attention as the average high-school student pays a grammar book—unless its contents commended it as helpful and trustworthy. This test assumes that anything *God* writes will commend itself to every soul energized by His Holy Spirit. A book lacking this widespread acceptance does not deserve recognition as the Word of God.

Conclusion

The Holy Spirit testifies to the authenticity of the books He has written. That testimony in the heart of believers is His "seal of approval." Is it possible that we have misunderstood that testimony? Hardly, for at every point in history when the question has come up and the evidence has been reviewed, the consensus of godly men and women concerning which books deserve a place in Scripture has consistently been the same. These books, and these alone, are inspired.

By now you should have a clear understanding of II Timothy 3:16, "All scripture is given by inspiration of God. . . ." The sixty-six books of our Bible, Genesis to Revelation, are the very words of God, written by men under His control, and free from all error.

Conclusion. Be sure to underscore the point that the New Testament is not inspired because certain men have determined it to be so; these men simply recognized the fact that it is inspired. Our present twenty-seven books were officially recognized at the Third Council of Carthage in A.D. 397. Before this time the church's proximity to the apostolic age made it possible to determine canonicity based simply on widespread use of various books, based in turn on common knowledge of their origin. But eventually questions began to arise, and by this time church leaders had gradually developed these tests, under the direction of the Holy Spirit, to reconfirm the prevailing faith and practice.

You should not give the impression, though, that these men were simply rubber stamping tradition. In fact, different segments of the church had conflicting views regarding some books, and the consensus was worked out through a process of extended controversy. At first glance this fact is disconcerting, but a little reflection can turn that around. After all, if the issue was thoroughly debated by the church's most capable scholars over a long period of time, during an age not far removed from a vast store of first-hand information about the writings and writers in question, our confidence about their conclusions can far exceed our confidence of our own ability to resolve the question after the passing of so many centuries.

Book	Date
Gospel according to the Hebrews	65-100
Epistle of Barnabas	70-135
I Clement	96
Epistles of Ignatius	100
The Didache	100-120
Gospel of Thomas	100
Epistle of Polycarp to the Philippians	108
Shepherd of Hermas	115-140
II Clement	120-140
Apocalypse of Peter	150
Acts of Paul and Thecla	170

An Excerpt from the New Testament Apocrypha

Appendix C (p. 132) contains a reading from the New Testament Apocrypha. (Note that "New Testament Apocrypha" refers to a different set of writings than the Apocrypha written during the intertestamental period and contained in the Catholic Bible. The New Testament Apocrypha has never been gathered into a single collection, because the comprised works number in the hundreds, many of them surviving only in fragments.) You can use this reading to illustrate the obvious difference in character between the canonical and the noncanonical books.

The Problem with Oral Tradition

Take a break to play a game where you whisper something to a person who whispers to someone else, and so on. See Appendix C (p. 134) for the story to spread by word of mouth and for further instructions.

Review Questions

1. What ancient author specifically described the Jews' beliefs regarding the Old Testament canon?

   Josephus

2. What is the "seal of approval" that God has put upon the inspired books?

   the testimony of the Holy Spirit

True or False

__T__ 3. The Bible refers to other books written during its own time.

__F__ 4. Once settled by the early church, the canon never again became a controversial issue.

__F__ 5. The Zechariah who was martyred wrote a book of the Bible.

Multiple Choice

__C__ 6. The canon of Scripture is

   A. the dozen or so books of the Bible that contain the key doctrines of salvation.
   B. the body of doctrine clearly taught in all the books of the Bible.
   C. the collection of books that give clear evidence of divine inspiration.
   D. the early church's decision that the New Testament is equal in authority to the Old.

_C_ 7. Which of the following is *not* one of the noncanonical books mentioned in this lesson?

    A. I Maccabees
    B. Bel and the Dragon
    C. The Testament of Hezekiah
    D. The Gospel of Thomas

_B_ 8. Which of the following was *not* used by the Jews of Jesus' day to designate a major section of the Old Testament?

    A. The Law
    B. The Wisdom Books
    C. The Psalms
    D. The Prophets

_A_ 9. Which of the following is *not* one of the criteria used to determine the canon of the New Testament?

    A. The book must contain Old Testament quotations.
    B. The book must have originated within the apostolic circle.
    C. The book must enjoy widespread acceptance.
    D. The book must not contradict scriptural teaching.

_A_ 10. The noncanonical books

    A. have some value but no authority.
    B. are the only books that Roman Catholics accept as Scripture.
    C. were written by companions of the apostles.
    D. were specifically pointed out and rejected by Jesus.

_D_ 11. The apocryphal books

    A. have never been printed as part of the Bible.
    B. were written by Roman Catholic monks.
    C. are biographies of early church leaders.
    D. contain both fact and fiction.

12. Explain the role of the apostles in determining which books are authoritative for the church. Is this role restricted to the New Testament writings? On what basis can a book not written by an apostle be considered apostolic? Name as many of these books as you can. What chronological limit does this test impose upon the New Testament canon?

[Key ideas: The apostles are the only ones to whom Jesus promised infallible guidance and binding authority. Whatever books they imposed upon the church are authoritative. Their role touches upon the Old Testament in that they imposed it as divinely authoritative. They also imposed their own teachings upon the church, teachings derived from Christ and written down in the books of the New Testament. The few New Testament books not written by an apostle derive their authority from their authors' close association with an apostle. The books not written by an apostle are Mark, Luke, Acts, Hebrews (unless it was written by Paul), James, and Jude. Since the last apostle died around A.D. 100, no book written after that date can be considered canonical.]

29

13. Explain how Jesus' statement about the martyrs "from Abel to Zechariah" confirms the traditional Old Testament canon of thirty-nine books.

[Key ideas: The Jews at the time of Christ accepted the same books we have in our Old Testament today, but they put them in a different order. Genesis was first; II Chronicles last (the order was according to time of writing rather than the period of history covered). With the books in this order, Abel would be the first martyr; Zechariah the last. In context, Jesus means to refer to all the martyrs of Scripture, so Abel and Zechariah put the beginning and ending limits on the number of books He accepted, confirming the traditional canon.]

14. Explain the difference between Martin Luther's questions about the canon and the unbelief of modern critics.

[Key ideas: Luther was committed to accepting the Scripture as God's inspired Word; modern critics dismiss all claims of inspiration. Luther wanted to be sure he knew which books he was obliged to obey; modern critics acknowledge only that some books have had great influence on Christian theology.]

15. Explain the key terms in this statement (the italicized words): "The *canon* of *Scripture* does not include the *Apocrypha*."

[Key ideas: The student should essentially reproduce the definitions given in the "Master the Terms!" box.]

16. What is the key test of canonicity? Defend this test against its most obvious objection.

the testimony of the Holy Spirit in the heart of the believer to the identity of His Word
[Key ideas: The most obvious objection to this test is its seeming subjectivity. However, upon further reflection one realizes that this means of confirming God's Word is the ideal means because it keeps man in his proper place. If God had ordained certain men to decide which books are canonical, men would stand in judgment over the text. God, however, has chosen to communicate to men what books are from Him by the testimony of His Spirit, who wrote the Scripture. Thus God's Word is not judged by men, but men are judged by His Word. Futhermore, history teaches us that this recognition is not a matter of personal preference or whim. In each generation believers have come to the same conclusion: these sixty-six books are God's Word.

17. Suppose tomorrow's newspaper contains the surprising headline: "Long lost New Testament book found, author claims to be the Apostle Peter." Would you consider this book canonical? Why or why not?

[Key ideas: This book should not be considered Scripture. The book fails to pass the test of widespread acceptance. According to our scenario, this work was unknown until its recent discovery. It is doubtful that God would inspire a book, but then not confirm its identity in the hearts of believers. Note that the test of widespread acceptance is really just another way of approaching the key test of canonicity: the testimony of the Holy Spirit in the heart of the believer. In the case of this recent discovery, we conclude that if for nearly two thousand years the Spirit has not been confirming the identity of this book as a part of Scripture, it must not be Scripture.]

CHAPTER THREE

Do You Have God's Word Today? *Part 1*

③

Memory Verses: I Peter 1:24, 25

Life Before Xerox

Imagine what life was like before someone invented the photocopier. Today, all you have to do to copy a document is find a copier, pay a small fee, and push a button. Instantly, your exact duplicate is ready. This process can sure help with library research!
Even more amazing is the fact that you can get thousands of copies with little effort if you have access to a printing press and know how to use it. Modern technology has made it possible for us to enjoy more newspapers, magazines, documents, and books than any previous generation. As a result, mass production of written materials has become something taken for granted, and we can hardly imagine a time when the case was otherwise.

But the case certainly was otherwise when the Bible was written. Furthermore, for nearly fourteen hundred years after John finished the Book of Revelation, the only way to copy the Scripture

GET THE BIG PICTURE

- ❏ Historical background
- ❏ The preservation of Scripture in the original languages: the science of textual criticism
  - • Goal of textual criticism
  - • Materials available for textual criticism
  - • Conclusion drawn by textual criticism: God has preserved His Word
    - - Preservation of the Old Testament
    - - Preservation of the New Testament
- ❏ The preservation of Scripture in translations

Note: The shaded portions appear in Part 2.

33

was to do it by hand. Do you suppose it would be humanly possible to copy the whole Bible without making a mistake? After all, if you're like most students, you sometimes have trouble even copying down your homework assignments correctly!

This lesson and the one following will explore some of the history and significance of the fact that for centuries the only way to reproduce the Bible was to copy it by hand. You probably thought the last lesson was a little more challenging than the first. These next two lessons will challenge you a little more yet. Perhaps it would be nice to leave out the hard things and stick to the simple. But people have a way of asking hard questions, and it is good for Christians to be able to answer them. In fact, you may have asked some of these questions yourself as you have worked your way through this book. So put your brain in gear and see what you can learn. We think you will be glad you did.

Facts and a Question

Let us put before you four historical facts and then raise an important question. The first fact is that God inspired every single word written down by the human authors of Scripture. The first lesson of this book established this crucial point of Christian doctrine. The second, third, and fourth facts are somewhat unsettling; they raise questions about whether God's Word has survived until today. The second fact is that the original documents of Scripture (called *autographs*) have disappeared. The third fact is that the handwritten copies (called *manuscripts*) by which the Bible has come to us over the centuries contain slightly different wording, and no manuscript is entirely free from copyists' errors. This is not a theory or a guess. Anyone who can read the original languages of Scripture can look at these manuscripts, or at reproductions of them, and see for himself that they occasionally differ from one another and that all evidence scribal mistakes. The fourth fact is that your Bible is a translation

God inspired every word in the autographs.

These autographs have disappeared.

No two existing manuscripts agree in every detail, and all contain some scribal errors.

Your Bible is a translation from these manuscripts.

from ancient languages; not a single word God originally inspired was in English.

The question, then, is obvious. How can you know that you have the Word of God today? How can you be sure that God's Word has not been defiled by the human hands that have copied and recopied it or by those who have translated it into your language? Can you really be certain that the Bible you hold in your hands is the Word of God?

This question deals with the issue of the *preservation* of God's Word. We have maintained that God inspired the sixty-six books of our Bible so that every word of them is His Word. The questions we raise in this lesson deal with what God has done to preserve His Word so that it remains available in every generation.

The preservation of God's Word is an important issue. Unbelievers have often seized upon the differences among the manuscripts as a reason not to believe that God inspired the Bible. If we wish to maintain our position, we cannot stop with showing that God inspired the words originally written. We also must show that those words survive today.

We will divide our discussion into two sections. First we will deal with the preservation of God's Word in its original languages by the process of manuscript copying. Later we will take up the preservation of God's Word in other languages by the process of translation.

Copy All You Want!

Your first reaction to the idea of copying someone else's work is probably negative. It sounds like cheating. Remember, though, that in the ancient world, the kind of copying we are discussing was the equivalent of today's book publishing. It was more than

35

an acceptable practice; it was a highly valued profession. The difference between "copying" then and now, of course, is that the ancient copyists were not representing the writings as their own; they were publishing the works of others.

The question we are dealing with is whether we can be sure that God's Word has survived intact over centuries and centuries of hand copying. If all the manuscripts were identical, there would be no question at all. But the manuscripts are not all the same, as we have observed. So how can we know that God's Word has been preserved for us in its original languages?

The first thing you need to realize about this question is that it involves issues that become quite complicated. The study of manuscript differences gets so complicated, in fact, that an entire field of scholarship has developed around it. Our purpose in discussing the issue with you is not to take you deep into these difficulties and the controversies that surround them. Instead, we want to help you understand some basic facts, and we want you to see how these facts support your faith that your Bible is God's Word.

Introduction to Textual Criticism

The field of scholarship that deals with differences in Bible manuscripts is known as *textual criticism*. In some ways this name is unfortunate, because it seems to suggest an attitude of disrespect toward the Bible. When we think of criticism, we think of jabs like these: "You're dumb." "Your clothes make you look fat." "What a terrible shot!" When you think about it a bit more,

DID YOU KNOW? While in college, Johann Albrect Bengel (1687-1752) encountered unbelievers who taught and wrote that tens of thousands of manuscript differences rendered the New Testament untrustworthy. Bengel decided he would study the preservation of the Greek text for himself before accepting these views. Contrary to what he was being taught, he concluded that the variations are remarkably few. He also discovered that no point of doctrine rests on an uncertain text. Bengel's work solidified his belief in verbal inspiration, and he went on to become a leading scholar in the field of textual criticism.

though, you realize that not all criticism is negative. Ten minutes before your date arrives, you may appreciate your mom's or dad's criticism concerning your appearance. And certainly we all like positive critical judgment: "I really like that dress." "You played a great game."

Whether positive or negative, criticism is basically the act of comparing one thing to another and making a decision or an evaluation. The people who give you compliments have judged your clothing or skills in comparison with others and have made a positive evaluation. A television critic judges programs by certain standards, compares them to other programs, and then forms an opinion, favorable or not. So criticism is simply an informed evaluation, a judgment passed by someone who is qualified to render it.

> *The textual critic seeks to determine what most likely was the original wording of the text by comparing the readings that differ.*

But who is qualified to pass judgment on the Bible? Of course, nobody is qualified to decide that something written in the Bible is false. But textual criticism does not deal with questions of truth or error in the Bible. There is another field of biblical criticism that does deal with those questions, and those critics *are* at fault for presuming to pass judgment on the Scripture. But textual criticism restricts itself to questions about what an author actually wrote. Where the manuscripts differ from one another, the textual critic compares the various readings

Higher Criticism and Textual Criticism. The field of study that often involves denying the truth of the Bible is called higher criticism; textual criticism is sometimes called lower criticism. Higher criticism deals with questions about how a piece of literature came into existence. These questions touch on issues such as whether ascriptions of authorship are true and whether the events of the book actually happened as recorded. Higher criticism, not lower criticism, is the field where skeptics and atheists show their unbelief.

37

(usually involving no more than a word or a brief phrase), formulates an educated opinion about which one is most likely the original, and makes a decision, which, by the way, is binding on absolutely no one.

Let's conclude our introduction to the field of textual criticism with two important observations. First, you should be aware that the science of textual criticism is not restricted to biblical studies. Serious study of any kind of literature involves questions about what a writer originally wrote in passages where various editions of his work contain different readings. Of course, textual criticism is especially important in the study of hand-copied literature, where such differences are especially numerous. Second, you should understand that textual criticism did not arise as a means of creating doubts about the Bible. Instead, it represents the natural response of people to the discovery that various copies of an important piece of literature contain differences in wording.

Sincere Christians have taken several approaches to some issues related to Bible manuscripts, and they have often entered into controversy over their positions. Without taking up these controversies, we can be thankful that so many scholars have spent so much time studying the differences between these manuscripts. The information they have collected and organized can help build our confidence in the trustworthiness of the Bible we use every day. A little later we will discuss some of this information. First, though, it will be helpful for you to learn more about the materials and methods for making books in ancient times. After all, neither Moses nor Paul could go out and buy a box of stationery or a ream of typing paper when he got ready to write something!

Ancient Books and Writing

No doubt your reaction to the words "Okay, class, take out a half sheet of paper" is something less than ecstatic. But paper itself really is a blessing. How would you like to carry a stack of heavy clay tablets to school every day? Teachers would have trouble, too, lugging home a briefcase full of homework to grade. To be fair, we must admit that clay would have its benefits: clay airplanes would fly farther and faster, and landings would be more

Egypt and Textual Criticism. Egypt has been an especially fruitful field for the discovery of ancient writings because its hot, dry climate has allowed papyrus to survive much better than in other regions. Much of our knowledge about history during Bible times has been gained from ancient manuscripts found in the caves and sands of Egypt.

38

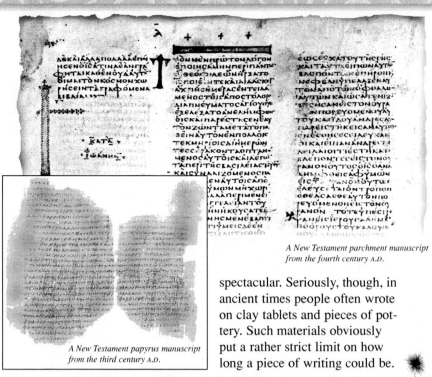

A New Testament parchment manuscript from the fourth century A.D.

A New Testament papyrus manuscript from the third century A.D.

spectacular. Seriously, though, in ancient times people often wrote on clay tablets and pieces of pottery. Such materials obviously put a rather strict limit on how long a piece of writing could be.

The most common material for literary writing in the ancient world was papyrus (from which we get our word *paper*). In fact, probably all the books of the Bible were written on papyrus. Papyrus is a reed found mainly along the Nile River in Egypt, growing as tall as twelve to fifteen feet. The manufacture of writing material involved cutting the reeds into sections about a foot long and slicing the pith (soft interior fibers) into thin strips. Two layers of moist strips, laid at right angles to one another, would be pressed together. After drying and smoothing, a sheet of papyrus became a very good writing surface. For long documents, sheets of papyrus would be glued together end to end and rolled up into a scroll.

The biggest problem with papyrus was that it would rot when exposed to

39

moisture. For this reason it is safe to assume that the original of each book perished shortly after it was written. A more durable writing surface, called parchment, was made of animal skins. The story is told of Eumenes II, king of Pergamum (in Asia Minor), who decided about 190 B.C. that he wanted a library to rival the one in Alexandria, Egypt. He hired the Alexandrian librarian to come to Pergamum to develop his library. Naturally, the pharaoh did not appreciate the competition and threw the librarian into jail. Also, he refused to sell papyrus to the king of Pergamum. Eumenes frantically sought an alternative. When he developed a high quality parchment, he began to promote it as an improvement over papyrus. Because it was durable and readily available, this new, improved parchment replaced papyrus for serious writing—though not until the fourth century A.D.

We mentioned earlier that ancient "books" were actually scrolls of papyrus or parchment, averaging twenty-five or thirty feet in length. Compared to today's books, the scroll format suffered from several serious drawbacks. The fact that one side remained blank represented a waste of writing material. Scrolls were bulky (the Old

1

Once cut into sections, the papyrus plant would be stripped of its outer sheath.

2

The remaining fibrous, pithy center was then sliced into strips.

3

The strips were then arranged in two layers at right angles to each other. After being hammered together, the layers would form a temporarily durable writing surface.

4

Papyrus sheets were commonly glued together in a scroll format until the second century.

Early in the second century, Christians began folding and gluing the sheets in a codex format.

DID YOU KNOW?

The side of a papyrus sheet with the grain running horizontally was easier to write on than the side with the grain running vertically. People would use the back side of a sheet only when necessary. This fact helps us understand the significance of the book of God's judgment that John saw, described in Revelation 5:1. This book, says John, was written "within and on the backside." This description suggests that these judgments are so extensive that one side of a scroll cannot contain them; the Lord had to continue writing on the back.

Testament filled fifteen to twenty scrolls—how many points do you suppose bringing your Bible to Sunday school was worth?), and they were cumbersome to use. Imagine a teacher saying to the class, "Open your scrolls to column fifty-three." You would have to unroll with one hand while rolling up with the other, never forgetting to count the columns as you went. Be thankful for the book format we enjoy today!

Let's move on now from the subject of book materials to that of writing itself. For much of the nineteenth and twentieth centuries, liberals have scoffed at the idea that Moses himself wrote the first five books of the Bible. They argue that Moses died long before writing existed in the ancient Near East. They also explain that what Moses taught was passed on orally from generation to generation until someone finally wrote it down.

We know now, however, that writing was widespread hundreds of years before Moses was born. Moses was writing in the late fifteenth century B.C. Archeologists have discovered the written law codes of Hammurabi, an ancient Babylonian king, dating three hundred years before Moses' birth. They have also discovered that slaves were writing on the walls of the salt mines in Egypt at the time of Moses. If slaves could write, certainly Prince Moses could. After all, Acts 7:22 mentions that "Moses was learned in all the wisdom of the Egyptians." Far from being illiterate, Moses probably knew three or four languages!

Manuscripts of the Bible

We come now to the question of how we know that, in spite of their differences, the ancient manuscripts preserve the Word of God. One way to answer this question would be to suggest that

41

one of the manuscripts should serve as the standard against which the others could be corrected. But we could make such a claim only if God guided us to select the right manuscript. In *any* question of truth, the only infallible guide is God Himself. God *has* given us clear leading on many subjects; we find His leading in the Bible. We learn there, for example, that Jesus is the Son of God, who lived a sinless life and died to pay the penalty for man's sin. There can be no question about this truth or about many others clearly taught in the Bible.

But does the Bible tell us which of its manuscripts contains the inspired text down to the smallest detail? Thankfully, it does not. We must search for our answer along other lines.

Are you surprised that we think this silence is a blessing? Think about this for a moment. Though such insight would simplify matters considerably, it would come at an awful price. We would have to conclude that God inspired an errant text, for no existing manuscript is perfect in every detail. But suppose God preserved a *perfect* manuscript that exactly preserved His Word.

> *The imperfections in the manuscripts are so minor that they have absolutely no bearing on the overall doctrines of Scripture.*

Wouldn't that be a blessing? No. Such a manuscript would present a strong temptation to idolatry. People in false religions often worship items such as bones, stones, and bits of cloth thought to have been associated with some godly saint or with the Lord Jesus Himself. People do this because human nature tends to venerate objects instead of worshiping God in spirit (John 4:20-24). A manuscript that was the Word of God in all its perfection would certainly become an object of worship, detracting from the glory of its author.

So we cannot claim that there is a single manuscript containing every single word, just as God inspired it. Instead, God has caused His Truth to spread throughout the world in copies that He has allowed to contain slight imperfections. The imperfections are so minor that they have absolutely no bearing on the doctrines of

MASTER the TERMS

- *Preservation:* God's work causing His Word to remain available in every generation
- *Textual Criticism:* the science of evaluating different manuscripts and forming opinions about which reading is most likely to be the original
- *Reading:* a specific form of a certain passage in a manuscript, usually restricted to a single word or a brief phrase.
- *Manuscript:* an ancient handwritten copy of some portion of Scripture

Scripture. There are no manuscripts that fail to present the essential truth about God's holiness, man's sin, and the gracious redemption provided in Christ.

These imperfections have never been an obstacle to faith for people who are inclined to believe. In fact, though God has not told us this in just so many words, it seems that He has purposely provided ammunition that people who hate Him can use to attack Him and to justify their refusal to believe. These minor difficulties, then, serve as a test of true faith that helps to separate the "sheep" from the "goats" (Matt. 25:32).

Looking Ahead to Part 2

It may seem uncomfortable for this lesson to end on a somewhat negative note. Remember, though, that this lesson is only Part 1 of the subject before us. In Part 2 we will help you recognize that lacking a perfect copy of God's Word need not rob us of our confidence in Scripture. God has preserved a great wealth of evidence supporting the conclusion that we do have God's Word today.

Review Questions

1. What two basic human activities has God used to preserve His Word in our language?

   copying and translation

2. Our word *paper* comes from the name of what ancient writing material?

   papyrus

3. The development of what writing material resulted from political and economic conflict between two nations?

   parchment

4. The law codes of Hammurabi prove what important point about the Bible's reliability?

   that writing was common in Moses' time

5. What is wrong with the following statement? "At the time of Christ, the biggest problem with books was their tendency to fall apart at the spine."

   Scrolls were used at the time of Christ, and they do not have spines.

_T_ 6. Differences among Bible manuscripts have been cited by unbelievers as proof that the wording of modern Bibles is unreliable.

_F_ 7. Our understanding of the Bible's preservation rests solely on the facts of history.

_F_ 8. There is no such thing as constructive criticism; criticism by its very nature is destructive.

Multiple Choice

_A_ 9. Which of the following is not true?

A. Only a few of the original manuscripts written by the Scripture writers themselves have survived until today.
B. The handwritten copies of the Bible that have come down to us from ancient times contain differences in wording.
C. Every single word that the Scripture writers themselves put on paper was exactly what God wanted, without error.
D. Copies of Scripture written on parchment were much more durable than those written on papyrus.

_D_ 10. In the ancient world, hand copying someone else's work for publication was

A. tolerated as a necessary evil.
B. punishable by imprisonment or death.
C. legal only if the copyist was a professional scribe.
D. a highly valued service.

A 11. Textual criticism is the field of scholarship that

    A. attempts to determine the original wording of passages where various copies or editions of a work differ from one another.

    B. examines the factual content of a piece of literature in order to determine its trustworthiness.

    C. attempts to determine whether an author is consistent with himself by comparing the ideas found in his various writings.

    D. compares the works of various authors in order to determine which authors are most reliable.

C 12. Textual criticism

    A. is a relatively simple and straightforward field of study.

    B. should be rejected by all who believe the Bible.

    C. has yielded results that increase our confidence that God has preserved His Word.

    D. has determined which ancient manuscripts of the Bible contain no errors.

    E. is a field of study that relates exclusively to the Bible.

B 13. Minor imperfections in Bible manuscripts

    A. make it difficult, but not impossible, to trust the Bible.

    B. do not change the character of the Scripture as the Word of God.

    C. have come about despite God's best efforts to prevent them.

    D. make it impossible to determine the message of the Bible.

14. Explain why J. A. Bengel became interested in textual criticism and how this study affected his thinking about the New Testament.

[Key ideas: See special box on Bengel on page thirty-seven in the student book. The most important ideas are that Bengel wanted to investigate the basis for unbelievers' claims that the New Testament had not been reliably preserved and that his faith was strengthened by what he found.]

15. When unbelievers compare manuscripts, they find differences that they take as justification for their unbelief. When believers compare manuscripts, they find a degree of similarity that strengthens their faith. Explain how these two groups can look at the same evidence and come to opposite conclusions.

[Key ideas: This is a challenging question that is not raised in the lesson. It arises from the facts given in the box on J. A. Bengel. Probably the best answer is that God has allowed many aspects of His creation to be ambiguous, as a test of men's willingness to respond positively to Him. Even the physical creation, such as the fossil record, works this way. God does not force people to acknowledge Him against their will, but He does give plenty of evidence to justify believing in Him and His Word. The evidence for faith is far greater than that against it, but God gives men the freedom to pursue their own inclinations.]

47

16. Explain why the term *textual criticism* does not imply an unbelieving attitude toward the Bible.

[Key ideas: The main point is the meaning of the word criticism. It does not necessarily signify an intent to disprove or belittle. The textual criticism of the Bible is simply the science of comparing various manuscript differences and attempting to decide what the writer originally wrote.]

17. Suggest two possible reasons for the Bible's not telling us which manuscripts preserve God's Word.

[Key ideas: First, if the Bible contained such a statement, that claim would ultimately impugn God's Word, since no perfect manuscript exists. Second, if the Bible contained such a statement and a perfect manuscript did exist, the manuscript would present a temptation to idolatry.]

CHAPTER FOUR

Do You Have God's Word Today? *Part 2*

④

Where We've Been and Where We're Going

In Part 1 of our discussion you explored some historical background about the hand copying of Bible manuscripts and learned something about the science of textual criticism. All this has focused on the issue of the preservation of God's Word in its original languages. In this lesson we will finish that aspect of the question of how we can know that we have God's Word today, and we will also go on to examine the second aspect of the question, which is how we can be sure that our translations preserve God's Word in our own language.

The Accuracy of Old Testament Manuscripts

Because of its age, the Old Testament has been especially criticized as inaccurate. The existing manuscripts are copies of copies of copies of copies, and each new copy not only perpetuated earlier copying errors but also added new errors of its own.

GET THE BIG
PICTURE

❏ Historical background
❏ The preservation of Scripture in the original languages: the science of textual criticism
  • Goal pursued by textual criticism
  • Materials available for textual criticism
  • Conclusion drawn by textual criticism: God has preserved His Word
    - Preservation of the Old Testament
    - Preservation of the New Testament
❏ The preservation of Scripture in translations

Note: The shaded portions appear in Part 1.

49

You can correct some copying errors by comparing newer copies with older ones, but the oldest Old Testament manuscripts that we have were produced up to thirteen hundred years after the original writings. Until recently, the oldest Hebrew manuscript we had was from the tenth century A.D., nearly twenty-three hundred years after the time of Moses. Bible-believing Christians' only response to these charges was simply to trust that God had accurately preserved His Word. Today two factors combine to bolster our confidence in the trustworthiness of the Old Testament text.

The Method of the Scribes

The first factor is the care with which the scribes copied the Old Testament. Jewish tradition relates that after Ezra the scribe finished II Chronicles and compiled the canonical books, he formed a school of scribes to be the guardians of the text. As time passed, the scribes developed an elaborate system of tests to insure the accuracy of their work. For example, they noted in the margin any word that occured only once in the Bible. If the word appeared elsewhere in a later copy, then the scribe knew there had been a mistake. The scribes also kept track of the number of letters and words in each book. For each book they knew the middle word and letter, and they even knew how many times each letter occurred. After finishing a book, they would check their work. If it did not pass and they could not find the problem, they would destroy the copy and begin again. Talk about frustration! Imagine having to recopy Isaiah!

Later Jews also had a high view of Scripture. Knowing that there was a curse on any who would add to or take away from the Word of God, they were extremely careful not to alter the text in any way. Only a trained scribe was allowed to copy the sacred

50

Care in Copying the Manuscripts

There are two exercises in Appendix C (p. 135) that would be helpful in reinforcing the principles of copying.

books. Thus the copying was left to an elite group with great skills, great care in checking their work, and an exalted view of the Word of God.

Christ Himself testified to these scribes' successful preservation of the Old Testament Scriptures. The Lord often quoted from the Old Testament, but He never designated a particular manuscript or group of manuscripts as corrupt or doctrinally incorrect. Had there been any cause for doubt, He certainly would have specified which text had the authority of Scripture. Thus, we are confident there was no significant change in the text during those four thousand years.

However, the Old Testament text had to pass through another fifteen centuries of hand copying before the age of movable type printing in Europe. How do we know it survived unchanged during that period? Critics often charged that the rate of change would have been so great that after a few centuries the text would have been unidentifiable with its prototype. After all, the oldest available manuscript went back to only the tenth century. Though that was one thousand years ago, it was still one thousand years *since* the time of Christ. But a startling discovery made just after World War II finally put this question to rest.

The Discovery of the Dead Sea Scrolls

In November or December of 1946, three Bedouin shepherds were tending their sheep in the Jordan Valley near the Dead Sea. One of the Bedouins had the habit of exploring caves, hoping to find treasure. As he walked along

The caves at Qumran

the base of a cliff, he threw a rock into a cave. To his amazement, he heard some pottery shatter. The shepherd called his two cousins over and described what had just happened. Because it was so late, they agreed to explore the cave together later. Being

The Discovery of the Dead Sea Scrolls. Various accounts of the discovery of the Dead Sea scrolls differ on some details. Our description follows that given by John Trever in *The Untold Story of Qumran* (Westwood, N.J.: Revell, 1965). We take Trever's first-hand involvement with the scrolls, nearly from the beginning, as our basis for confidence in the reliability of his account.

51

One of the Dead Sea Scrolls

too busy the next day, they delayed the exploration further.

Early on the third day the youngest cousin, Muhammed the Wolf, arose before dawn and slipped away to the cave alone. He slid in through a small opening and found several large earthen jars and some broken pottery. Only one jar contained anything of interest—three leather scrolls. Muhammed pulled out the scrolls and returned to camp. When his older cousins found out that he had sneaked off without them to explore the cave, they became angry and would not allow him to have anything more to do with the "treasure." The following March the two older cousins traveled to Bethlehem, where they eventually sold Mohammed's scrolls for $68.47. Later these three scrolls and one other were sold for $250,000 to the nation of Israel and are now displayed in the Shrine of the Book Museum in Jerusalem.

Since then tens of thousands of fragments from hundreds of manuscripts have been discovered in various caves around the Dead Sea. Part or all of every book of the Old Testament except Esther has been found. Many other documents have also been found, including books from the Apocrypha. All these finds date back to between 200 B.C. and A.D. 100.

The Shrine of the Book Museum, which houses some of the Dead Sea Scrolls

One of the most impressive manuscripts is the Isaiah scroll, one of Muhammed's original three. It is a leather scroll in good condition, containing almost the entire prophecy. This scroll dates back to 100 B.C., about a thousand years earlier than any Hebrew manuscript previously known. Here was the real test. How closely would the modern text match this old manuscript? *The texts were almost identical.* In fact, a committee using the scroll to translate Isaiah for a new English version found only thirteen points at which they preferred the scroll's wording over that of the traditional text.

These manuscript finds near the Dead Sea are among the most significant archeological discoveries of the century, and perhaps of all time. They forever shattered the view of liberal scholars that the original text of the Old Testament was hopelessly lost through centuries of copying. Now we possess physical evidence demonstrating that the Hebrew text used in Jesus' day agrees with the text we currently use.

The Accuracy of New Testament Manuscripts

The manuscript evidence for the New Testament has an entirely different complexion. In some respects it is even stronger than the evidence for the Old Testament, while in other respects it is not. Like the Old Testament evidence, it gives us strong assurance that God has preserved His Word.

Number and Age of the Manuscripts

The evidence for the text of the New Testament is far superior to that of the Old in terms of nearness to the time of writing. Among the more than five thousand Greek manuscripts (not to mention thousands of copies of early translations into other languages), more than a few date to within two hundred years of the original. The oldest known manuscript, containing a small portion of John 18, was copied perhaps as soon as twenty-five years after John died.

The oldest New Testament manuscript, containing a portion of John 18 (A.D. 125)

53

Number and Age of the Manuscripts. Here is a striking fact regarding the preservation of the text of the New Testament. Every other work of ancient literature contains passages where none of the surviving manuscripts gives a sensible reading. Textual critics of classical literature must often engage in "conjectural emendation," which is a fancy term for making an educated guess at what the author originally wrote. A few of the more radical textual critics of the New Testament have been dissatisfied enough with a few passages that they have conjectured a reading found in none of the manuscripts. But the vast majority of critics maintain that there is not a single passage for which none of the existing readings is acceptable. The bottom line of this view is that every single word of the original text has been preserved in some manuscript. In this respect, the New Testament is unique among all ancient literature.

That we have so many manuscripts of the New Testament from so early a period sets it apart from all other books as unique. For example, Homer's *Iliad*, the most popular book of the Greek speaking world, exists in only 647 manuscripts. Aristotle wrote around 340 B.C., and we have only five Greek manuscripts of any of his works, the earliest dating around A.D. 1100. Some lengthy passages from ancient authors have come down to us in only a single manuscript. Yet no one seriously questions whether we have the words of these authors. Why, then, should we question whether we have the Word of God? The manuscripts are so abundant that the New Testament scholar who compares his field to that of any other ancient literature feels almost guilty about the wealth of evidence available to him.

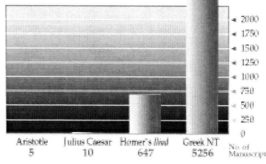

	No. of Manuscripts
Aristotle	5
Julius Caesar	10
Homer's *Iliad*	647
Greek NT	5256

Care in Copying the Manuscripts

Although New Testament manuscripts approach more closely the time of writing than do those of the Old, they contain more differences in wording. For several reasons the New Testament copyists were not as careful as the Jewish scribes. First, the copying was not restricted to a certain class of people and, as a result, was not regulated. There was no systematic testing for accuracy.

54

Copyists used various handwriting styles and abbreviations. While many copyists were painstakingly careful, a few were very sloppy and careless. Most, of course, simply did the best they could within practical limits.

A second reason for inaccuracy was the haste with which many books were copied. When Paul wrote a letter to a church, other churches in the area wanted copies as soon as possible. As Christianity spread, the demand for copies exceeded the supply. Wealthy patrons would spend great amounts of money for personal copies. The faster one could copy, the richer one became.

Yet another reason for mistakes in some copies arose from a method of copying that was developed to increase efficiency. In this method, one person would read a manuscript to a room full of copyists who wrote what they heard. To minimize errors, a corrector would check the work afterward. Still, some copying errors escaped notice.

You should not get the idea, though, that New Testament manuscripts are hopelessly at odds with one another. Repeatedly textual critics have observed that in over ninety-five percent of the text, these manuscripts agree with each other in the smallest details. Furthermore, no manuscript differs from another in the essential teachings of the New Testament. When we consider that the copying took place throughout Europe, North Africa, and

Western Asia over a period of some fourteen hundred years, the remarkable thing is not that these five thousand manuscripts differ from one another but that they are so strikingly alike.

Summary of Manuscript Evidence

God did not choose to do a miracle and preserve a perfect text of Scripture. When you think about it, though, the preservation of God's Word in the mass of manuscripts is for all practical purposes miraculous. Centuries of painstaking textual criticism have yielded results that give us absolute assurance regarding more than ninety-five percent of the individual words of the New Testament; the percentage for the Old is even higher. Most of the five percent in question are matters of word order and other differences that have little or no effect on the meaning. Even the few passages in which the meaning is questionable do not leave us in any doubt about any doctrine of Scripture. The doctrines in those passages in question are clearly taught in other passages in which the manuscripts agree. The textual evidence for the New Testament is so strong that if you constructed a Bible from the very worst manuscripts (those that differ most extensively from all the others), you would still have overwhelming testimony to the character of God and the way of salvation.

Think about how God works. Sometimes He does something that defies the laws of nature. Miracles of this type include Israel's crossing the Red Sea, Jesus' turning the water into wine, and so on. At other times, though, God simply engineers natural processes to achieve His goals. The story of Esther seems

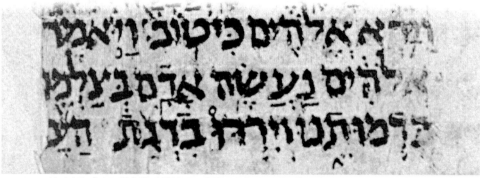

56   *A portion of the Leningrad Codex (A.D. 1000) showing Genesis 1:25-26*

Heretical Manuscripts?

It is fair to say that if Satan tried to corrupt the teaching of the Bible by prompting unbelievers to tamper with the manuscripts, his attempt was a miserable failure. Controversialists who love to point out instances of supposed doctrinal tampering ought to be fair enough also to point out the even greater number of passages where the so-called tamperers left the doctrines intact.

To demonstrate this fact to your stu-dents, engage them in an activity in which they must compare supposed heretical readings with readings found in the KJV. First, have them turn to Mark 1:1 and call on someone to read the verse. Then read the following, which is a translation of the same verse from certain manuscripts claimed by some to be heretical.

Mark 1:1, "The beginning of the gospel of Jesus Christ."

Ask your students how these two read-ings differ, and then have them list possible explanations for the differ-ence. Here are the possibilities they should mention.

1. The KJV preserves the original reading, and some scribes chose to remove the final phrase because they did not believe in Christ's deity.

2. The shorter reading is the original reading, and certain scribes added the final phrase to make Jesus' identity clearer (either on purpose or by mistake).

designed to emphasize this fact. None of that book's events appears to be miraculous. Yet the way the circumstances work together to secure the deliverance of God's people makes it clear that God Himself was at work. In the same way, God seems to have used "natural" circumstances and processes to preserve such a wealth of textual evidence supporting our Bible that, in hindsight, we realize that something supernatural has taken place.

Translations

What we have discussed so far relates to the preservation of God's Word in its original languages. Very few teenagers, however, have ever seen a copy of the Scripture in its original languages. We hope you have found our discussion of the ancient manuscripts profitable, but we realize that you are probably more concerned about the trustworthiness of your English Bible than about that of the manuscripts. Can you say with confidence that the Bible you hold in your hands is the Word of God?

Lost in Translation?

The issue, you recall, is whether God has preserved the words of Scripture. Of course, by its very nature, translation involves changing words. Sometimes the change is simple; the translator merely substitutes for a word in one language a simple equivalent in the other. If we could translate every word of Scripture this way, there would be no question about whether the resulting translation is truly the Word of God. But if you are taking a foreign language course, you know that you often cannot translate

A portion of Codex Sinaiticus (A.D. 350) showing John 1:18

57

The Challenge of Word Play. Word play is especially difficult to translate, since it usually involves a dual meaning of a single word (e.g., saying that a couple on a tennis date is "courting"). An interesting example of the difficulty of translating word play arose in the nineteenth century, in connection with the Congress of Vienna. This congress was intended to restore Europe's political order after the Napoleonic wars, but at one point it disintegrated into a social extravaganza. A witty Frenchman commented, *"Le Congrés danse, mais il ne marche pas."* The words literally mean "The Congress dances, but it does not work." The point is clear enough, but the translation loses the humor that springs from the dual meaning of the French verb *marcher:* "to walk" and "to function properly."

Another example of word play comes from the Old Testament. In chapter 1 of Jeremiah, God calls a young man to be His prophetic spokesman. While explaining the nature of his ministry, the Lord gives Jeremiah a vision:

---

3. The KJV preserves the original reading, and some scribes failed to include the final phrase by mistake.

Now ask your students, "Of these three possibilities, which one is least likely to be true?" The explanation least likely to be true is number one. Explain that the reason for this conclusion is that all these manuscripts clearly uphold Christ's deity in other places. For example, the same manuscripts that lack "the Son of God" in Mark 1:1 state very clearly Christ's

deity in John 1:1. To further demonstrate this point, have your students turn to John 1:18. After a volunteer reads the verse in the KJV, read the following, which is a translation of the same verse found in some of the same manuscripts that have the shorter version of Mark 1:1.

"No man hath seen God at any time. The only begotten God, who is in the bosom of the Father, he hath declared him."

Ask them what the variation is between these two verses. The "heretical" manuscripts read, "God" (refering to Jesus), and the KJV reads simply "Son." If the shorter reading in Mark 1:1 must be considered heretical because it lacks a clear statement of deity found in other manuscripts, then the KJV reading in John 1:18 must also be considered heretical for the same reason.

Your purpose in this exercise is not to prove that one reading is superior to the other. Your goal is simply to word-for-word without losing the meaning. For example, the English comment on the weather "It's cold" does not transfer word-for-word into Spanish. The Spanish expression for that idea, translated literally into English, is "Makes cold." For a biblical example, consider Matthew 1:18, which says that Jesus was conceived "before they [Mary and Joseph] came together." A strictly literal translation of this phrase would read "before than to come together them." You would quickly become frustrated with Bible reading if your Bible contained such confusing language every few verses!

A translator, then, cannot avoid changing some words, based on his understanding of what the text says and how the languages work. Since human understanding and decisions are imperfect, the only way for a translation to avoid all imperfection would be for God to control the translator just as He controlled the original writer.

Some Christians believe this is exactly what God did in 1611 when the King James Version was translated. If this is so, then our question is answered, for the translation itself is just as inspired as the original writings. While this position seems to simplify the issue of preservation, in the end it produces greater problems. For example, on what basis can we claim that these translators were inspired and others were not? Such a claim is complicated by the fact that the King James translators themselves did not believe they were inspired. Indeed, they recognized their own fallibility. Furthermore, if these men were inspired in the same sense the biblical authors were, how can we account for the fact that sometimes the meaning communicated by the KJV is different from that of the original languages? Should we correct the Greek and Hebrew manuscripts by the KJV? Admittedly, such a difference does not occur on every page, but it need occur only once to make this position quite problematic.

If all translations are subject to human error, can we still say that we have God's Word in our own language? Before we look at some pertinent Scripture portions, let's think about our own experience with translation. Have you ever watched the evening news and observed a newsman interview someone through an interpreter? Did it seem that they could understand each other?

58

demonstrate that there are no "heretical" readings among the more than five thousand Greek manuscripts. Though there are many variations among these many documents, all teach the same doctrine. This exercise has given only a couple examples; however, these examples are typical of the many readings supposed to be heretical.

In their preface, "The Translators to the Reader," those that produced the King James Version make some significant observations concerning the preservation of God's Word in translations.

"We do not deny, nay, we affirm and avow, that the very meanest translation of the Bible in English, set forth by men of our profession [Protestant religious viewpoint], (for we have seen none of their's [Roman Catholics'] of the whole Bible as yet) containeth the word of God, nay, is the word of God: as the King's speech which he uttered in Parliament, being translated into French, Dutch, Italian, and Latin, is still the King's speech, though it be not interpreted by every translator with the like grace."

Though the situation may have been somewhat awkward, each person was probably able to express his thoughts to the other quite well. While visiting Israel, I spent an evening with some Christians living in Bethlehem. Just before we left, one man, who didn't know English, prayed for all of us in Arabic. As I was leaving, I asked my host what the man prayed, and with apparent ease he listed several of the requests. It never occurred to me to question whether those ideas were in fact mentioned in the prayer. Why? I assumed—as we all do—that successful translation is not only possible, but that it is also a normal activity among those that know two languages well.

Now consider the New Testament and its world. In the first century A.D., the dominant translation of the Old Testament was the Septuagint. This translation was made around 150 B.C. from Hebrew into Greek, and it was far from ideal by today's standards. Some portions offer a good rendering of the Hebrew. Others, however, are very interpretive and not at all literal. Still other portions are so literal that the sense cannot be understood without comparing the Greek to the original Hebrew. Yet this was the Bible of the early church. In fact, Christ and His apostles frequently quoted from it and never criticized it. In one place the apostle Paul exhorts his Greek-speaking readers to "let the word of Christ dwell in you richly" (Col. 3:16). Since the only Bible these believers could read was the Septuagint, the apostle must have been encouraging Christians to read the Septuagint as "the word of Christ."

But what about the Septuagint? Are Christ and the apostles denying that these problems existed? No, their recommendation of

59

No Translation Can Be Entirely Literal

Appendix C (p. 138) contains a very literal translation of Genesis 1:1-5 and Matthew 1:18-25 that you may wish to use to illustrate this point further.

The Problem with an "Inspired Translation"

If we accept the King James Version as inspired, we encounter textual problems similar to what we encounter in the original language manuscripts. Just as the manuscripts differ from one another, so do various editions and printings of the King James Version. Some of these differences result from intentional revisions, but others result from printing errors much like scribal slips. Consider, for example, the following information, taken from David

Beale's *A Pictorial History of our English Bible* (Greenville, S.C.: BJU Press, 1982), p. 47. This book provides a great deal of enlightening information, much of which you could share with your class.

"A 1631 edition [of the King James Version was] dubbed the 'Wicked Bible' for its rendering of the seventh commandment as 'Thou shalt commit adultery.' A similar type of error led to the naming of a 1653 edition, the 'Unrighteous Bible,' which says in

What About Mistakes in Translations? Though the Word of God cannot be destroyed by the mistakes of translators, the individual words of Scripture are still important, and we do not have license to change them to suit ourselves. God inspired the very words of Scripture because He knew which words would best communicate His message. We are interested in recovering these individual words from the manuscripts to the greatest possible extent, and likewise we want our translations to reflect them as clearly as possible. But unless we are prepared to argue that God has inspired the very words of a particular translation, we must maintain that the Word of God transcends the individual words and survives intact even when some of those words have suffered imperfect handling by men.

Aramaic in the Old Testament. The passages written in Aramaic are Daniel 2:46–7:28, Ezra 4:8–6:18, 7:12-26, Jeremiah 10:11, and two words in Genesis 31:47.

this translation simply demonstrates what Christians throughout history have maintained—that minor mistakes in translation do not harm the character of God's Word. The Word of God is a message and a body of truth that so thoroughly saturates the stories, poetry, preaching, and personal correspondence of Scripture that it simply cannot be destroyed by any faithful attempt to copy or translate it. If the Word of God were so fragile that the slightest human touch could ruin it, we would be in big trouble, and God would be no remarkable author. The miracle and wonder of the Scripture is that God has given it to us in an indestructible form.

Do you own a Bible? Read it! It is God's Word to you. Obey it! Do not be troubled if a preacher or teacher suggests occasionally that a word or two might be understood differently, as long as the suggestion fits well with the Bible's overall teaching. Be thankful for that insight, and don't let it rob you of your confidence that you can trust the Bible you hold in your hands.

Which Translation?

But which Bible should you hold in your hands? You are probably aware of several English translations; perhaps you have wondered what the differences are and which one you should use. The King James Version has long been the standard translation for English-speaking Christians, but newer translations are easier to understand. Is there anything wrong with using a newer translation? This is a controversial question, and you will do well to respect the views of your spiritual leaders. In addition to their advice, here is some general information that can help you on this issue.

Always remember that the original writers of the Bible did not write in English. Nor did they write in Spanish, German, or French. Their language was Hebrew, Aramaic, or Greek. You should be sure that the translation you use reflects accurately the wording of the original languages. Of course, unless you learn these languages yourself, you will be dependent upon someone else's assessment of that accuracy. Learn as much as you can and learn whom to trust.

Also remember that "new" does not automatically mean "lib-

I Corinthians 6:9, 'the unrighteous shall inherit the kingdom of God.' Cotton Mather, complaining in 1702 of 'Scandalous Errors of the Presswork,' through which 'The Holy Bible itself . . . hath been affronted,' mentions one edition which expresses the problem very artistically: it makes Psalm 119:161 read, 'Printers [the true reading is *Princes*] have persecuted me without a cause.'"

These slips are remarkable because they result in surprising readings, and we can consider them unfortunate in that they cause people to make light of the Bible. But no one would seriously maintain that they destroy the character of the King James Version, because we can easily identify and correct them. The same principle applies to the vast majority of scribal slips among the original language manuscripts.

eral." Still, many new translations do push a certain agenda or deny a specific doctrine. Because they do not accurately preserve the meaning of the original texts, they are to be rejected. Beware of a new translation unless you have good reason to trust it.

On the other hand, the "old" translations (of which the King James Version is by far the most important) spring from orthodox theology and are therefore reliable. Their biggest problem is that they are hard to understand. But who said reading the Bible should be easy? We certainly do not want to confine people to a Bible they cannot understand, but the study of Scripture will always require discipline and diligent effort. A translation that takes the work out of Bible study is doing too much work for you and robbing you of the benefit. Furthermore, it probably does some of that work incorrectly and robs you of the most accurate meaning.

In closing, let us reiterate what we said above. If you have confidence that the Bible you hold in your hand accurately preserves the meaning of the Greek and Hebrew, there is no reason to wonder whether you have the Word of God. Thank God for it. Read it. Trust it. Obey it.

Conclusion

We have now covered the theological and historical portion of the question "How do I know the Bible is true?" Paul's declaration that "All scripture is given by inspiration of God" (II Tim. 3:16) means that the Holy Spirit supernaturally guided the writers of the sixty-six canonical books so that the words they wrote were the very words God intended. Furthermore, we can have confidence that God has preserved the wording of these books for us today.

At this point you may be saying, "You've been using the Bible to prove itself. Isn't this circular reasoning?" Up to this point, the material presented is specifically for you, the Christian teenager. But what if you were defending the Bible to someone who didn't believe its claims in the first place? Would they accept these verses? Probably not. In the next lesson we will look at some evidences outside the Bible that support its claims to be the Word of God.

61

Imperfections and the KJV Translators

Appendix D (p. 145ff.) contains a lengthy quotation from the King James translators' preface. The preface explains that the translators recognized the imperfections of translations yet maintained that the translations were nonetheless truly the Word of God.

Review Questions

1. According to tradition, what Old Testament character gave very careful attention to the preservation of the exact wording of the Hebrew text?

   Ezra

2. In order for a translation to be perfect in every word, God must have

   miraculously controlled the translators just as He controlled the original writers.

F 3. The accuracy of Old Testament manuscripts has never been seriously questioned, because some of the existing manuscripts were copied within a few years of the original writing.

B 4. Which of the following statements about Bible manuscripts is true?

   A. False religions have arisen based on a few manuscripts that are full of doctrinal errors.
   B. Each manuscript presents the same essential truths and doctrines.
   C. The oldest manuscripts in existence are no nearer to the time of writing than five hundred years.
   D. A few existing manuscripts contain the original text precisely as God inspired it.

B 5. Which of the following statements about Bible translations is false?

A. It is impossible to translate from one language to another without changing words.

B. Textual critics concentrate their study on evaluating the accuracy of the translations.

C. Some Bible translations are untrustworthy and should be rejected.

D. The most important point on which to evaluate a Bible translation is the accuracy with which it reflects the wording of the original languages.

D 6. The Dead Sea Scrolls

A. are the only manuscripts ever discovered that are actually older than the original writings.

B. have revolutionized the textual criticism of the New Testament.

C. guided the translators of the King James Version in resolving textual questions.

D. have confirmed the trustworthiness of the traditional text of the Hebrew Old Testament.

B 7. The Isaiah Scroll

A. finally revealed the true text of many obscure passages in the book.

B. is nearly identical in wording to manuscripts copied one thousand years later.

C. was destroyed by vandals before scholars studied it.

D. is written in Isaiah's own handwriting.

A 8. If a New Testament were put together from the manuscripts copied most poorly, it would

A. differ very little from the New Testament as you know it.

B. be full of dangerous errors found in heretical manuscripts.

C. obscure the character of God and the way of salvation.

D. be easier to understand than the New Testament as you know it.

63

B 9. A translation so easy to read that it takes the work out of Bible study would be

    A. welcomed by all Christians.

    B. doing too much work for the reader.

    C. easy to create if Christians would stop arguing about translation philosophy.

    D. impossible to create without the insights of modern textual criticism.

A 10. What should be your attitude toward the Bible translation you are expected to use?

    A. Read, believe, and obey it.

    B. Be suspicious of its teaching since no translation is perfect.

    C. Never consider the possibility that even a single word of it could be improved.

    D. Be ready to replace it with a newer version since newer versions are better than older ones.

A 11. Which of the following statements compares most accurately the strength of manuscript evidence for the Old Testament and that for the New?

    A. The New Testament evidence is stronger in terms of the number of manuscripts and their age but not as strong in terms of the manuscripts' similarity to one another.

    B. The New Testament evidence is stronger in every way.

    C. The legibility of Old Testament manuscripts makes up for what they lack in attention to detail.

    D. There is no significant difference between them.

B 12. Which of the following attitudes toward new translations is most dangerous?

    A. Reject them without questioning.

    B. Accept them without questioning.

    C. Accept them if they prove accurate to the original Greek and Hebrew.

    D. Reject them if they are viewed by some Christians as defective.

_C_ 13. The past two lessons devote more space to the subject of the preservation of God's Word in the original languages than to the subject of Bible translations. Which of the following statements seems to give the best reason for this emphasis?

   A. Since the original languages are the more obscure subject, they are more suitable for academic study.
   B. The original languages are the more controversial subject, requiring more detailed discussion.
   C. The preservation of the original languages is the fundamental issue, since a translation can be no more accurate than the original-language manuscripts.
   D. The original languages are the more commonly discussed subject, requiring you to be more prepared to defend your position.

Essay

14. Contrast the manuscript evidence for Aristotle's writings with the manuscript evidence for the New Testament.

[Key ideas: Aristotle's writings have survived in five manuscripts compared to more than five thousand for the New Testament. The oldest manuscript of Aristotle was copied about fourteen hundred years after the original writing, while several manuscripts of the New Testament date to within two hundred years of the original.]

65

15. Discuss several reasons that the New Testament manuscripts differ from one another more than those of the Old.

[Key ideas: The copyists were not professional scribes. Books were copied hastily, sometimes for profit. The method of reproduction in which a reader read the text to a room full of copyists also resulted in numerous copying errors.]

16. Is the preservation of Scripture miraculous or not? Explain.

[Key ideas: It is not miraculous in the sense that God does not seem to have set aside laws of nature and of everyday human behavior in preserving His Word. He has used the natural processes of copying and translation, and He has allowed people to make mistakes in their handling of the Scripture. Yet, as we look back, and as we compare the preservation of the Bible to that of other ancient literature, we realize that God has providentially allowed the Bible to survive in an amazingly trustworthy fashion. As a result, we can have far more confidence about its very words than we could reasonably expect these natural processes alone to yield. In this sense, the preservation of God's Word is miraculous.]

CHAPTER FIVE

More Evidence? Read On!

⑤

Memory Verses: Matthew 16:16-17

Keeping Evidence in Its Proper Place

Let's start this lesson by summarizing what we have covered so far. Everyone wants reliable information, especially regarding life-and-death issues. We have claimed that the Bible is reliable because it comes from the ultimate reliable source. When it comes to life and death, God is the expert because He created all, sees all, and controls all. He is infallible, and so is His book. But the question "How do you *really* know?" keeps nagging us. We have used the Bible to prove itself, but if the Bible is not entirely reliable, we cannot trust its claim to be God's Word. How can you know that the Bible is true?

"Proving" the trustwortiness of the Bible should be no different than proving any book's reliability: we collect evidence, weigh that evidence, and then draw reasonable conclusions—or is it different? We must remember that if the Bible is God's Word, it is the supreme authority by which all evidence and arguments must be judged. Furthermore, if the Bible's explanation of man's spiritual condition is correct, human beings cannot accurately evaluate the proof for the Bible's reliability. Men are sinners, unwilling to face the truth about themselves and the holy God that made them. Evidence alone—no matter how compelling—cannot convince fallen humans to believe the Bible.

Kinds of Evidence. Theologians often refer to the Bible's own testimony to its reliability as *internal evidence,* while those evidences found outside the Bible are called *external evidences.* This lesson focuses on external evidences.

67

Believing It All

The evidence presented in this lesson reminds us of the Bible's reliability in areas of science, history, and geography. Since many people believe that the Bible is true only in areas of "faith and practice," you may want to take some time during this lesson to remind your students of the importance of believing that all of the Bible is inerrant. We have already dealt with some of the implications of denying inerrancy in the case study of Clark Pinnock. At this point, however, a more thorough discussion of inerrancy is in order. Use the section entitled "Believing It All" (found in Appendix C, p. 139) to guide your class through this important discussion.

GET THE BIG PICTURE

❑ Evidence from Science
  • Biology
  • Medicine
  • Earth Science
❑ Evidence from Archeology
  • Geography
  • History

❑ Evidence from Prophecy
  • Daniel
  • Isaiah
❑ Evidence from Personal Testimony
  • A Chicago Gangster
  • Down-and-Outers
  • Those on the Deathbed

Our Lord's earthly ministry demonstrated this truth in a striking way. Two groups of people observed Jesus closely for three years: Christ's disciples and the Pharisees. The disciples were common, uneducated fishermen, and the Pharisees were well-trained biblical scholars. Both groups had heard that Jesus of Nazareth was God's Messiah (John 1:41; Matt. 26:63-64), and both saw many miracles designed to prove that claim. They knew that Jesus could heal the crippled, give sight to the blind, and even raise the dead. Each group, however, responded differently to Jesus' ministry. Amazingly, those most familiar with the Scripture rejected Him as a demon-possessed blasphemer and therefore demanded His crucifixion. The uneducated fishermen, on the other hand, died martyrs' deaths because they proclaimed Him as the Son of God. Why did these two groups respond differently?

In His conversation with a Pharisee, Jesus indicated the reason these religious leaders rejected Him. Nicodemus approached Jesus one night and willing acknowledged Him as "a teacher come from God" (John 3:2). But he resisted being born again. Nicodemus claimed that Christ's message was difficult to understand and needed to be clarified and validated: "How can a man be born when he is old?" he inquired (John 3:4). Jesus, however, knew that Nicodemus's quandary was due not to a lack of information or evidence. His problem was sin. Without qualification Christ asserted, "He that believeth not is condemned. . . . And this is the condemnation, that light is come into the world, and men loved darkness rather than light, because their deeds were evil" (John 3:18-19). People reject the gospel not because evidence for belief is inconclusive. They reject the truth because they love the darkness of their sin rather than Jesus Christ, the Light of the world.

Why, then, did the disciples receive Jesus as the Messiah? God changed them. As His earthly ministry neared its close, Jesus asked the disciples who they thought He was. Peter, speaking for the disciples, responded confidently, "Thou art the Christ, the Son of the living God" (Matt. 16:16). Interestingly, Christ did not attribute Peter's correct confession to the miracles he saw, his unusual spiritual insight, or even his willingness to obey God's will. Jesus explained that Peter had grasped His true identity because God had revealed Himself to him: "Blessed art thou, Simon Barjona: for flesh and blood hath not revealed it unto thee, but my Father which is in heaven" (Matt. 16:17).

Think about your conversion. Did you become a Christian because someone proved to you that the Bible is true? Most likely you received the Lord because you were overwhelmed with your own sinfulness. Since the Scripture offered you forgiveness and eternal life, you repented and believed the gospel. It wasn't the "undeniable evidence" that moved you. Through the Holy Spirit, the Father convicted and changed your heart.

Now let's return to our original question: "How do you know the Bible is true?" We know the Bible is true because God has convinced us that it is true. How do we know He has convinced us? *The Scripture captivates our hearts.* Every time the Bible is attacked, our souls leap to its defense. Whenever it is vindicated, we swell with joy and satisfacton. When it speaks comfort, we take comfort. Whenever it calls us to action, we are moved.

Consequently, when witnessing, we must not tell an unbeliever that evidence alone will convince him to trust the Bible. He, like the Pharisees, may carefully consider our "proofs" and still find them unconvincing because he can think of another way to account for the evidence. Before our carefully crafted arguments can be effective, the skeptic must experience the Father's mysterious yet powerful work in his heart. Then the evidence will become as compelling for him as it is for us. Until he knows that change, we must focus on calling him to forsake his sin and believe the gospel, as Christ dealt with Nicodemus.

Nevertheless, both the saved and unsaved can profit from the four kinds of evidence presented in this lesson. The apostles themselves regularly appealed to the fact that they were eyewitnesses of Jesus' miracles (Acts 2:32; I Cor. 15:1-11; II Pet. 1:16).

69

God frequently uses such proofs when He brings a person to conversion, though it is God that changes the person—not the evidence. This evidence can also help us as believers. Because we have believed, we can effectively evaluate the evidence for believing. "Through faith we understand" because faith is "the evidence of things not seen" (Heb. 11:1, 3). By reviewing the objective bases for our faith, we grow in the confidence that the Bible's teachings are not "cunningly devised fables" (II Pet. 1:16). Thus, we realize anew that embracing Christ is not a leap in the dark but a leap into the light.

Evidence from Science

Have you ever looked at an old science textbook? Along with pictures of people in funny clothes with weird hairstyles, you will find concepts and theories that are out-of-date. For example, scientists have recently changed their ideas concerning the nature of the atom. The idea of the nucleus surrounded by orbiting electrons is now obsolete. Protons and neutrons, formerly considered the smallest particles of matter, can now be subdivided into quarks. Someday this "knowledge" is likely to give way to further discoveries. Genetics is another area of technological explosion. Scientists can now clone living organisms, something thought impossible a short time ago. Man broadens his horizons when he develops stronger microscopes and telescopes or arrives at a better system for collecting and analyzing data. As communications technology allows information to spread faster and more widely, mankind is continually revising scientific theories to match new discoveries. In such an advanced age, ancient literature seems almost absurd when it comes to science and medicine—ancient literature, that is, other than the Bible. The Bible rises above the thinking of its day both by avoiding errors and by stating facts that the ancient world seems not to have known. Some of its teachings are so advanced that they were not even understood until fairly recently. Here are some examples from various branches of science.

Strange Examples from History

In the field of medical science, Galen (second century A.D.) was second in importance only to Hippocrates. Yet Galen thought that blood was formed in the liver and then flowed through the veins, which also originated in the liver. He also believed that the blood vessels brought blood near the body's surface, where the blood was transformed into flesh.

Strange ideas about medicine appear in every age. Martin Luther encouraged the eating of horse dung for health reasons, and even today there is no dearth of quackery. But the Bible never stoops to absurdities. When it does recount something unusual, such as Jesus' putting mud in a blind man's eyes, it is recording a miracle, not recommending a medical remedy.

Biology

Leviticus 17:11 states, "For the life of the flesh is in the blood." Moses made this statement about 1445 B.C. Thousands of years later, physicians believed that many diseases should be treated by letting out "bad" blood. But, for some reason, the patients kept dying. Now we know how important blood is for sustaining life. Organizations like the Red Cross hold blood drives regularly in order to have blood available for people who have lost too much. Rather than take blood away, we put blood in. Modern science has been a little slow in "discovering" this truth stated by Moses more than three thousand years ago.

How did Moses know that blood was necessary for life? We cannot know whether God told Moses directly or whether Moses learned this fact from some human source. What we do know is that Moses, under divine inspiration, wrote the truth.

Medicine

The Bible helped Scottish doctor James Simpson to bring about a major advance in medicine. As a surgeon in the nineteenth century, he was troubled over the trauma endured by patients undergoing surgery. Often the pain was so great that the patient died on the operating table. Simpson wanted to find a way for his patients to be unconscious during the ordeal. One day he called some friends together to try out a new gas he had discovered. As they talked, Dr. Simpson uncorked the bottle. Sometime later when the doctor regained consciousness, he noticed that all of his friends had passed out too. Within a week, Dr. Simpson had used this anesthetic, chloroform, in several operations and childbirths.

At first there was strong opposition to the use of chloroform during childbirth. Many argued that God intended for women to

More on Simpson. For more information on James Simpson, see Robert H. Curtis, *Triumph Over Pain* (New York: David McKay Company, Inc., 1972), pp. 74-78.

DID YOU KNOW? George Washington was a victim of the practice of bleeding sick patients. On December 12, 1799, he traveled by horseback for several hours through cold and snow. Doctors treated the resulting severe case of laryngitis by bleeding him. After four heavy bleedings, Washington died on December 14.

71

suffer in childbirth and that chloroform circumvented God's purposes. It was then that James Simpson realized that putting a patient to sleep before surgery was not new. Genesis 2:21 reads, "And the Lord God caused a deep sleep to fall upon Adam, and he slept: and he took one of his ribs, and closed up the flesh instead thereof." Thousands of years before 1847, God had put His patient to sleep before operating on him. This argument was enough to convince Queen Victoria. She gave birth to her seventh child under the influence of this anesthetic. For the English, the matter was settled, and Dr. Simpson was knighted for his discovery.

Earth Science

Job, who lived probably about the time of Abraham, declared that God "hangeth the earth upon nothing" (Job 26:7). How did he know this? Obviously, he did not have access to telescopes, satellites, or space shuttles. The theory commonly accepted by the ancients pictured the earth as a circular plate supported by four elephants standing on a big sea turtle. We know the truth today because we now have the benefit of Galileo's telescope, Johannes Kepler's discoveries regarding the orbit of the earth around the sun, and many observations made from outer space. But how did Job know? God must have told him.

In contrast to other ancient literature, the Bible is strikingly accurate in its statements about various matters of science and medicine. For a book that is thousands of years old, it is remarkably up-to-date. This book can be only God's doing.

Evidence from Archeology

Within the past one hundred years, archeology has unearthed a number of finds that validate the accuracy of God's Word in matters of geography and history. Christian archeologists have rejoiced at these findings, which have forced even their non-Christian colleagues to respect the accuracy of the biblical record.

W. F. Albright

Many scholars consider William Foxwell Albright (1891-1971) the greatest archeologist of his generation—a generation that witnessed an explosion of archeological discoveries relating to the Bible. Though Albright never changed many of his unbelieving positions concerning the Scripture, archeology did force him to reconsider much of the liberalism he had been taught.

"I defend the substantial historicity of patriarchal tradition [the narratives in Genesis]. . . . I have not surrendered a single position with regard to early Israelite monotheism but, on the contrary, consider the Mosaic tradition as even more reliable than I did. . . . I now recognize that Israelite law and religious institutions tend to be older and more continuous than I had supposed—in other words, I have grown more conservative in my attitude to Mosaic tradition."
—*From the Stone Age to Christianity,* (Garden City, New York: Doubleday, 1957), p. 2.

Geography

When the nation of Israel was established in 1948, Jews who were displaced during World War II flooded the tiny country of Palestine. Because the country was practically a desert, there was a dire need for more water sources. To find new water supplies, the state of Israel hired an archeologist named Nelson Glueck, well known for his success in using the Bible to locate ancient sites. Mr. Glueck simply took his Bible in hand and looked for texts describing water sources. He found these locations and instructed his men to dig there. Wherever they dug, they found water.

Glueck made another important contribution to Israel's economy based on Deuteronomy 8:9, which describes Israel as "a land whose stones are iron, and out of whose hills thou mayest dig brass." At the time, Israel was not known for its vast mineral deposits. In fact, many thought Glueck was on a wild goose chase in trying to prove that verse accurate. But Glueck's conviction was strengthened by other verses in I Kings and I Chronicles indicating that copper mining and metal working took place in Israel. After a lengthy search, he discovered the ancient copper mines in the south of Israel dating back to the time of Solomon. These mines had vast mineral resources that were far from exhausted.

More on Glueck. For more information about Nelson Glueck's discovery, see George S. Syme and Charlotte U. Syme, *The Closer You Look the Greater the Book* (Denver: Accent Books, 1976), p. 48.

Copper in the Old Testament. First Chronicles 4:14 reveals that there was a "valley of *Charashim* [smiths]." First Chronicles 4:12 refers to *Irnahash*, which literally means "city of copper." There is also a brief reference to coppersmith work in I Kings 7:45-46.

Copper would have been a tremendous source of wealth for Solomon. For more information see Nelson Glueck, "The Bible as Divining Rod," *Horizon* 2 (November 1959): p. 52.

73

History

Archeology has also been helpful in validating the historical accuracy of biblical accounts. At one time, liberals believed that there was no such person as King Belshazzar. Daniel 5 records that Belshazzar, the son of Nebuchadnezzar, was the king of Babylon on the night the city fell to the Persians. On that evening, God had written a message on a palace wall, announcing the inevitable doom of the kingdom. Unable to interpret the writing, Belshazzar summoned Daniel and promised him the third highest position in the kingdom if he could explain what the writing meant. Until recently the Bible's record of a king named Belshazzar was unsupported by any other historical source. Nebuchadnezzar's son, ancient historians tell us, was Evil-Merodach, and the king when Babylon fell was Nabonidus. Obviously, the biblical account did not match historical records.

A cuneiform tablet that mentions Belshazzar by name

A recent archeological discovery of an ancient library has cleared up this apparent discrepancy. From it we learn that although Nabonidus was king of Babylon when the city fell, he had been away from the city for some time, down in the southern part of his empire. In his absence, he had appointed his son, Belshazzar, to rule in his stead. This explains why Daniel was awarded the *third* highest position in the kingdom; it was the highest position Belshazzar could give. Furthermore, ancient Egyptian records indicate that "son" did not have to mean the actual son or even a descendant of the king. It could simply refer to kingly succession.

Apparently, the person who wrote the book of Daniel had a firsthand account of the court life in Babylon, since accounts written in antiquity seem unaware of Belshazzar. These finds strengthen our faith that Daniel himself wrote the book that bears his name.

Another example of archeology's importance in disproving the critics' view that the Bible is a collection of myths and legends was the discovery of Boghazkoy, the capital city of the Hittite Empire. The Bible mentions the Hittites several times and indicates that they were a powerful people. Until the last hundred years or so, however, historians could not find one scrap of evidence (outside the Bible) that this empire existed. The discovery of Boghazkoy confirms that the Hittites were a powerful people located in the region of modern-day Turkey. Once again, the Bible proves to be correct.

So we see that the Bible is uniquely accurate in areas of science and medicine thousands of years prior to modern theories. The accuracy of details concerning geography and history indicates that the writers were writing firsthand accounts at the time the books were reported to have been written.

The evidences we have studied so far demonstrate the Bible's reliability, but most of them do not deal directly with the issue of divine origin. We will now examine two other kinds of evidence that go further in showing that God must be the author of this inerrant book.

Evidence from Prophecy

The first supernatural evidence we will consider deals with the accuracy with which Old Testament prophets foretold future events. We will focus our attention on one prophecy from Daniel and one from Isaiah.

Daniel

Daniel 8 records a vision of a ram and a goat, a vision given to Daniel during the third year of the reign of Belshazzar, king of

The Bible Superior to Herodotus. Herodotus, a famous Greek historian born about 484 B.C., wrote *History,* a detailed account of the Persian wars. He makes no mention of Belshazzar in his book.

More on Daniel. See Merrill Unger, *Archeology and the Old Testament* (Grand Rapids: Zondervan, 1954), pp. 297-300. Unger discusses the historicity of Daniel at length. See Unger, pp. 91-92.

More on Daniel 8
For more detail on the prophecy in Daniel 8, see Appendix C (p. 141).

Babylon. In verses 20-22, an angel explains to Daniel the meaning of the dream. The ram stands for the Medo-Persian Empire; the goat stands for the kingdom of Greece that arose and destroyed the Persian Empire. The goat sports a single horn that is broken at the peak of its power; this horn represents Alexander the Great. Alexander died at the age of thirty-three, despairing that he had no more worlds to conquer. His kingdom was then divided among four of his generals, just as the prophecy predicted by picturing four horns sprouting in place of the broken one.

Since Daniel lived about two hundred years prior to Alexander the Great, it is obvious that he could not have predicted these political developments on his own. Granted, he might have been able to guess that Babylon would soon fall. He probably could see "the handwriting on the wall" that Persia was gaining power. But in Daniel's time, Greece was nothing but a collection of tiny city-states engaged in constant war with one another. For Daniel to foresee that Greece would become a world power would be like someone today foreseeing that Rwanda, a small nation whose recent history is filled with civil strife, will one day dominate the world. But Daniel did not stop there; he also predicted that Greece would come to power under the leadership of a single individual whose reign would be cut short and whose kingdom would be divided among four successors.

The facts of history leave us with only three possible conclusions: either Daniel was an incredible guesser, someone else wrote the "prophecy" after the fact, or God revealed the information to Daniel. The first option is in fact incredible, in the strict sense of the word ("impossible to believe"). We can also rule out the second possibility because the historical details and the writing style signal that the book was written at the time of Daniel. We are left with the third answer: God must have revealed this prophetic information to Daniel. The Bible is the Word of God.

Isaiah

Isaiah 45:1 reveals in another remarkable prophecy that God had anointed a king named Cyrus to do great things. Isaiah 44:28 reveals that Cyrus would permit Israelite captives to return to their

---

The Unbelievers' Dilemma. Theological liberals find themselves facing the same three possible conclusions that we have presented here. However, they opt for the second solution. The date of Daniel is one of the major dividing lines between liberals and conservatives. There is simply no rational way to believe that a mere human wrote Daniel prior to Alexander's death. One viewpoint or the other must give.

The liberal assumption that the book of Daniel could not have been written before 167 B.C. falls flat when one considers linguistic evidence from the Dead Sea Scrolls. Aramaic scrolls found in the Dead Sea caves were considerably different linguistically from the Aramaic portions of Daniel. In fact, the Aramaic in Daniel matches the style of the fifth century B.C.

For further research see William Sanford LaSor, "The Dead Sea Scrolls," in the *Expositor's Bible Commentary*, vol. 1 (Grand Rapids: Zondervan, 1979), p. 403.

land and rebuild the city of Jerusalem. Isaiah wrote about 150 years before Cyrus was even born. The Jews were still in the land of Palestine; none of them were captives in another land. The Babylonian Empire that would conquer Judah did not yet exist.

How could Isaiah know that all this would happen and even identify the deliverer by name? Could it have been coincidence? It would be as though one might guess that a George Snowcroft will be president of the United States two hundred years from now. We cannot even be positive that the United States will still exist then as we know it today. Can *you* name a person who, in two hundred years, will lead a nation? *God* must have spoken to Isaiah.

The Bible's claims are further strengthened when we consider that no one has ever proved a prophecy to be false. Many skeptics have sought to discredit the Bible and would jump at the chance to exploit a false prophecy, but they cannot do so. All these fulfilled prophecies lead to an obvious conclusion. A human prophet may hit a few guesses, but no man guesses right every single time. Only God can accurately foretell the future.

Cuneiform cylinder seal similar to the one that records Cyrus's release of the Jewish captives

Evidence from Personal Testimony

Since people cannot observe these fulfilled prophecies first-hand, they may excuse such evidence as inconclusive. People demand visible proof that they can see today. This demand leads us to the most powerful external evidence of the Bible's claims as the Word of God—the testimony of changed lives.

A Chicago Gangster

George Mensik was a right-hand man of Chicago gangster Al "Scarface" Capone. From 1925-31, Capone controlled the

More About Mensik. George Mensik died on October 29, 1974. He was extremely reluctant to share the details of his conversion. Whenever he shared his testimony, he would not allow his family members to remain in the service. Therefore, it is difficult to get information on his life. The facts of this story are taken from a cassette recording of his testimony, a written interview, and the testimony of friends.

Ironside's Story. George and Charlotte Syme record this incident in the life of Harry Ironside in their book *The Closer You Look the Greater the Book*, p. 146.

George Mensik

underworld of Chicago crime. As wicked as George Mensik was, God began to work in his heart. Mensik's wife and five-year-old daughter trusted Jesus Christ as Savior and started praying for Mensik's salvation. Burdened with guilt over their pleas, he came home drunk one day, determined to shoot them both. He picked up a loaded pistol and walked into his daughter's room. As he pointed the gun at the kneeling figure of the girl beside her bed, he heard her small voice crying up to God to save her dad. Mensik broke down and shortly thereafter received Christ.

George Mensik's life changed dramatically. His life was in great danger for a few years. Thugs would jump from black limousines and shoot at his house. But even in the midst of the persecution, he had joy and peace in his heart. He had a prison ministry and was able to lead many souls to Christ. The state of Illinois completely cleared his criminal record. Once able to eat ice cream and laugh while his henchmen tortured somebody, as a Christian he would weep over lost souls and the effects of sin in people's lives.

Down-and-Outers

Another story is told of the famous preacher Harry Ironside. He was visiting a street meeting in San Francisco and was asked to preach. While on the platform, Dr. Ironside was handed a card on which a well-known agnostic had written a challenge for a debate the following Sunday afternoon. The topic would be "Agnosticism versus Christianity." After Ironside read the challenge out loud to the crowd, he agreed to the debate on one condition. The agnostic must bring with him one man who had been saved from a life of alcohol and one lady rescued out of a life of prostitution due to their belief in agnosticism.

Harry Ironside

For his part, Ironside would bring one hundred such converts to Christ from San Francisco alone. With a smirk on his face and a wave of his hand, the agnostic quietly slipped his way out of the cheering crowd. The Bible is powerful, able to transform the most wicked sinner.

Those on the Deathbed

Voltaire

The Bible is also able to provide peace in a person's heart. Have you ever heard of anyone who, on his deathbed, lamented the fact that he had lived his life as a Christian? On the other hand, many atheists have died discontented, realizing that they had rejected the truth. Consider, for example, the French philosopher Voltaire. One of the most celebrated figures of his day, he used his wit and worldly wisdom to ridicule Christianity and the Bible. But as he lay on his deathbed for two months, he turned against his flatterers with rage: "Begone! It is you that have brought me to my present condition. Leave me, I say; begone! What a wretched glory is this which you have produced to me!" After his death, his nurse is reported to have said often, "For all the wealth in Europe I would not see another infidel die."

On the other hand, consider the last words of Joseph Barker, an American infidel who came to Christ and became a preacher of

Where to find the quotations. These quotations are from S. B. Shaw, ed., *Dying Testimonies of Saved and Unsaved: Gathered from Authentic Sources* (Berwyn, Ill.: Shaw, 1898) and Herbert Lockyer, *Last Words of Saints and Sinners* (Grand Rapids: Kregel, 1969).

DID YOU KNOW?

Voltaire once said that within a century of his death, the Bible would be studied only as an antiquarian relic. At another time he said, "In twenty years Christianity will be no more. My single hand shall destroy the edifice it took twelve apostles to rear."

If you were God, how would you deal with such a man? Here's what God did. Within fifty years of Voltaire's death, his house and printing press were in the hands of the Geneva Bible Society, playing a key role in the printing and distribution of the very book Voltaire had scorned!

79

the gospel. A few days before his death, he spoke these words to his son and two friends: "I wish you to witness that . . . I die in the full and firm belief in Jesus Christ. I am sorry for my past errors; but during the last years of my life I have striven to undo the harm I did, by doing all that I was able to do to serve God, by showing the beauty and religion of His Son, Jesus Christ. I wish you to write and witness this, my last confession of faith, that there may be no doubt about it."

Test Yourself!

Someone has well said that your life is the only Bible some people will ever read. Those who read the Bible itself will find there a clear picture of a holy and loving God. What about those who read only your life? What portrait of God do your words and deeds paint? How much holiness is evident? How much genuine love?

Here is a man who started out like Voltaire, but God's grace reached him and changed him, and his deathbed was entirely different from Voltaire's. The value of an investment lies not in its short-term performance but in what it is worth at its end. A human life is an investment, and the final outcome tells a convincing story: lives lived in rebellion against God's Word end in total loss, but those lived in obedience and faith yield an immeasurable return of peace and satisfaction in Christ. What the Bible accomplishes in the life of a believer is perhaps the strongest testimony to its identity as the Word of God.

Conclusion

What you have learned about external evidences supporting the Bible will help you to face Bible critics with greater confidence. No amount of evidence, however, will force somebody to believe the Bible. Satan has blinded the minds of this world to the light of God's Word. God's gift of faith is necessary for one truly to accept the Bible as God's Word. Certainly our faith is not a leap in the dark since there is much evidence to support it, but faith is necessary nonetheless. If you must defend what you believe to somebody who is searching, pray hard that the Holy Spirit will guide that person to the truth.

God Can Change Unbelieving Scholars

You may wish to climax the discussion of personal testimonies with the testimony of Eta Linnemann, a famous, once-liberal theologian. Her journey to faith in Christ is included in Appendix C (p. 144, "From Proud Denial to Humble Faith").

What About You?

You should consider concluding this course with your own testimony of how the Bible has changed you. This testimony will help show the students that the power of the Scripture is active also among people close to them.

If you say that you really believe the Bible is God's Word, then you are acknowledging its power to change lives. Can you list changes in your own life that have come about because of the influence of God's Word? Can you name a bad habit that the Holy Spirit has helped you break through the commands and encouragement of the Scripture? Can you name a good habit that God has helped you to establish in obedience to His Word? Do you sincerely desire that your day-to-day conduct will measure up to God's standards for His own glory and for the good of yourself, your family, and your friends?

This study cannot end as a mere academic exercise. If you accept what we have written as true, you cannot avoid making a decision. The Book that we have argued is true and infallible demands your submission to God. The next move is yours, and what you decide will either confirm or change the course of your life, a course that is headed for one of only two possible outcomes. Which will it be for you?

Review Questions

1. What ancient empire was totally unknown outside biblical records until the nineteenth century?

   the Hittites

2. What famous historical figure was pictured in Daniel's vision as a single goat's horn?

   Alexander the Great

3. What Persian king does Isaiah name, 150 years before the king's birth, who would restore captive Jews to their homeland?

   Cyrus

4. How many of the Bible's prophecies have ever been proved false?

   zero

5. What medical practice commonly accepted two hundred years ago ignores a specific Bible teaching?

   bleeding or bloodletting

6. Name two valuable resources that archeologist Nelson Glueck was able to locate in Palestine based on biblical records.

   water and copper

_T_ 7. Evidence alone cannot convince a person that the Bible is true.

_F_ 8. The reason Belshazzar could not offer Daniel the second position in the kingdom is that Persian law did not allow foreigners to have such high authority.

_F_ 9. Most of the specific charges of inaccuracy brought against the Bible one or two hundred years ago are still being brought against it today.

Multiple Choice

_A_ 10. Using the Bible to prove itself is an example of

A. circular reasoning.
B. misguided reasoning.
C. rectangular reasoning.
D. historical reasoning.

_C_ 11. Peter became convinced that Jesus of Nazareth was the Son of God because

A. he heard Jesus teach day after day.
B. he saw Jesus' many miracles.
C. God the Father revealed it to him.
D. he could not deny that Jesus was a sinless man.

_D_ 12. What statement did Job make that was advanced far beyond the common beliefs of his day?

A. The earth pulls on the moon.
B. The planet Saturn has rings.
C. The planets revolve around the sun.
D. The earth hangs on nothing.

_B_ 13. What does archeology confirm about Belshazzar?

    A. the spelling of his name
    B. that a king by this name did rule Babylon
    C. that he conquered the Assyrian empire
    D. the dates of his birth and death

_B_ 14. Two or three centuries ago, skeptics charged that the Bible did not agree with science, history, or geography. The best response to such claims was

    A. to redefine the doctrine of inspiration to allow for such errors in the Bible while keeping the doctrine of salvation intact.
    B. to maintain that either the findings of these sciences can be harmonized with the Bible's teachings or else the critics are wrong.
    C. to remain uncommitted on the doctrine of inerrancy until the critics' charges could be answered.
    D. to discredit the critics by publicizing their evil lifestyles.

Essay

15. Explain why prophecy would be stronger than archeology as an external evidence supporting the divine claims of Scripture.

[Key ideas: Many ancient documents are accurate in their accounts of historical events. Historical or geographical accuracy does not prove divine inspiration; it simply lends credibility to its contents. Prophecy cannot be explained away as a coincidence. The accuracy of prophecy demands an all-knowing source.]

16. Explain why personal testimony could be a stronger argument than prophecy in proving the Bible's claims.

[Key ideas: Though prophecy is a powerful testimony to the Bible's claims to be divinely inspired, unbelievers can come up with rationalizations to explain them away. For example, they would claim that the prophecies in Daniel were written after the events they foretold had occurred. Another example might be that they would claim that Christ knew what the prophecies said concerning a Messiah so He set out to fulfill them. But critics cannot so easily explain away the testimony of a changed life. The constant reminder of a transformed Christian life lived side by side with the liberal's cannot be so easily dismissed.]

17. Why are critics so intent on proving that Daniel was written around the second century B.C.?

[Key ideas: The accuracy of Daniel's prophecies concerning the Persian and Greek empires make it impossible for liberals to accept that the book was written hundreds of years before the events surrounding the rise and fall of those empires occurred. If Daniel foretold the events, then the only explanation is that God inspired these writings, and skeptics are not willing to accept this fact. The only alternative they have is to believe that the prophecies were written after the events and published under Daniel's name.]

85

18. How would you respond to the following statement?

"The fact that many people have found joy and victory through devotion to the Bible is, to me, not a compelling reason for becoming a Christian. Not that I oppose their devotion—it certainly has changed their lives for the better. However, only the weak-minded need such a remedy. Many people are not able to cope with their own addictions or fear of the unknown—particularly their fear of death. Those, on the other hand, that have been adequately educated and properly trained in dealing with life's challenges do not need such 'props' to hold them up mentally and emotionally."

[Key ideas: The person who would make such a statement remains unconvinced by the gospel because he loves the darkness of his sin rather than Jesus Christ, the Light of the world (John 3:18-19). More evidence will not convince him that the Scriptures are true because evidence alone cannot convert a man. The Pharisees saw Christ's miracles but still denied Christ's claims. They acknowledged that His works were supernatural, but they excused those signs as demonic. For such a person to be saved he must let go of his sin and pride and bow before the Lord Jesus Christ. Such people must experience the Father's self-revelation. That supernatural revelation alone can convince a person that Jesus is the Christ and that the Bible is God's Word (Matt. 16:16-17).]

87

Notes

89

Photograph Credits

The following agencies and individuals have furnished materials to meet the photographic needs of this textbook. We wish to express our gratitude to them for their important contribution.

American Schools of Oriental Research
Bowen Bible Lands Collection
Consulate General of Israel, NY
Israel Ministry of Tourism
Library of Congress
Marquette Manor Baptist Church
Bryan Smith
Unusual Films

Chapter 1
Unusual Films 6

Chapter 3
Unusual Films 39 (top)

Chapter 4
Bryan Smith 51; Consulate General of Israel, NY 52 (top); Israel Ministry of Tourism 52 (bottom both); Unusual Films 56, 57

Chapter 5
American Schools of Oriental Research 73; Unusual Films, courtesy of Bowen Bible Lands Collection, Bob Jones University 77; photo courtesy of Marquette Manor Baptist Church 78 (top); Unusual Films 78 (bottom); Library of Congress 79

Appendix A

Transparency Masters

The following pages contain lesson outlines and other materials to be photocopied onto transparencies or used as you see fit.

The Inspiration of Scripture

Introduction

I. The Source of Inspiration

II. The Process of Inspiration

    A. Inspiration is something the Holy Spirit did.

    B. Inspiration involves human activity.

    C. Inspiration is essentially divine control.

    D. Inspiration guarantees perfection.

III. Some Questions About Inspiration

    A. The questions asked

        1. Don't the New Testament references to inspiration apply only to the Old Testament?

        2. How could the apostles recall perfectly what Jesus did and taught?

    B. The questions answered

        1. The New Testament teaches the inspiration of both testaments.

        2. The Holy Spirit gave the New Testament authors perfect recall.

Conclusion

Memory Verses
Lesson 1

II Timothy 3:16

All scripture is given by inspiration of God, and is profitable for doctrine, for reproof, for correction, for instruction in righteousness:

II Peter 1:20-21

20 Knowing this first, that no prophecy of the scripture is of any private interpretation.
21 For the prophecy came not in old time by the will of man: but holy men of God spake as they were moved by the Holy Ghost.

The Canon of Scripture

Introduction

 I. Testimony of the Holy Spirit

 II. Testimony to the Old Testament Canon

   A. Jewish view

   B. Jesus' teaching

 III. Tests to determine the New Testament Canon

   A. Apostolic origin

   B. Scriptural contents

   C. Widespread acceptance

Conclusion

Memory Verses
Lesson 2

Luke 24:44

And he said unto them, These are the words which I spake unto you, while I was yet with you, that all things must be fulfilled, which were written in the law of Moses, and in the prophets, and in the psalms, concerning me.

II Peter 3:2

That ye may be mindful of the words which were spoken before by the holy prophets, and of the commandment of us the apostles of the Lord and Saviour:

The Preservation of Scripture

Introduction

I. The Facts About the Text

   A. God inspired every word.

   B. The originals have disappeared.

   C. Existing manuscripts differ slightly.

   D. We read translations rather than the original words.

   Question: In what sense can we say that we have God's Word today?

II. Transmission of the Text

   A. Introduction to Textual Criticism

      1. Its goal

      2. Its materials

   B. The trustworthiness of biblical manuscripts

      1. Old Testament: supported by

         a. the method of the scribes

         b. the discovery of the Dead Sea Scrolls

      2. New Testament: supported by

         a. the number and age of the manuscripts

         b. the similarity of the manuscripts

      3. Summary of manuscript evidence

III. The Translation of the Text

   A. Difficulties in translation

   B. Assurances concerning translation

   C. Selection of a translation

Conclusion

Memory Verses

Lessons 3-4

I Peter 1:24-25

24 For all flesh is as grass, and all the glory of man as the flower of grass. The grass withereth, and the flower thereof falleth away:

25 But the word of the Lord endureth for ever. And this is the word which by the gospel is preached unto you.

Scribal Copying Exercise

INANTIQUITYNONLITERARYEVERYDAYDOCUMENTSWERE
CUSTOMARILYWRITTENINACURSIVEHANDINWHICHMOST
OFTHELETTERSWEREFORMEDWITHOUTLIFTINGTHEPENAND
ABBREVIATIONSWEREFREQUENTLYUSEDWEREANYBOOKSOF
THEGREEKBIBLEEVERCIRCULATEDINCURSIVESCRIPT
SCHOLARSARGUETHATITISHIGHLYUNLIKELYTHATTHE
ORIGINALTEXTSWEREEVERWRITTENINCURSIVESCRIPT
ITWASDIFFICULTTOUSETHATFORMOFWRITINGBECAUSE
OFTHEROUGHSURFACEOFTHEPAPYRUSONTHEOTHERHAND
ONESCHOLARPOINTEDOUTTHATINTHEBOOKOFCHRONICLES
CODEXVATICANUSHADHADCERTAINCHANGESOFLETTERS
WHICHCANNOTBEEXPLAINEDINTERMSOFCONFUSIONOF
UNCIALSCRIPTINWHICHTHESELETTERSAREVERY
DIFFERENTFROMONEANOTHERBUTWHICHAREREADILY
EXPLAINABLEINCURSIVESCRIPTWHERETHEYRESEMBLE
EACHOTHERCLOSELYONEVERYSIDE.

Scribal Copying Exercise

1. In antiquity non-literary, everyday documents were

2. customarily written in a cursive hand in which most

3. of the letters were formed without lifting the pen and

4. abbreviations were frequently used. Were any books of

5. the Greek Bible ever circulated in cursive script?

6. Scholars argue that it is highly unlikely that the

7. original texts were ever written in cursive script.

8. It was difficult to use that form of writing because

9. of the rough surface of the papyrus. On the other hand,

10. one scholar pointed out that in the book of Chronicles,

11. Codex Vaticanus had had certain changes of letters

12. which cannot be explained in terms of confusion of

13. uncial script, in which these letters are very

14. different from one another but which are readily

15. explainable in cursive script, where they resemble

16. each other closely on every side.

Evidence Confirming Scripture

Introduction

  I. Natural Evidences

    A. From science

      1. Biology

      2. Medicine

      3. Earth science

    B. From archeology

      1. Geography

      2. History

  II. Supernatural Evidences

    A. From prophecy

      1. Daniel

      2. Isaiah

    B. From personal testimony

      1. A converted Chicago gangster

      2. Down-and-outers

      3. Those on their deathbeds

Conclusion

Memory Verses
Lesson 5

Matthew 16:16-17

16 And Simon Peter answered and said, Thou art the Christ, the Son of the living God.
17 And Jesus answered and said unto him, Blessed art thou, Simon Bar-jona: for flesh and blood hath not revealed it unto thee, but my Father which is in heaven.

TEST ONE

Memory Verses

1-3. Write II Timothy 3:16. _____

_____

_____

4-6. Write Luke 24:44. _____

_____

_____

_____

7-9. Write I Peter 1:24-25. _____

_____

_____

_____

True or False

_____ 10. Peter called Paul's writings Scripture.

_____ 11. Though Jesus did not teach the inerrancy of Scripture, Paul makes it clear that Scripture is inerrant.

_____ 12. The Gospel writers were able to recall the words of Jesus with complete accuracy.

_____ 13. When evaluating any information, you should first consider the source of the information.

_____ 14. The Bible avoids references to nonbiblical books.

_____ 15. The "seal of approval" God put on the Bible is actually the testimony of the Holy Spirit.

_____ 16. Different ancient Bible manuscripts have some differences in wording.

_____ 17. Our understanding of the Bible's preservation rests solely on the facts of history.

_____ 18. Textual criticism applies only to the Bible.

Short Answer

19. What member of the Trinity was specially involved in the work of inspiration?_____

20. What doctrine teaches that God inspired each word of the Bible?_____

21. The collection of divine books that give clear evidence of divine inspiration is the _____ of Scripture.

22. A group of Jewish and Christian works dated in or near biblical times but not accepted as Scripture

   is the _____.

23-24. What two writing materials were used for ancient manuscripts?_____

   _____

25. The field of scholarship that attempts to determine the original wording of passages where various

   copies or editions of a work differ from one another is _____.

Multiple choice

_____ 26. Why are inspiration and inerrancy foundational doctrines?

   A. Scripture defines them as foundational doctrines.
   B. The validity of all other doctrine depends on them.
   C. The Lord Jesus began his teaching ministry with them.
   D. The church has always considered them foundational.

_____ 27. Which of the following is not one of the criteria used to determine the canon of the New Testament?

   A. The book must not contradict other books of the Bible.
   B. The book had to be written by an apostle or a close associate of an apostle.
   C. The book must have clear quotes from the Old Testament scriptures.
   D. The book must have had widespread acceptance in the early church.

_____ 28. Which is the best description of the noncanonical books?

   A. The Roman Catholic Church accepts them all as Scripture.
   B. Although the apostles wrote them, they have no other evidence of inspiration.
   C. The Lord Jesus specifically rejected them.
   D. Though they have some value, they have no divine authority.

_____ 29. In the ancient world, what was hand copying someone else's work for publication considered?

    A. a task for professionals only   C. plagiarism

    B. a highly valuable service   D. a job for slaves

Short essay

30-31. What is dangerous about the following statement? "The Bible contains the Word of God."

_____

_____

32-33. What was the difference between Martin Luther's questions about the canon and the unbelief of

modern critics?_____

_____

_____

34-35. Why did J. A. Bengel become interested in textual criticism of the New Testament?

_____

_____

_____

Matching

Match each of the following definitions of *inspiration* with the description that best suits it.

    A. good definition   B. weak on inerrancy   C. unacceptable

_____ 36. Inspiration is that influence of the Spirit of God upon the minds of the Scripture writers which made their writings the record of a progressive divine revelation, sufficient, when taken together and interpreted by the same Spirit who inspired them, to lead every honest inquirer to Christ and to salvation.

_____ 37. Inspiration is that inexplicable power which the Divine Spirit put forth of old on the authors of holy Scripture, in order to guide them even in the employment of the words they used, and to preserve them alike from all error and from all omission.

_____ 38. We call our Bible inspired, by which we mean that by reading and studying it we find our way to God, we find His will for us, and we find how we can conform ourselves to His will.

Discussion

39-41. Explain how the description of a ship caught in a storm (Acts 27:15) contributes to our understanding of the meaning of *inspiration*._____

_____

_____

42-43. Give at least two possible reasons that God has not miraculously designated which manuscripts preserve God's Word exactly._____

_____

_____

44-46. Why is it impossible for the Bible to be a good book if it is not the Word of God?

_____

_____

_____

_____

47-50. Suppose tomorrow's newspaper contains this surprising headline: "Long Lost New Testament Book Found, Author Claims to Be the Apostle Peter." How would you evaluate that claim?_____

_____

_____

_____

ANSWERS—TEST ONE

Memory Verses

1-3. Write II Timothy 3:16. ___*All scripture is given by inspiration of God, and is profitable for doctrine, for*___

___*reproof, for correction, for instruction in righteousness.*___

___

4-6. Write Luke 24:44. ___*And he said unto them, These are the words which I spake unto you, while I was yet*___

___*with you, that all things must be fulfilled, which were written in the law of Moses, and in the prophets, and in*___

___*the psalms, concerning me.*___

___

7-9. Write I Peter 1:24-25. ___*For all flesh is as grass, and all the glory of man as the flower of grass. The grass*___

___*withereth, and the flower thereof falleth away: But the word of the Lord endureth for ever. And this is the*___

___*word which by the gospel is preached unto you.*___

___

True or False

___*True*___ 10. Peter called Paul's writings Scripture.

___*False*___ 11. Though Jesus did not teach the inerrancy of Scripture, Paul makes it clear that Scripture is inerrant.

___*True*___ 12. The Gospel writers were able to recall the words of Jesus with complete accuracy.

___*True*___ 13. When evaluating any information, you should first consider the source of the information.

___*False*___ 14. The Bible avoids references to nonbiblical books.

___*True*___ 15. The "seal of approval" God put on the Bible is actually the testimony of the Holy Spirit.

___*True*___ 16. Different ancient Bible manuscripts have some differences in wording.

___*False*___ 17. Our understanding of the Bible's preservation rests solely on the facts of history.

___*False*___ 18. Textual criticism applies only to the Bible.

Short Answer

19. What member of the Trinity was specially involved in the work of inspiration? *the Holy Spirit*

20. What doctrine teaches that God inspired each word of the Bible? *verbal inspiration*

21. The collection of divine books that give clear evidence of divine inspiration is the *canon* of Scripture.

22. A group of Jewish and Christian works dated in or near biblical times but not accepted as Scripture

    is the *Apocrypha*.

23-24. What two writing materials were used for ancient manuscripts?

    papyrus and parchment

25. The field of scholarship that attempts to determine the original wording of passages where various

    copies or editions of a work differ from one another is *textual criticism*.

Multiple choice

B 26. Why are inspiration and inerrancy foundational doctrines?

   A. Scripture defines them as foundational doctrines.
   B. The validity of all other doctrine depends on them.
   C. The Lord Jesus began his teaching ministry with them.
   D. The church has always considered them foundational.

C 27. Which of the following is not one of the criteria used to determine the canon of the New Testament?

   A. The book must not contradict other books of the Bible.
   B. The book had to be written by an apostle or a close associate of an apostle.
   C. The book must have clear quotes from the Old Testament scriptures.
   D. The book must have had widespread acceptance in the early church.

D 28. Which is the best description of the noncanonical books?

   A. The Roman Catholic Church accepts them all as Scripture.
   B. Apostles wrote them, but they have no other evidence of inspiration.
   C. The Lord Jesus specifically rejected them.
   D. Though they have some value, they have no divine authority.

<u>__B__</u> 29. In the ancient world, what was hand copying someone else's work for publication considered?

        A. a task for professionals only   C. plagiarism
        B. a highly valuable service   D. a job for slaves

Short essay

30-31. What is dangerous about the following statement? "The Bible contains the Word of God."

It allows the possibility that some things in the Bible are not God's Word.

32-33. What was the difference between Martin Luther's questions about the canon and the unbelief of

modern critics?   *Luther was committed to accepting the Scripture as God's inspired Word, but*

modern critics do not believe any of the Bible is God's Word.

34-35. Why did J. A. Bengel become interested in textual criticism of the New Testament?

He wanted to investigate the basis for unbelievers' claims that the New Testament had not been

reliably preserved.

Matching

Match each of the following definitions of *inspiration* with the description that best suits it.

    A. good definition   B. weak on inerrancy   C. unacceptable

<u>__B__</u> 36. Inspiration is that influence of the Spirit of God upon the minds of the Scripture writers which made their writings the record of a progressive divine revelation, sufficient, when taken together and interpreted by the same Spirit who inspired them, to lead every honest inquirer to Christ and to salvation.

<u>__A__</u> 37. Inspiration is that inexplicable power which the Divine Spirit put forth of old on the authors of holy Scripture, in order to guide them even in the employment of the words they used, and to preserve them alike from all error and from all omission.

<u>__C__</u> 38. We call our Bible inspired, by which we mean that by reading and studying it we find our way to God, we find His will for us, and we find how we can conform ourselves to His will.

Discussion

39-41. Explain how the description of a ship caught in a storm (Acts 27:15) contributes to our understanding of the meaning of *inspiration*. *The same word used to describe the ship's being carried by the wind also describes the Scripture writers' being carried along by the Holy Spirit. The writers were under the Spirit's control, much as the ship was moved by the wind.*

42-43. Give at least two possible reasons that God has not miraculously designated which manuscripts preserve God's Word exactly. *First, this would have required some sort of continual revelation beyond the completion of the Bible. Second, people would be tempted to worship a perfect manuscript as an idol.*

44-46. Why is it impossible for the Bible to be a good book if it is not the Word of God?

The Bible repeatedly claims to be the Word of God, so if it is not, then it is full of lies and falsehoods. A book full of lies is not a good book. If the Bible is a good book at all, it must be God's Book as well.

47-50. Suppose tomorrow's newspaper contains this surprising headline: "Long Lost New Testament Book Found, Author Claims to Be the Apostle Peter." How would you evaluate that claim?

The book cannot be canonical because it has not passed the test of time and has not been confirmed to the hearts of many generations of believers. The Holy Spirit would not have inspired a book two thousand years ago and kept it unavailable to the entire church ever since. The early church did not acknowledge it. It has no more evidence of inspiration than apocryphal books.

Test Two

Memory Verses

1-4. Write I Peter 1:24-25. _____

_____

_____

_____

_____

5-8. Write II Peter 1:20-21. _____

_____

_____

_____

9-12. Write Matthew 16:16-17. _____

_____

_____

_____

True or False

_____ 13. The Gospel writers were able to recall the words of Jesus with complete accuracy.

_____ 14. When evaluating any information, you should first consider the source of the information.

_____ 15. Our understanding of the Bible's preservation rests solely on the facts of history.

_____ 16. The accuracy of Old Testament manuscripts has never been seriously questioned because some of the existing manuscripts were copied within a few years of the original writing.

_____ 17. Most of the specific charges of inaccuracy brought against the Bible one or two hundred years ago are still being brought against it today.

Short Answer

18. What doctrine teaches that God inspired each word of the Bible?_____

19. A group of Jewish and Christian works dated in or near biblical times but not accepted as Scripture

    is the _____.

20. The collection of divine books that give clear evidence of divine inspiration is the _____
    of Scripture.

21. According to tradition, what Old Testament character gave very careful attention to the preservation

    of the exact wording of the Hebrew text?_____

22. What ancient empire was totally unknown outside biblical records until the nineteenth century?

    _____

23. What famous historical figure was pictured in Daniel's vision as a single goat's horn?_____

    _____

24. What Persian king does Isaiah name 150 years prior to the king's birth?_____

Multiple choice

_____ 25. The Isaiah Scroll

   A. finally revealed the true text of many obscure passages in the book.
   B. is nearly identical in wording to manuscripts copied one thousand years later.
   C. was destroyed by vandals before scholars finished studying it.
   D. is written in Isaiah's own handwriting.

_____ 26. Which of the following statements about Bible manuscripts is true?

   A. False religions have arisen based on a few manuscripts that are full of doctrinal errors.
   B. Each manuscript presents the same essential truths and doctrines.
   C. The oldest manuscripts in existence are no nearer to the time of writing than five hundred years.
   D. A few existing manuscripts contain the original text precisely as God inspired it.

_____ 27. Which of the following statements about Bible translations is false?

   A. It is impossible to translate from one language to another without changing words.
   B. Textual critics concentrate their study on evaluating the accuracy of the translations.
   C. Some Bible translations are untrustworthy and should be rejected.
   D. The most important point on which to evaluate a Bible translation is the accuracy with which it reflects the wording of the original languages.

_____ 28. Using the Bible to prove itself is an example of

    A. circular reasoning.   C. rectangular reasoning.
    B. misguided reasoning.   D. historical reasoning.

_____ 29. What does archeology confirm about Belshazzar?

    A. the spelling of his name
    B. that he conquered the Assyrian empire
    C. that a king by that name did indeed rule Babylon
    D. the dates of his birth and death

_____ 30. A translation so easy to read that it takes the work out of Bible study would be

    A. welcome to most Christians.
    B. doing too much work for the reader.
    C. easy to create if Christians would stop arguing about translation philosophy.
    D. impossible to create without the insights of modern textual criticism.

Discussion

31-32. What is dangerous about the following statement? "The Bible becomes God's Word when it

speaks to you personally." _____

_____

_____

_____

_____

33-34. How can a believing Christian also be a textual critic? _____

_____

_____

_____

_____

35-36. Describe the way in which God preserved the New Testament up until the invention of the

printing press. _____

_____

_____

_____

37-39. Contrast the evidence for Aristotle's writings with the manuscript evidence for the New Testament.

_____

_____

_____

_____

40-42. Discuss several reasons that the New Testament manuscripts differ from one another more than

those of the Old Testament. _____

_____

_____

_____

43-46. Explain why fulfilled prophecy is a stronger external evidence of the divine claims of

Scripture than support from archeology. _____

_____

_____

_____

47-50. Why are higher critics so intent on proving that Daniel was written around the second century before Christ?

_____

_____

_____

_____

_____

ANSWERS—Test Two

Memory Verses

1-4. Write I Peter 1:24-25. *For all flesh is as grass, and all the glory of man as the flower of grass. The grass*

withereth, and the flower thereof falleth away: But the word of the Lord endureth for ever. And this is the

word which by the gospel is preached unto you.

_____

_____

5-8. Write II Peter 1:20-21. *Knowing this first, that no prophecy of the scripture is of any private*

interpretation. For the prophecy came not in old time by the will of man: but holy men of God spake as

they were moved by the Holy Ghost.

_____

_____

9-12. Write Matthew 16:16-17. *And Simon Peter answered and said, Thou art the Christ, the Son of the*

living God. And Jesus answered and said unto him, Blessed art thou, Simon Bar-jona: for flesh and blood

hath not revealed it unto thee, but my Father which is in heaven.

_____

_____

True or False

True 13. The Gospel writers were able to recall the words of Jesus with complete accuracy.

True 14. When evaluating any information, you should first consider the source of the information.

False 15. Our understanding of the Bible's preservation rests solely on the facts of history.

False 16. The accuracy of Old Testament manuscripts has never been seriously questioned because some of the existing manuscripts were copied within a few years of the original writing.

False 17. Most of the specific charges of inaccuracy brought against the Bible one or two hundred years ago are still being brought against it today.

Short Answer

18. What doctrine teaches that God inspired each word of the Bible? __*verbal inspiration*__

19. A group of Jewish and Christian works dated in or near biblical times but not accepted as Scripture

    is the _____*Apocrypha*_____.

20. The collection of divine books that give clear evidence of divine inspiration is the ____*canon*____ of Scripture.

21. According to tradition, what Old Testament character gave very careful attention to the preservation

    of the exact wording of the Hebrew text? ____*Ezra*____

22. What ancient empire was totally unknown outside biblical records until the nineteenth century?

    _____*the Hittites*_____

23. What famous historical figure was pictured in Daniel's vision as a single goat's horn? _____

    _____*Alexander the Great*_____

24. What Persian king does Isaiah name 150 years prior to the king's birth? ____*Cyrus*____

Multiple choice

__*B*__ 25. The Isaiah Scroll

   A finally revealed the true text of many obscure passages in the book.
   B. is nearly identical in wording to manuscripts copied one thousand years later.
   C. was destroyed by vandals before scholars finished studying it.
   D. is written in Isaiah's own handwriting.

__*B*__ 26. Which of the following statements about Bible manuscripts is true?

   A. False religions have arisen based on a few manuscripts that are full of doctrinal errors.
   B. Each manuscript presents the same essential truths and doctrines.
   C. The oldest manuscripts in existence are no nearer to the time of writing than five hundred years.
   D. A few existing manuscripts contain the original text precisely as God inspired it.

__*B*__ 27. Which of the following statements about Bible translations is false?

   A. It is impossible to translate from one language to another without changing words.
   B. Textual critics concentrate their study on evaluating the accuracy of the translations.
   C. Some Bible translations are untrustworthy and should be rejected.
   D. The most important point on which to evaluate a Bible translation is the accuracy with which it reflects the wording of the original languages.

__*A*__ 28. Using the Bible to prove itself is an example of

A. circular reasoning. C. rectangular reasoning.
B. misguided reasoning. D. historical reasoning.

_____C_____ 29. What does archeology confirm about Belshazzar?

A. the spelling of his name
B. that he conquered the Assyrian empire
C. that a king by that name did indeed rule Babylon
D. the dates of his birth and death

_____B_____ 30. A translation so easy to read that it takes the work out of Bible study would be

A. welcome to most Christians.
B. doing too much work for the reader.
C. easy to create if Christians would stop arguing about translation philosophy.
D. impossible to create without the insights of modern textual criticism.

Discussion

31-32. What is dangerous about the following statement? "The Bible becomes God's Word when it

speaks to you personally." __It implies that the Bible can mean something different to every person,__

__meaning that it is not absolutely true. It makes all authoritative preaching and teaching impossible and__

__allows every person to decide for himself what God says.__

33-34. How can a believing Christian also be a textual critic? __A textual critic is not necessarily someone__

__who disbelieves the Bible, but is someone who tries to determine by sound reasoning and careful__

__examination of the evidence what the original wording of a passage is. "Critic" does not mean that he__

__criticizes in the negative sense.__

35-36. Describe the way in which God preserved the New Testament up until the invention of the

printing press. *Scribes copied from existing manuscripts. As old manuscripts wore out from*

use, new copies were made. Many copies were made, and the copies were spread over a wide geograph-

ical area, so any minor mistakes made in copying would have affected only a part of the manuscripts.

37-39. Contrast the evidence for Aristotle's writings with the manuscript evidence for the New Testament.

Aristotle's writings survived in five manuscripts, while the New Testament has over five thousand

manuscripts. The oldest copy of Aristotle's work was copied fourteen hundred years after its

composition; some New Testament manuscripts date from within two centuries of the originals.

40-42. Discuss several reasons that the New Testament manuscripts differ from one another more than

those of the Old Testament. *The copyists were not professional scribes, and the books were*

sometimes produced in a hasty manner.

43-46. Explain why fulfilled prophecy is a stronger external evidence of the divine claims of

Scripture than support from archeology. *Archeology supports only historical or geographic accuracy,*

which does not prove the writing is supernatural. Fulfilled prophecy demands an all-knowing author.

47-50. Why are higher critics so intent on proving that Daniel was written around the second century before Christ?

The highly accurate prophecies are unacceptable to higher critics, who deny the supernatural. If Daniel

was written when conservatives maintain, then the only explanation is that Daniel was shown by God

what was going to happen in the future.

Appendix B

Reproducible Masters

The following pages contain activity exercises that you may photocopy and distribute to your class. The readings from the apocryphal books go with Chapter 2; ideas for class discussion appear in Appendix C. The word-find exercise would work well for seat work; it goes with Chapter 5. If you think your students would feel demeaned by being asked to do a word find, you may want to omit these activities. There are plenty of other activities to fill time both in and out of class with meaningful work.

A Selection from Bel and the Dragon

Now there was a great serpent in that place, and the Babylonians worshiped it. And the king said to Daniel,

"You cannot deny that it is a living god, so worship it."

And Daniel said, "I will worship the Lord my God, for he is a living God. But with your permission, O King, I will kill this serpent without sword or stick."

And the king said, "You have my permission."

And Daniel took pitch, fat, and hair and boiled them together, and made lumps of them, and he put them into the serpent's mouth, and it ate them and burst open. And he said, "See the objects of your worship!"

When the Babylonians heard it, they were very indignant and made a conspiracy against the king, saying, "The king has become a Jew! He has overturned Bel, and killed the serpent, and slaughtered the priests."

So they went to the king and said, "Give Daniel up to us, or else we will kill you and your household."

And the king saw that they were pressing him hard, and he was forced to give Daniel up to them. And they threw him into the lions' den, and he remained there six days. There were seven lions in the den; and they had been given two human bodies and two sheep every day; but now these were not given them, so that they might devour Daniel.

Now the prophet Habakkuk was in Judea, and he had cooked a stew and crumbled bread into a bowl, and was going into the field to carry it to the reapers, when the angel of the Lord said to Habakkuk, "Carry the dinner that you have to Babylon, to Daniel, in the lions' den."

And Habakkuk said, "Sir, I have never seen Babylon, and I do not know the den."

Then the angel of the Lord took hold of the crown of his head, and lifted him up by his hair and with the speed of the wind set him down in Babylon, right over the den. And Habakkuk shouted, "Daniel! Daniel! Take the dinner which God has sent you."

And Daniel said, "You have remembered me, O God, and have not forsaken those who love you."

Then Daniel arose and ate. And the angel of God immediately put Habakkuk back in his own place again.

On the seventh day, the king came to mourn for Daniel; and he came to the den and looked in, and there sat Daniel. Then the king shouted loudly, "You are great, Lord God of Daniel, and there is no other beside you!"

And he lifted him out, and the men who had tried to bring about his destruction he threw into the den; and they were instantly devoured before their eyes.

A Selection from The Shepherd of Hermas

The master, who reared me, had sold me to one Rhoda in Rome. After many years, I met her again, and began to love her as a sister. After a certain time I saw her bathing in the river Tiber; and I gave her my hand, and led her out of the river. So, seeing her beauty, I reasoned in my heart, saying, "Happy were I, if I had such an one to wife both in beauty and in character." I merely reflected on this and nothing more. After a certain time, as I was journeying to Cumae, and glorifying God's creatures for their greatness and splendour and power, as I walked I fell asleep. And a Spirit took me, and bore me away through a pathless tract, through which no man could pass: for the place was precipitous, and broken into clefts by reason of the waters. When then I had crossed the river, I came into the level country, and knelt down, and began to pray to the Lord and to confess my sins.

Now, while I prayed, the heaven was opened, and I see the lady, whom I had desired, greeting me from heaven, saying, "Good morrow, Hermas."

And, looking at her, I said to her, "Lady, what doest thou here?"

Then she answered me, "I was taken up, that I might convict thee of thy sins before the Lord."

I said to her, "Dost thou now convict me?"

"Nay, not so," said she, "but hear the words that I shall say to thee. God, Who dwelleth in the heavens, and created out of nothing the things which are, and increased and multiplied them for His holy Church's sake, is wroth with thee, for that thou didst sin against me."

I answered her and said, "Sin against thee? In what way? Did I ever speak an unseemly word unto thee? Did I not always regard thee as a goddess? Did I not always respect thee as a sister? How couldst thou falsely charge me, lady, with such villainy and uncleanness?"

Laughing she saith unto me, "The desire after evil entered into thine heart. Nay, thinkest thou not that it is an evil deed for a righteous man, if the evil desire should enter into his heart? It is indeed a sin and a great one too," saith she; "for the righteous man entertaineth righteous purposes. While then his purposes are righteous, his repute stands stedfast in the heavens, and he finds the Lord easily propitiated in all that he does. But they that entertain evil purposes in their hearts, bring upon themselves death and captivity, especially they that claim for themselves this present world, and boast in its riches, and cleave not to the good things that are to come. Their souls shall rue it, seeing that they have no hope, but have abandoned themselves and their life. But do thou pray unto God, and He shall heal thine own sins, and those of thy whole house, and of all the saints."

As soon as she had spoken these words the heavens were shut; and I was given over to horror and grief. Then I said within myself, "If this sin is recorded against me, how can I be saved? Or how shall I propitiate God for my sins which are full-blown? Or with what words shall I entreat the Lord that He may be propitious unto me?"

While I was advising and discussing these matters in my heart, I see before me a great white chair of snow-white wool; and there came an aged lady in glistening raiment, having a book in her hands, and she sat down alone, and she saluted me, "Good morrow, Hermas."

Then I, grieved and weeping, said, "Good morrow, lady."

And she said to me, "Why so gloomy, Hermas, thou that art patient and good-tempered, and art always smiling? Why so downcast in thy looks, and far from cheerful?"

And I said to her, "Because of an excellent lady's saying that I had sinned against her."

Then she said, "Far be this thing from the servant of God! Nevertheless the thought did enter into thy heart concerning her. Now to the servants of God such a purpose bringeth sin. For it is an evil and mad purpose to overtake a devout spirit that hath been already approved, that it should desire an evil deed, and especially if it be Hermas the temperate, who abstaineth from every evil desire, and is full of all simplicity and of great guilelessness. Yet it is not for this that God is wroth with thee, but that thou mayest convert thy family, that hath done wrong against the Lord and against you their parents. But out of fondness for thy children thou didst not admonish thy family, but didst suffer it to become fearfully corrupt. Therefore the Lord is wroth with thee. But He will heal all thy past sins, which have been committed in thy family; for by reason of their sins and iniquities thou hast been corrupted by the affairs of this world. But the great mercy of the Lord had pity on thee and thy family, and will strengthen thee, and establish thee in His glory. Only be not thou careless, but take courage, and strengthen thy family. For as the smith hammering his work conquers the task which he wills, so also doth righteous discourse repeated daily conquer all evil. Cease not therefore to reprove thy children; for I know that if they shall repent with all their heart, they shall be written in the books of life with the saints."

After these words of hers had ceased, she saith

unto me, "Wilt thou listen to me as I read?"

Then say I, "Yes, lady." She saith to me, "Be attentive, and hear the glories of God." I listened with attention and with wonder to that which I had no power to remember; for all the words were terrible, such as man cannot bear. The last words however I remembered, for they were suitable for us and gentle. "Behold, the God of Hosts, Who by His invisible and mighty power and by His great wisdom created the world, and by His glorious purpose clothed His creation with comeliness, and by His strong word fixed the heaven, and founded the earth upon the waters, and by His own wisdom and providence formed His holy Church, which also He blessed—behold, He removeth the heavens and the mountains and the hills and the seas, and all things are made level for His elect that He may fulfil to them the promise which He promised with great glory and rejoicing, if so be that they shall keep the ordinances of God, which they received, with great faith."

When then she finished reading and arose from her chair, there came four young men, and they took away the chair, and departed towards the East. Then she calleth me unto her, and she touched my breast, and saith to me, "Did my reading please thee?"

And I say unto her, "Lady, these last words please me, but the former were difficult and hard."

Then she spoke to me, saying, "These last words are for the righteous, but the former are for the heathen and the rebellious." While she yet spoke with me, two men appeared, and took her by the arms, and they departed, whither the chair also had gone, towards the East. And she smiled as she departed and, as she was going, she saith to me, "Play the man, Hermas."

Word Search

1. The Word of God changed my life from a Chicago gangster into a Christian missionary._____

2. I was a famous preacher who won a debate with an agnostic before it even started because of the life-changing power of the gospel._____

3. Due to faulty medical theories, I was bled to death._____

4. An argument based on Genesis 2:21 convinced Queen Victoria to try my chloroform._____

5. For more than two thousand years, I was thought to be a king without a history._____

6. I died as a miserable atheist._____

7. My copper mines brought me much wealth._____

8. I knew the importance of blood long before medical science._____

9. I became famous by using my Bible as a guide to discover archeological sites._____

10. I am very glad I changed my mind and trusted God's Word before I died._____

11. The Bible prophesied my greatness long before I was born, even calling me by name._____

12. When I had nothing, I mentioned that the earth was hung on nothing._____

13. Though considered a fraud by liberals, my book has survived many a lion's den._____

14. As prophesied, I conquered the Persian empire in a few short years._____

```
D R A Z Z A H S L E B D
R U E H D Y F K E D A R
D H J D M A I R N D A E
R L O B N S N A E N A R
Z E B N N A S I I I G I
I N K E O I X R E L N A
S C M R M M O E U L S T
N R S P A N O E L N N L
E S S N S B C L E A A O
M O E I O K E E O V S V
N D D C Y R U S E S O M
L E W A S H I N G T O N
```

Answers

1. Mensik
2. Ironside
3. Washington
4. Simpson
5. Belshazzar
6. Voltaire
7. Solomon
8. Moses
9. Glueck
10. Barker
11. Cyrus
12. Job
13. Daniel
14. Alexander

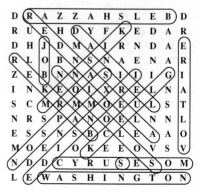

Appendix C

Supplement for Teacher Notes

The following pages contain supplementary information referred to in the teacher notes. Much of this material can be used for classroom enrichment as you see fit.

Chapter 1

John Wesley's Proof of Divine Inspiration

"I beg leave to propose a short, clear, and strong argument to prove the divine inspiration of the holy Scriptures.

"The Bible must be the invention either of good men or angels, bad men or devils, or of God.

"1. It could not be the invention of good men or angels; for they neither would nor could make a book, and tell lies all the time they were writing it, saying 'Thus saith the Lord,' when it was their own invention.

"2. It could not be the invention of bad men or devils; for they would not make a book which commands all duty, forbids all sin, and condemns their souls to hell to all eternity.

"3. Therefore, I draw this conclusion, that the Bible must be given by divine inspiration."

(From "A Clear and Concise Demonstration of the Divine Inspiration of the Holy Scriptures," published in 1789.)

Case Study on Clark Pinnock

What happens when one gives up the doctrine of inerrancy? The life of a well-known evangelical scholar, Clark Pinnock, provides an example for us concerning the pathway that follows this decision.

Clark Harold Pinnock was born on February 3, 1937, in Toronto, Ontario. He made a profession of faith at an early age and was reared in a fundamentalist Baptist church. After completing his education, he began teaching at New Orleans Baptist Seminary, a Southern Baptist school. Pinnock's early writings were noteworthy for their strong defense of inerrancy. In 1966, while at New Orleans, he wrote a book entitled *A Defense of Biblical Infallibility,* coming out strongly for a Bible without error. Pinnock writes, "If the biblical writers were liable to err in one particular, what guarantee have we that they were not equally fallible in another?" (12). In 1968, he appealed to the Southern Baptist denomination to return to complete confidence in the Word of God in his treatise *A New Reformation: A Challenge to Southern Baptists.*

In 1971, while at Trinity Evangelical Divinity School, Pinnock wrote a book entitled *Biblical Revelation,* which attacked "limited inerrancy" and again upheld verbal inspiration. Here he affirms, "The result of denying inerrancy, as skeptics well know, is the loss of a trustworthy Bible. Limited inerrancy is a slope, not a platform. Although we are repeatedly assured that minor errors in unimportant matters would not greatly affect the substance of the Christian faith nor the authority of Scripture, this ad-

mission has the effect of leaving us with a Bible which is a compound of truth and error, with no one to tell us which is which" (80). In 1974 he went on to state, "We are driven to acknowledge that, according to Jesus' own conviction, the Scriptures are of divine origin, and therefore completely trustworthy, inerrant and infallible." In the same article he concludes, "If we abandon the high view of Scripture [as Jesus held], we are in effect abandoning Him in His authority over us" ("The Inspiration of Scripture and the Authority of Jesus Christ," *God's Inerrant Word,* 1974).

When Clark Pinnock returned to Canada in 1974 as a professor at Regent College, his thinking began to change. In a 1976 article ("Inspiration and Authority: A Truce Proposal"), he began to backpedal on his position concerning inerrancy. He pled with Christians not to waste time arguing over inerrancy but to move on to other more important issues.

In 1979 he wrote "The Ongoing Struggle Over Biblical Inerrancy" for the *Journal of the American Scientific Affiliation.* In this article he criticized those who would fight for complete inerrancy of the Bible or who would promote a partial inerrancy view. Knowing he would be criticized by Fundamentalists, Pinnock assured that "even though the strict inerrancy assumption is lacking [among some Evangelicals including Pinnock], there remains strong confidence in God speaking infallibly in the Scriptures, so that fears about unhindered drifting into heresy from this position should seldom be realized" (73).

But drift he did. In December of 1980, Pinnock was involved in a dialogue with a liberal. At the end of the dialogue, they found many areas of agreement. In fact, the liberal said afterwards, "He [Pinnock] and I pretty much view the Bible in the same way, and apparently we have found that out, which means either he's going to lose his credibility as a conservative or I am going to lose mine as a liberal." The liberal was not the loser.

In 1981 Pinnock praised the World Council of Churches for their Christian values and goals for world evangelism. Later, in 1987, Pinnock maintained that the Bible does not teach eternal punishment for unbelievers. He concludes, "Where then, did the everlasting-torment view come from? . . . I believe it arose from the unbiblical Greek view of the natural immortality of the soul. . . . But if one thinks biblically, and sees human beings as mortal, needing to be given eternal life if they are to have it, then no such awful consequence follows" (*Christianity Today,* Mar. 20, 1987). In July of the same year, Pinnock concedes that Jonah is a book of "didactic fiction that intends to teach something other than historical facts" (*The Scripture Principle,* 117).

Inevitably, even Pinnock's view of God changed. An article in *The Grace of God, The Will of Man,* published in 1989, reveals that Pinnock does not believe that God knows "all that the future holds, because much of that future will be determined by the choices available to human freedom, and these choices are, even to God, presently shrouded in mystery" (26). Pinnock has also adopted the view that salvation is available within non-Christian religions, writing, "I welcome the Saiva Siddhanta literature of Hinduism, which celebrates a personal God of love, and the emphasis on grace that I see in the Japanese Shin-Shu Amida sect. I also respect the Buddha as a righteous man (Matt. 10:41) and Mohammed as a prophet figure in the style of the Old Testament" (*More Than One Way?* 110-11).

Pinnock has proved himself right. Denying inerrancy is a slope, not a platform. In fifteen years, he went from biblical inerrancy to denying basic Bible doctrines. As a result, he and his followers now have an unreliable Bible and a very small God. Worse, there is no evidence that they have yet reached the bottom of the slope.

Lesson 2

A Selection from Bel and the Dragon

The apocryphal book Bel and the Dragon describes what purports to be a fascinating incident from the life of Daniel. The first part of the story relates Daniel's encounter with the idol Bel and its priests. It is a tale of mystery and intrigue, providing the first "locked room" case in literary history. Because of his great wisdom, Daniel proves to King Cyrus that his god Bel is not real and that the priests are charlatans. As a result, the idol is destroyed and the priests and their families are killed. (The actual story may be found in any copy of the Apocrypha or on page 59, Level E, of the BJU Bible curriculum.) The subsequent story of Daniel and the dragon (recounted below) continues the plot.

This story is included here as an illustration of the contents of the Apocrypha that should both interest your students and confirm the difference in character between these books and genuine Scripture.

. . .

Now there was a great serpent in that place, and the Babylonians worshiped it. And the king said to Daniel, "You cannot deny that it is a living god, so worship it."

And Daniel said, "I will worship the Lord my God, for he is a living God. But with your permission, O King, I will kill this serpent without sword or stick."

And the king said, "You have my permission."

And Daniel took pitch, fat, and hair and boiled them together, and made lumps of them, and he put them into the serpent's mouth, and it ate them and burst open. And he said, "See the objects of your worship!"

When the Babylonians heard it, they were very indignant and made a conspiracy against the king, saying, "The king has become a Jew! He has overturned Bel, and killed the serpent, and slaughtered the priests."

So they went to the king and said, "Give Daniel up to us, or else we will kill you and your household."

And the king saw that they were pressing him hard, and he was forced to give Daniel up to them. And they threw him into the lions' den and he remained there six days. There were seven lions in the den; and they had been given two human bodies and two sheep every day; but now these were not given them, so that they might devour Daniel.

Now the prophet Habakkuk was in Judea, and he had cooked a stew and crumbled bread into a bowl, and was going into the field to carry it to the reapers, when the angel of the Lord said to Habakkuk, "Carry the dinner that you have to Babylon, to Daniel, in the lions' den."

And Habakkuk said, "Sir, I have never seen Babylon, and I do not know the den."

Then the angel of the Lord took hold of the crown of his head, and lifted him up by his hair and with the speed of the wind set him down in Babylon, right over the den. And Habakkuk shouted, "Daniel! Daniel! Take the dinner which God has sent you."

And Daniel said, "You have remembered me, O God, and have not forsaken those who love you."

Then Daniel arose and ate. And the angel of God immediately put Habakkuk back in his own place again.

On the seventh day, the king came to mourn for Daniel; and he came to the den and looked in, and there sat Daniel. Then the king shouted loudly, "You are great, Lord God of Daniel, and there is no other beside you!"

And he lifted him out, and the men who had tried to bring about his destruction he threw into the den; and they were instantly devoured before their eyes.

Class Discussion and Observations

1. Could Habakkuk have been living at the time of Daniel's adventure in the lions' den?

   Habakkuk had prophesied about 609 B.C. concerning the coming judgment of Judah at the hands of the Chaldeans. Daniel was probably thrown into the lions' den about 535 B.C.; King Cyrus had no jurisdiction over Daniel prior to about 539 B.C. This is an interval of at least seventy years. We have no way of knowing Habakkuk's age at the time he wrote his book, but an age over 20 would make him quite old at the date of this incident. While it is possible that he could have been alive at the time of this event, it is not likely.

2. Was there really a great serpent or dragon in Babylon that was worshiped?

   The idol Bel, in the first part of the story, is the well-known Babylonian god Marduk.

Strangely, nothing is mentioned in history of a huge, living serpent being worshiped in Babylon. This was not an unimportant city in some out-of-the-way place. We would expect a phenomenon such as this to be mentioned in other literature.

3. How do the details in the Apocrypha concerning the incident with the lions' den correspond to Daniel's version?

Apocrypha	Daniel
1. Thrown in because of killing the serpent	1. Thrown in because of praying to God instead of the king
2. Motivation was anger	2. Motivation was jealousy
3. Length of time was seven days	3. Length of time was one night

4. Why did God send Habakkuk to Daniel with food? Was it necessary?

Daniel's reaction was that he was encouraged that God had not forsaken him. Certainly he would have felt that way already since he was surrounded by rapacious lions in a confined area and was not touched. Daniel would have survived one more day without food, so starvation does not seem to be the issue. There really does not appear to be any reason for such a fantastic miracle to have occurred.

5. Some may say that this story was not meant to be historical or factual. Rather, it is an allegory which teaches a truth or lesson. The lesson taught is that there are no other gods but Jehovah, and He will take care of His faithful ones. If it was meant to be historical, there are serious problems with the facts. If it was meant to be an allegorical book, this intention itself sets it apart from all other inspired books. Besides, if God wanted to assure His children that He will take care of them, He would not fabricate some story to prove that He does. An example from real life would be much more convincing.

A Selection from The Shepherd of Hermas

The Shepherd of Hermas is one of the New Testament apocryphal books, probably written somewhere near the end of the first century. It is a lengthy work (longer than any canonical book) consisting of a series of five visions, twelve fairly short commandments, and ten lengthy parables. Its state of preservation is one indication that it does not deserve a place in the canon. J. B. Lightfoot, in his collection of the writings of the Apostolic Fathers, published in 1891, says that about three-fourths of the Greek original exists in only a single fourteenth-century manuscript. The last portion of the book (about 5 percent of its whole length) simply did not exist in Greek; Lightfoot had to supply this portion from a Latin translation, of which there were about twenty manuscripts. We supply here Lightfoot's translation of the first vision.

. . .

The master, who reared me, had sold me to one Rhoda in Rome. After many years, I met her again, and began to love her as a sister. After a certain time I saw her bathing in the river Tiber; and I gave her my hand, and led her out of the river. So, seeing her beauty, I reasoned in my heart, saying, "Happy were I, if I had such an one to wife both in beauty and in character." I merely reflected on this and nothing more. After a certain time, as I was journeying to Cumae, and glorifying God's creatures for their greatness and splendour and power, as I walked I fell asleep. And a Spirit took me, and bore me away through a pathless tract, through which no man could pass: for the place was precipitous, and broken into clefts by reason of the waters. When then I had crossed the river, I came into the level country, and knelt down, and began to pray to the Lord and to confess my sins.

Now, while I prayed, the heaven was opened, and I see the lady, whom I had desired, greeting me from heaven, saying, "Good morrow, Hermas."

And, looking at her, I said to her, "Lady, what doest thou here?"

Then she answered me, "I was taken up, that I might convict thee of thy sins before the Lord."

I said to her, "Dost thou now convict me?"

"Nay, not so," said she, "but hear the words, that I shall say to thee. God, Who dwelleth in the heavens, and created out of nothing the things which are, and increased and multiplied them for His holy Church's sake, is wroth with thee, for that thou didst sin against me."

I answered her and said, "Sin against thee? In what way? Did I ever speak an unseemly word unto thee? Did I not always regard thee as a goddess? Did I not always respect thee as a sister? How couldst thou falsely charge me, lady, with such villainy and uncleanness?"

Laughing she saith unto me, "The desire after evil entered into thine heart. Nay, thinkest thou not that it is an evil deed for a righteous man, if the evil desire should enter into his heart? It is indeed a sin and a great one too," saith she; "for the righteous man entertaineth righteous purposes. While then his purposes are righteous, his repute stands stedfast in the heavens, and he finds the Lord easily propitiated in all that he does. But they that entertain evil purposes in their hearts, bring upon themselves death and captivity, especially they that claim for themselves this present world, and boast in its riches, and cleave not to the good things that are to come. Their souls shall rue it, seeing that they have no hope, but have abandoned themselves and their life. But do thou pray unto God, and He shall heal thine own sins, and those of thy whole house, and of all the saints."

As soon as she had spoken these words the heavens were shut; and I was given over to horror and grief. Then I said within myself, "If this sin is recorded against me, how can I be saved? Or how shall I propitiate God for my sins which are full-blown? Or with what words shall I entreat the Lord that He may be propitious unto me?"

While I was advising and discussing these matters in my heart, I see before me a great white chair of snow-white wool; and there came an aged lady in glistening raiment, having a book in her hands, and she sat down alone, and she saluted me, "Good morrow, Hermas."

Then I, grieved and weeping, said, "Good morrow, lady."

And she said to me, "Why so gloomy, Hermas, thou that art patient and good-tempered, and art always smiling? Why so downcast in thy looks, and far from cheerful?"

And I said to her, "Because of an excellent lady's saying that I had sinned against her."

Then she said, "Far be this thing from the servant of God! Nevertheless the thought did enter into thy heart concerning her. Now to the servants of God such a purpose bringeth sin. For it is an evil and mad purpose to overtake a devout spirit that hath been already approved, that it should desire an evil deed, and especially if it be Hermas the temperate, who abstaineth from every evil desire, and is full of all simplicity and of great guilelessness. Yet it is not for this that God is wroth with thee, but that thou mayest convert thy family, that hath done wrong against the Lord and against you their parents. But out of fondness for thy children thou didst not admonish thy family, but didst suffer it to become fearfully corrupt. Therefore the Lord is wroth with thee. But He will heal all thy past sins, which have been committed in thy family; for by reason of their sins and iniquities thou hast been corrupted by the affairs of this world. But the great mercy of the Lord had pity on thee and thy family, and will strengthen thee, and establish thee in His glory. Only be not thou careless, but take courage, and strengthen thy family. For as the smith hammering his work conquers the task which he wills, so also doth righteous discourse repeated daily conquer all evil. Cease not therefore to reprove thy children; for I know that if they shall repent with all their heart, they shall be written in the books of life with the saints."

After these words of hers had ceased, she saith unto me, "Wilt thou listen to me as I read?"

Then say I, "Yes, lady." She saith to me, "Be attentive, and hear the glories of God." I listened with attention and with wonder to that which I had no power to remember; for all the words were terrible, such as man cannot bear. The last words however I remembered, for they were suitable for us and gentle. "Behold, the God of Hosts, Who by His invisible and mighty power and by His great wisdom created the world, and by His glorious purpose clothed His creation with comeliness, and by His strong word fixed the heaven, and founded the earth upon the waters, and by His own wisdom and providence formed His holy Church, which also He blessed—behold, He removeth the heavens and the mountains and the hills and the seas, and all things are made level for His elect, that He may fulfil to them the promise which He promised with great glory and rejoicing, if so be that they shall keep the ordinances of God, which they received, with great faith."

When then she finished reading and arose from her chair, there came four young men, and they took away the chair, and departed towards the East. Then she calleth me unto her, and she touched my breast, and saith to me, "Did my reading please thee?"

And I say unto her, "Lady, these last words please me, but the former were difficult and hard."

Then she spoke to me, saying, "These last words are for the righteous, but the former are for the heathen and the rebellious." While she yet spoke with me, two men appeared, and took her by the arms, and they departed, whither the chair also had gone, towards the East. And she smiled as she departed and, as she was going, she saith to me, "Play the man, Hermas."

Class Discussion and Observations

The general flavor of this writing is much different from that of Scripture; it features the author's personal experience far more extensively than the canonical writings. The only possible comparisons are with John's visions in the Revelation and with some of the autobiographical sections of Paul's writings. But John's visions do not reveal his inner psychology to any great extent; such psychology is the main focus of this vision. Paul's autobiographical details are intended to meet the needs of his readers; he says what he says about himself because his readers need to hear it. This writer seems simply to enjoy talking about himself and his experience.

Your students may think it a problem that Hermas says he fell asleep as he walked. It is indeed hard to understand how this could happen, and it seems to suggest that what we are reading is fiction rather than fact. But your students must be careful with this reasoning. The same reasoning is used by unbelievers to discredit miracles in the Bible. God could certainly cause someone to fall asleep while walking, if it suited His purpose to do so. This detail alone does not discredit the book.

More serious objection to the book can be raised on the basis of its incompatibility with Scripture. For example, Hermas says that he always viewed Rhoda as a goddess. A goddess? Such language seems to reflect the spirit of an idolatrous age rather than the Spirit of the God who hates idolatry. Hermas also seems to think that he must somehow earn God's pardon for his sins: "How shall I propitiate God for my sins . . . ? Or with what words shall I entreat the Lord that He may be propitious unto me?" Hermas seems to lack the simple confidence expressed in I John 1:9: "If we confess our sins, He is faithful and just to forgive us our sins, and to cleanse us from all unrighteousness." Someone might argue, though, that this is presented as Hermas's faulty understanding rather than as divine truth. But the woman speaking from heaven seems to confirm Hermas's view by saying, "While then [the righteous man's] purposes are righteous, his repute stands stedfast in the heavens, and he finds the Lord easily propitiated in all that he does."

While literature such as this may be interesting and may reflect certain aspects of biblical truth, it has about it the marks of human frailty rather than divine infallibility, and it clearly does not deserve a place in the Scripture.

Chapter 3

Oral Tradition Exercise

This exercise is designed to show the danger of saying that part of the Bible was transmitted orally over a number of years before actually being written down. Have the class (or you yourself) select the ten students with the best memories. Read the following apocryphal story of Judith quietly to the first student. That student must then turn and repeat the story to the best of his memory to the next student and so on. If each student represents a generation and if a generation is approximately 30 years, then this exercise represents what can be expected to happen to a story transmitted orally over a period of 300 years.

One day the Assyrians decided to attack the Jews. The commander-in-chief of the Assyrians was Holofernes. Holofernes laid seige to Bethulia, a town lying on the route to Jerusalem, and cut off its water supply. After 34 days the exhausted Jewish defenders began to lose heart, but reluctantly agreed to resist 5 more days before surrendering.

A young woman by the name of Judith, a beautiful and pious widow, promised, with God's help, to defeat the Assyrians. After praying for divine help, she put on her best clothes and, accompanied by her maid, went to the Assyrian camp. Here she convinced Holofernes that soon he would be able to conquer the Jews because they had provoked their God by proposing to eat the offerings set aside for the temple. On the fourth day Holofernes invited her to a private banquet in his tent. As he was lying in a drunken stupor, Judith prayed, took his own sword, and cut off his head, which she then put into a sack and carried back to the elders of Bethulia. The enemy, having found their leader dead, fled in panic and were slaughtered and spoiled by the Jews.

Taken from Bruce Metzger's summary of Judith in the *Expositor's Bible Commentary,* vol.1, p. 165.

Lesson 4

Scribal Copying Exercise

This exercise is designed to illustrate to the students the difficulty of accurate manuscript copying.

INANTIQUITYNONLITERARYEVERYDAYDOCUMENTSWERE

CUSTOMARILYWRITTENINACURSIVEHANDINWHICHMOST

OFTHELETTERSWEREFORMEDWITHOUTLIFTINGTHEPENAND

ABBREVIATIONSWEREFREQUENTLYUSEDWEREANYBOOKSOF

THEGREEKBIBLEEVERCIRCULATEDINCURSIVESCRIPT

SCHOLARSARGUETHATITISHIGHLYUNLIKELYTHATTHE

ORIGINALTEXTSWEREEVERWRITTENINCURSIVESCRIPT

ITWASDIFFICULTTOUSETHATFORMOFWRITINGBECAUSE

OFTHEROUGHSURFACEOFTHEPAPYRUSONTHEOTHERHAND

ONESCHOLARPOINTEDOUTTHATINTHEBOOKOFCHRONICLES

CODEXVATICANUSHADHADCERTAINCHANGESOFLETTERS

WHICHCANNOTBEEXPLAINEDINTERMSOFCONFUSIONOF

UNCIALSCRIPTINWHICHTHESELETTERSAREVERY

DIFFERENTFROMONEANOTHERBUTWHICHAREREADILY

EXPLAINABLEINCURSIVESCRIPTWHERETHEYRESEMBLE

EACHOTHERCLOSELYONEVERYSIDE.

This cutting was taken from Bruce Metzger's book *New Testament Textual Criticism,* p. 188, and modified for the purposes of this exercise. Here is the text of the passage in a more readable format.

1. In antiquity non-literary, everyday documents were

2. customarily written in a cursive hand in which most

3. of the letters were formed without lifting the pen and

4. abbreviations were frequently used. Were any books of

5. the Greek Bible ever circulated in cursive script?

6. Scholars argue that it is highly unlikely that the

7. original texts were ever written in cursive script.

8. It was difficult to use that form of writing because

9. of the rough surface of the papyrus. On the other hand,

10. one scholar pointed out that in the book of Chronicles,

11. Codex Vaticanus had had certain changes of letters

12. which cannot be explained in terms of confusion of

13. uncial script, in which these letters are very

14. different from one another but which are readily

15. explainable in cursive script, where they resemble

16. each other closely on every side.

Statistics of lines (letters/words): Line 1 (43/6), line 2 (43/9), line 3 (45/10), line 4 (45/8), line 5 (42/8), line 6 (42/9), line 7 (43/8), line 8 (43/10), line 9 (43/11), line 10 (45/10), line 11 (43/8), line 12 (42/9), line 13 (38/8), line 14 (41/8), line 15 (43/7), line 16 (27/6).

Notes:

This exercise is designed to recreate the difficulties of the ancient scribe. The early manuscripts were written in uncials (capital letters), with no break between words or sentences. Terms describing common errors are **homeoteleuton** (skipping material between lines that have the same ending—notice lines 5 and 7), **haplography** (writing something once which should be written twice—notice line 11), and **dittography** (writing something twice which should be written only once). Another common error that your students might make is the writing of "one very" instead of "on every" in line 16.

The fact that the text being copied is unfamiliar makes this exercise somewhat different from the work of the biblical scribes, and it may affect the students' accuracy. They may feel that they could copy something familiar more accurately than they can copy this passage. But remind them that, when copying familiar text, they may be tempted to write what they remember instead of copying what is written. Many manuscript differences in the Gospels, for instance, tend to assimilate differences between the Gospels. It is easy to see how a scribe especially familiar with an account in one Gospel might accidentally use some of that Gospel's wording when copying the slightly different account of the same incident in another Gospel.

You may wish to distribute photocopies instead of using the overhead projector, in order to minimize the need for head movement during copying. (The section of transparency masters includes pages for this exercise; reduce the size if photocopying instead of projecting.) Give the students about 12-13 minutes to copy the exercise, enough time to get through it if they hurry. When time is up, show the easy-to-read transparency and have the students exchange papers to check each other's accuracy, marking any errors. Point out the common errors that they, as well as scribes, made. But also point out how easy it is to figure out what the errors are and how they were made. A very large percentage of manuscript differences can be traced back to these kinds of simple mistakes.

Variations:

1. Appoint a few conscientious students to be Masoretic scribes. As they copy, they will need to keep the words on the same lines and will need to know the number of lines and the number of words and letters per line. This way they will be able to count what they've copied in order to check their work. They should be much more accurate than the average student. Of course, they will need more time.

2. Don't show the original on the screen, and collect any photocopied originals. Have the students check their work among themselves to see if they can come up with an accurate copy. This process is very similar to what we must do today because the originals are no longer available.

The Scriptorium Exercise

This is a variation of the written Scribal Copying Exercise and is designed to show the students the special difficulties connected with copying in a scriptorium setting, where many scribes write what they hear one person (the lector) reading. At a reasonable pace read the paragraph only once. Make sure that when the students correct the exercise, they check the punctuation.

> Jon and Bryan went to the store. There they bought a sum of goods totalling $5.50. They pulled out their wallets only to find they had no money. They did not know what to do. A policeman came and led them away to Jael. She took their fingerprints and sent them home. They're going to be more careful tomorrow.

Note: You must be careful how you read certain words. You should pronounce "Jael" so that it could be confused with "jail." Also, be sure to read "they're" as written, rather than expanding it to "they are"; you want to see how many students write "their" or "there."

Extreme Literalism in Translation

Here is some material to illustrate what the Bible would sound like if translated extremely literally, with very little liberty taken to smooth out the language. The cause of the roughness is not that the original languages are defective; the original reads very smoothly to a native speaker. The cause of the roughness is the simple fact that languages differ from one another, and word-for-word translation from any language into any other language is very difficult to read.

We chose these passages, not because they yield especially rough translations, but because they represent the beginning of each testament, and because they are familiar to your students. In our translation we have not overplayed the point by being unnecessarily awkward; we have simply tried to present an accurate sample of what the whole Bible would sound like if translators allowed themselves no liberty to change minor details of wording in order to maintain good English idiom.

Genesis 1:1-5

1 In beginning God created the heavens and the earth.

2 And the earth was empty and waste, and darkness upon face of ocean, and the Spirit of God hovering upon the face of the water.

3 And God said, Be light. And light was.

4 And God saw the light, that good, and God divided between the light and between the darkness.

5 And God called to the light day and to the darkness he called night. And it was evening and it was morning, day one.

Matthew 1:18-25

18 And of Jesus Christ the birth thus was. His mother Mary having been engaged to Joseph, before than to come together them, she was found having in womb by Holy Spirit.

19 And Joseph, her husband, being righteous and not wishing to make her an example, thought secretly to divorce her.

20 And these things he thinking, behold an angel of Lord according to a dream appeared to him saying, Joseph son of David, do not fear to take Mary your wife, for the thing in her begotten of Spirit is Holy.

21 And she shall bear a son, and you shall call his name Jesus, for he shall save his people from their sins.

22 And all this has happened in order that it might be fulfilled, the thing spoken by Lord through the prophet saying,

23 Behold, the virgin shall have in womb and shall bear a son, and they shall call his name Emmanuel, which is translated, with us the God.

24 And having arisen Joseph from the sleep, he did as commanded him the angel of Lord, and he took his wife,

25 And he was not knowing her until which she brought forth a son, and he called his name Jesus.

Chapter 5

Believing it *All!*

The evidence presented in this lesson adds another important dimension to our study: assurance that everything the Bible teaches is true.[1] Some people have marked out a middle position between sound doctrine and total rejection of truth by claiming that the Bible is infallible in matters of salvation but not in nonessential matters such as science, history, and geography. This kind of thinking became common during the eighteenth and nineteenth centuries, when scientists and historians began to point out passages where the Bible teaches something that was inconsistent with what was "known" in other fields of study. Uncomfortable with simply declaring the critics wrong, some Christians restated the doctrine of inspiration to apply only to the essential doctrines of salvation, allowing for errors in other areas.

This position is extremely dangerous. It is not always possible to distinguish between science, history, geography, and salvation. The work of Christ includes miracles that defy science; and His life, death, and resurrection took place in a definite historical and geographical context. If we let unbelievers take away certain portions of our Bible, where will we draw the line? In fact, the very first portion they want to take away is the Creation account, which they see as unscientific. But if we give up the biblical record of Creation, we lose the very foundation of every other Bible doctrine. For example, the Bible's teaching about salvation requires us to believe that death is the result of man's sin. But how can this be true if Darwinian evolution is true? If evolution is true, death must have been in existence for millions of years before the first man ever existed. If we give unbelievers the first inch on this point, we will have no basis on which to resist their taking away everything else we believe.

Chapter 5 looks at a few evidences for accepting all the Bible as true. Many of the objections that arose more than one hundred years ago have evaporated in the light of further discoveries. Today we have no reason for hesitating to declare that every word God inspired is true, no matter what field of knowledge it touches upon.

Someone in your class may ask how this position differs from the position we put forth in the previous lesson that manuscript copying errors are no problem, since they do not undermine biblical doctrines. The difference is this: the errors we accepted in the previous lesson are slips of the pen or mind during the copying process. What we deny here is that Moses or Paul wrote something that was not true. The former can happen without compromising the doctrine of inspiration, since we do not claim that God inspired the manuscript copyists. But if a Scripture writer himself wrote something that was not true, we cannot claim that God controlled the very wording of what was originally written, and our doctrine of inspiration disintegrates. A person who allows for copyist errors has a relatively narrow range of choices regarding what a particular passage of Scripture requires him to believe. But someone who allows for mistakes in the original writing gives himself almost unlimited freedom to pick and choose what he will believe.

Engage your students in an exercise that will demonstrate to them the importance of this distinction. First, have them turn to a familiar passage of Scripture, Luke 1:26-38. After someone reads the passage, read the following section, which is the same passage with some of the variations from different manuscripts. Before you begin reading, have your students close their Bibles so they must *listen* for the variants. At three points this passage differs from the wording of the text used by the KJV translators. Those variations are indicated in bold-italic font.

26 And in the sixth month the angel Gabriel was sent from God unto a city of Galilee, named Nazareth,

27 To a virgin espoused to a man whose name was Joseph, of the house of David; and the virgin's name [was] Mary.

28 And the angel came in unto her, and said, Hail, [thou that art] highly favoured, the Lord [is] with thee: blessed [art] thou among women. ***Blessed art thou among women, and blessed is the fruit of thy womb.***

29 And when she saw [him], she was troubled at his saying, and cast in her mind what manner of salutation this should be.

30 And the angel said unto her, Fear not, Mary: for thou hast found favour with God.

31 And, behold, thou shalt conceive in thy womb, and bring forth a son, and shalt call his name JESUS.

32 He shall be great, and shall be called the Son of the Highest: and the Lord God shall give unto him the throne of his father David:

33 And he shall reign over the house of Jacob for ever; and of his kingdom there shall be no end.

34 Then said Mary unto the angel, How shall this be, seeing I know not a man?

35 And the angel answered and said unto her, The Holy Ghost shall come upon thee, and the power of the Highest shall overshadow thee: therefore also

that holy thing which shall be born *["of thee" does not occur in some manuscripts]* shall be called the Son of God.

36 And, behold, thy cousin Elisabeth, she hath also conceived a son in her old age: and this is the sixth month with her, who was called barren.

37 For **nothing from God** shall be impossible.

38 And Mary said, Behold the handmaid of the Lord; be it unto me according to thy word. And the angel departed from her.

First, ask them to state (to the best of their recollection) the variants from the KJV. Second, ask them how these variations could change the meaning of the passage.

Though the first variant is lengthy, it does not affect the message. Someone may complain that it makes the passage sound "Roman Catholic," because it includes two phrases found in the often-recited rosary that are not found in this passage in the KJV. However, there is nothing untrue about those phrases. The problem with these phrases in the rosary is their use in the Catholic Church, not their content. In fact, these very words are found without variant readings in verse 42 of the same chapter.

The second variant is less noticeable: the KJV has "of thee" in verse 35, but the second passage does not. The only difference here is that the KJV's reading is a bit clearer. The context, however, renders the absence of these two words no problem for our understanding.

The third variant is even more minor: "from" instead of "with." Sometimes a preposition can make quite a difference in meaning. In this context, however, both prepositions mean basically the same thing: "God can do anything."

It is true that the original reading for this passage could have been only one of each of these variations. However, the meaning of the autograph is clear in each variant. We may not know for certain the exact wording of God's inspired original for this passage, but we do know the meaning of the autograph.

Now ask your students how a non-inerrantist might explain this passage. They should note, first of all, what a non-inerrantist is: a person who believes there were mistakes in the autographs of the Scripture—usually or exclusively in the areas of science, history, and geography. Second, they should note that such a person would grant that the meaning of the autograph in this passage is the same as we would observe: An angel came to Mary and assured her that she would, as a virgin, miraculously give birth to the divine Messiah. Third, the non-inerrantist might refuse to believe that Mary, as a virgin, actually gave birth to Jesus. Why? A virgin-birth is a biological impossibility.

Prophecy and Fulfillment in Daniel 8

The major source of information for this section is Leon Wood, *A Commentary on Daniel* (Grand Rapids: Zondervan, 1973).

Prophecy in the Text

1 In the third year of the reign of king Belshazzar a vision appeared unto me, even unto me Daniel, after that which appeared unto me at the first.

2 And I saw in a vision; and it came to pass, when I saw, that I was at Shushan in the palace, which is in the province of Elam; and I saw in a vision, and I was by the river of Ulai.

3 Then I lifted up mine eyes, and saw, and, behold, there stood before the river a ram which had two horns: and the two horns were high; but one was higher than the other, and the higher came up last.

4 I saw the ram pushing westward, and northward, and southward; so that no beasts might stand before him, neither was there any that could deliver out of his hand; but he did according to his will, and became great.

5 And as I was considering, behold, an he goat came from the west on the face of the whole earth, and touched not the ground: and the goat had a notable horn between his eyes.

6 And he came to the ram that had two horns, which I had seen standing before the river, and ran unto him in the fury of his power.

7 And I saw him come close unto the ram, and he was moved with choler against him, and smote the ram, and brake his two horns: and there was no power in the ram to stand before him, but he cast him down to the ground, and stamped upon him: and there was none that could deliver the ram out of his hand.

8 Therefore the he goat waxed very great: and when he was strong, the great horn was broken; and for it came up four notable ones toward the four winds of heaven.

9 And out of one of them came forth a little horn, which waxed exceeding great, toward the south, and toward the east, and toward the pleasant land.

Fulfillment in History

Daniel received this vision about 551 B.C.

Verse 20 identifies this ram as the Medo-Persian empire; the Persians came on the scene later than the Medes and, through Cyrus, came to dominate. This process was already well underway at the time of the vision, and would continue for about 200 years. The three directions of expansion are listed in the correct order chronologically; in Daniel's day the westward phase was just beginning.

Verse 21 identifies this goat as Greece (located on the westward edge of the Persian empire) and the horn as Greece's first king, which was Alexander the Great. The imagery suggests the tremendous speed with which Alexander would conquer huge territories as well as the motive of revenge ("moved with choler"); we know from history that the Greeks sought revenge against Persia because of earlier Persian attacks upon Greece. The fulfillment of these verses took place around 333 B.C.

Alexander suddenly died of a fever at the height of his power, in 323 B.C. Verse 22 explains that his domain would be divided among four kings and that their kingdoms would not match the power of his. This happened when the territories conquered by Alexander were divided among four of his generals. Cassander received Greece and Macedonia; Thrace and Asia Minor went to Lysimachus; Seleucus took Syria and the eastern territories, and Ptolemy took Egypt. This was not an orderly division; it took shape over a period of about twenty years as these generals fought with one another over their territories.

The little horn symbolizes Antiochus Epiphanes, who ruled the Seleucid domain from about 175 to 164 B.C. The little horn's becoming great reflects the fact that Antiochus was not even a rightful heir to the throne but gained it through flattery and bribery. This passage also predicts his atrocities against

10 And it waxed great, even to the host of heaven; and it cast down some of the host and of the stars to the ground, and stamped upon them.

11 Yea, he magnified himself even to the prince of the host, and by him the daily sacrifice was taken away, and the place of his sanctuary was cast down.

12 And an host was given him against the daily sacrifice by reason of transgression, and it cast down the truth to the ground; and it practised, and prospered.

13 Then I heard one saint speaking, and another saint said unto that certain saint which spake, How long shall be the vision concerning the daily sacrifice, and the transgression of desolation, to give both the sanctuary and the host to be trodden under foot?

14 And he said unto me, Unto two thousand and three hundred days; then shall the sanctuary be cleansed.

15 And it came to pass, when I, even I Daniel, had seen the vision, and sought for the meaning, then, behold, there stood before me as the appearance of a man.

16 And I heard a man's voice between the banks of Ulai, which called, and said, Gabriel, make this man to understand the vision.

17 So he came near where I stood: and when he came, I was afraid, and fell upon my face: but he said unto me, Understand, O son of man: for at the time of the end shall be the vision.

18 Now as he was speaking with me, I was in a deep sleep on my face toward the ground: but he touched me, and set me upright.

19 And he said, Behold, I will make thee know what shall be in the last end of the indignation: for at the time appointed the end shall be.

20 The ram which thou sawest having two horns are the kings of Media and Persia.

21 And the rough goat is the king of Grecia: and the great horn that is between his eyes is the first king.

22 Now that being broken, whereas four stood up for it, four kingdoms shall stand up out of the nation, but not in his power.

23 And in the latter time of their kingdom, when the transgressors are come to the full, a king of fierce countenance, and understanding dark sentences, shall stand up.

24 And his power shall be mighty, but not by his own power: and he shall destroy wonderfully, and shall prosper, and practise, and shall destroy the mighty and the holy people.

Israel ("the pleasant land" and "the host of the stars") and against the temple service (v. 12). He tried to force the Jews to adopt Greek ways in disobedience to Scripture; when they refused, he persecuted them, profaned the temple, and destroyed Jerusalem.

The cleansing of the temple, after Antiochus profaned it, took place under Judas Maccabeus on December 25, 165 B.C. Working back 2,300 days would place the beginning of this persecution in the year 171 B.C. Historical data are not precise enough to pin down an exact day, but we do know that this was the year when Antiochus's persecution of the Jews began.

These verses provide basic interpretation for the prophecies given earlier in the chapter. Details are given above.

This passage refers both to Antiochus (who ruled toward the end of the Greek period, just before Rome absorbed the Greek Empire) and to the future king who will persecute God's people during the tribulation period, as prophesied elsewhere, particularly in the book of Revelation. As bad as he was, Antiochus was only a foreshadowing of the horrors the Jewish people will have to experience in order to prepare them to accept Jesus as their Messiah.

25 And through his policy also he shall cause craft to prosper in his hand; and he shall magnify himself in his heart, and by peace shall destroy many: he shall also stand up against the Prince of princes; but he shall be broken without hand.

26 And the vision of the evening and the morning which was told is true: wherefore shut thou up the vision; for it shall be for many days.

27 And I Daniel fainted, and was sick certain days; afterward I rose up, and did the king's business; and I was astonished at the vision, but none understood it.

From Proud Denial to Humble Faith

Eta Linnemann was no dummy. She had well distinguished herself in climbing the ladder of higher education in Germany. Taught by such famous liberal theologians as Rudolf Bultmann and Friedrich Gogarten, she enjoyed the best education that twentieth-century liberal theology could offer. After finishing her degree, she began a life of teaching and writing—her first book became a best-seller. She secured a position as professor of theology and religious education at Braunschweig Technical University, received an honorary professorship at another university, and was inducted into the Society for New Testament Studies.

She had found her niche in life as a respected member of the theological and educational community. Her job was to inform her students and her readers concerning the nature of God's message to mankind. But since Dr. Linnemann did not believe that the Bible was the inspired Word of God, she first had to explain away the miracles in the Scripture as well as its many "unhistorical" events. For her, the core of God's message lay buried under layers of human misunderstandings. These layers could be discerned by human reason, which was to her the primary means of apprehending God. In time, however, she came to some disturbing conclusions. Human reason was not at all a satisfying means of finding God because it had repeatedly proved itself incapable as a flawless guide to truth. In Linnemann's own words: "I was forced to concede two things I did not wish: (1) no 'truth' could emerge from this 'scientific work on the biblical text,' and (2) such labor does not serve the proclamation of the gospel."

The more she thought about these inescapable conclusions, the more depressed she became. To dull her disillusionment, Linnemann buried herself in excessive television watching and alcohol abuse. But God in His grace led her to a group of "vibrant Christians" whose testimonies of a personal relationship with Jesus Christ opened her eyes. "By God's grace and love," she later confessed, "I entrusted my life to Jesus." The Lord freed this proud professor from her addictions and taught her the reality of sin and of His victory for believers: "I can still remember the delicious joy I felt when for the first time black was once more black and white was once more white; the two ceased to pool together as indistinguishable gray."

In time Linnemann realized that she could not continue to teach and write from a historical-critical perspective. "Suddenly it was clear to me that my teaching was a case of the blind leading the blind. I repented for the way I had misled my students." Now she had to decide how she would study the Bible. Would she let her intellect stand over the text, accepting as true only those things that made sense to her fallen, humanistically-educated mind? Or would she accept the Scripture as truth from the outset and change her intellectual perspective any time it conflicted with biblical statements? The thing that compelled her to choose the latter was a verse she had only recently truly grasped—John 3:16. "My life now consisted of what God had done for me and for the whole world—He had given his dear Son." She accepted that Jesus is the Son of God, that He was born of a virgin, and that He is God's Messiah. In short, she became convinced that the Bible was God's inspired Word.

Since that time she has often been asked why she no longer teaches the historical-critical theology she was taught. She responds that she had to reject liberal theology because she had accepted Jesus Christ. At the feet of her Savior she found no place for her former sinful fame. "I regard everything that I taught and wrote before I entrusted my life to Jesus as refuse," she has reflected. "Whatever of these writings I had in my possession I threw into the trash with my own hands in 1978. I ask you sincerely to do the same thing with any of them you may have on your own bookshelf." As of 1992, Eta Linnemann was teaching at a Bible institute in Batu, Indonesia.

—Taken from Eta Linnemann's introduction to her exposé of twentieth-century higher criticism, *Historical Criticism of the Bible: Methodology or Ideology?* Translated by Robert W. Yarbrough (Grand Rapids: Baker Book House, 1990) pp. 17-20.

---

[1]This is not quite the same thing as saying "Everything in the Bible is true." Some things in the Bible are false, because the Bible records lies told by Satan, Abraham, Jacob, Samson, and many others. But the Bible's teaching is true in these places, in that it accurately records the lies. The Bible does not teach that these lies are true; it teaches that these lies were told.

[2]It has been well observed that the Bible is not designed as a textbook of science or history. Therefore it can omit parts of the truth without being considered faulty. What we claim is that what the Bible *does* say on every subject *is* true; none of its teachings is either false or misleading.

Appendix D

The Translators' Preface to the King James Version of the Bible

Introductory Notes

The King James Version of the Bible has been the dominant Bible of the English-speaking world since shortly after its introduction in 1611. Its dominance has been so thorough that it is hard to imagine a time when it did not exist. The authors of this course have attempted to give a historical overview of the processes by which the Bible has come down to our generation, beginning with the inspiration of the original writings and continuing through the processes of manuscript copying and translation. The *Preface* contained in this appendix demonstrates that the approach we have taken is no innovation. So our approach represents the thinking of Christian people at least back to the time of the Reformation. You will find the author of the *Preface* arguing that the translators' views are consistent with the views of the earliest fathers of the church. If the translators' word is reliable, then the approach taken by this course reflects the main flow of Christian thought throughout the history of the church.

The *Preface* is rarely printed anymore, no doubt because the material it contains and the language it uses put it beyond both the interest and the ability of today's average Bible reader. The interest and ability of a Bible *teacher,* though, ought to be above average. We believe the *Preface* deserves your attention for several reasons. We have already mentioned the fact that it supports the approach we have taken in the lessons. In addition, it contains valuable historical information about the dissemination of the Scriptures, both in the early years of the church and in the time of the Catholic/Protestant battles resulting from the Reformation.

A few notes are in order regarding this presentation of the translators' *Preface.* To make the message of the *Preface* clearer, a few of the paragraph breaks have been changed. The headings have also been changed and stated in more familiar English. In the parallel columns you will find the *Preface* in both its original form (left column) and in a modern-language paraphrase (right column; prepared by Randy Leedy). Various Bibles differ slightly in their presentation of the *Preface.* Most of the differences are simply matters of spelling and punctuation. The version reproduced here in the left column is from *The Comprehensive Bible* (London: Samuel Bagster and Sons), 7-18.

The paraphrasing process presented several challenges. In the first place, the *Preface* contains many references to obscure authors and literature. Many of the names do not appear in the major reference sources on church history. These names appear in the Latin form (just as the King James Bible often uses "Esaias" instead of "Isaiah," for example). Wherever the modern English form of a name could be located in the reference works available to the paraphraser, the modern form was used. In other cases the paraphrase retains the original form. The citations contained in the original are recorded verbatim in a section of notes at the end of the *Preface*; Latin titles have not been modernized or translated into English.

Another challenge was to determine the extent to which the language should be paraphrased. At times the original wording yields such clear meaning even to the modern reader that no paraphrase at all was necessary. At other times the obscurity was so great that only a total rewrite could clarify it. Some of the sentences are extremely long, and the only way to break them up involved some reordering of thoughts. However, none of this was done in a haphazard manner; instead, the paraphraser first identified all the interconnections between ideas, then set about to reconstruct a more readable presentation of those ideas and their relationships to one another. The main goal has not been to preserve the wording of the original (after all, there is no absolute requirement to change it at all) but rather to make the meaning as clear as possible to the modern reader who might be daunted by the complexity of the original. One other feature introduced by the paraphraser toward this goal is the section headings. These headings will help the reader follow the flow of main ideas and keep his place in the discussion.

One of the more interesting challenges relates to determining the exact meaning of words. Some of the words seemed not to present a problem at first glance, but more careful thought raised doubt about exactly what the word meant. Regular consulting sessions with the *Oxford English Dictionary* revealed many cases where a word familiar to modern readers is used with a different meaning in the *Preface,* similar to many words in the King James Bible itself (e.g., *prevent, let,* and *conversation.*) One such example is the word *preposterous,* used in the statement "it is a preposterous order to teach first, and to learn after." Careful reading suggests that the modern meaning, denoting absurdity, does not seem to fit the context very well. The *O.E.D.,* though, reveals what might have been apparent in the etymology had the paraphraser had eyes to see it: in the seventeenth century the word could mean "backwards" (note *pre-* and *post-*).

The Latin and Greek quotations presented yet another challenge, since sometimes the author of the

Preface did not think it necessary to translate them. The paraphraser is fairly confident that he has rendered them accurately; however, as with the original English, he has striven for clarity of meaning as a higher priority than word-for-word correspondence. Recognition is due to Carl Conrad, of the Department of Classics of Washington University, St. Louis, Missouri, for help with the Latin quotations. The English quotations given in the original have for the most part been maintained word-for-word rather than being paraphrased; most of these quotations are from the Bible, and the paraphraser did not feel at liberty to meddle with their wording.

On a personal level, the exercise has brought the paraphraser to a deeper appreciation of the difficulties faced by a translator. Sometimes it is impossible to conserve the beauty or the force of the original while also communicating the meaning clearly. Something has to give. On the other hand, sometimes the modern language has a nice way to express something that the original seems to labor over. In such cases it is tempting to depart from the wording of the original in the interest of being clever, and it is a hard temptation to resist. The paraphraser is glad that he was dealing with the words of mere men. This project has brought him to a deeper respect for those who have maintained a careful set of working principles in translating the Scriptures.

One other word is in order about the content of the *Preface*. It is not the Word of God, and it is therefore fallible. Not every point of history and theology contained in it is maintained among most Bible believers today. Nevertheless its message is clear, and it is correct.

We have presented the *Preface* in parallel columns in order to meet the needs of a variety of readers. Those thoroughly familiar with the English of the seventeenth century will want to ignore the paraphrase and simply read the original. But even these readers will profit from an occasional glance at the right-hand column; they will be surprised at nuances of meaning uncovered there. Others may wish to read the original as much as possible, expecting to get stuck fairly often. They can seek help from the paraphrase as often as necessary. The easiest method for most people would be to read the paraphrase instead of the original. If you read this way, though, you will certainly find yourself sometimes wondering, "Did they really say *that?*" Check it out for yourself; you will find that they did, even if they perhaps put it a little differently. But however you read it, please read it. Your effort will be well rewarded.

THE TRANSLATORS TO THE READER[1]

Innovation Always Greeted with Resistance

Zeal to promote the common good, whether it be by devising any thing ourselves, or revising that which hath been laboured by others, deserveth certainly much respect and esteem, but yet findeth but cold entertainment in the world. It is welcomed with suspicion instead of love, and with emulation instead of thanks: and if there be any hole left for cavil to enter, (and cavil, if it do not find an hole, will make one) it is sure to be misconstrued, and in danger to be condemned. This will easily be granted by as many as know story, or have any experience. For was there ever any thing projected, that savoured any way of newness or renewing, but the same endured many a storm of gainsaying or opposition? A man would think that civility, wholesome laws, learning and eloquence, synods, and Churchmaintenance, (that we speak of no more things of this kind) should be as safe as a sanctuary, and[2] out of shot, as they say, that no man would lift up his heel, no, nor dog move his tongue against the motioners of them. For by the first we are distinguished from brute beasts led with sensuality: by the second we are bridled and restrained from outrageous behaviour, and from doing of injuries, whether by fraud or by violence: by the third we are enabled to inform and reform others by the light and feeling that we have attained unto ourselves: briefly, by the fourth, being brought together to a parley face to face, we sooner compose our differences, than by writings, which are endless: and lastly, that the Church be sufficiently provided for is so agreeable to good reason and conscience, that those mothers are holden to be less cruel, that kill their children as soon as they are born, than those nursing fathers and mothers, (wheresoever they be) that withdraw from them who hang upon their breasts (and upon whose breasts again themselves do hang to receive the spiritual and sincere milk of the word) livelihood and support fit for their estates. Thus it is apparent, that these things which we speak of are of most necessary use, and therefore that none, either without absurdity can speak against them, or without note of wickedness can spurn against them.

Yet for all that, the learned know, that certain worthy men[3] have been brought to untimely death for none other fault, but for seeking to reduce their countrymen to good order and discipline: And that in some Commonweals[4] it was made a capital crime, once to motion the making of a new law for the abrogating of an old, though the same were most pernicious: And that certain, which would be counted pillars of the State, and patterns of virtue and prudence, could not be brought for a long time to give way to good letters and refined speech; but bare themselves as averse from them, as from rocks or boxes of poison: And fourthly, that he was no babe, but a great Clerk,[5] that gave forth, (and in writing to

Zeal to promote the benefit of society, whether by producing something new or by improving that which already exists, certainly deserves much respect and esteem; nevertheless, the world grants it no better than an icy reception. Such zeal is greeted with suspicion rather than love, and with jealousy rather than thanks. If a benefactor of mankind leaves any point open to frivolous objection (and when no such opening exists the objectors will always make one), he is sure to be misrepresented, and he runs the risk of being condemned. Anyone who either knows history or has experience will quickly recognize this truth. Has anything new or improved ever been introduced without provoking storms of controversy? One would think that the ideals of civility, good government, education, and communication, orderly assemblies for the administration of church affairs, and provision for the clergy (along with many other such things) would be so far beyond objection that no man would raise a hand nor would a dog move its tongue against those desiring to promote them. After all, civility distinguishes us from brute beasts who know nothing beyond their appetites. Good government bridles us and restrains us from offensive behavior and from injuring one another, whether by fraud or by violence. Education and communication enable us to inform and reform others by the knowledge and sensitivity we ourselves have gained, and ecclesiastical assemblies bring us together face to face so that we settle our differences sooner than we could do by writing books, which multiply themselves to infinity. Finally, provision for the clergy commends itself irresistibly to common sense and to conscience, for those who would deprive their pastors (from whom, ironically, they themselves receive their spiritual sustenance) are like a mother who, even worse than killing her child at the moment of birth, starves him to death over time. It is apparent, then, that these things of which we speak are most necessary and, therefore, that nobody can speak against them without absurdity or kick at them without branding himself an evil man.

In spite of all this, the learned know that certain worthy men have been brought to untimely death for no other fault than that of promoting civility by seeking to bring their countrymen to good order and discipline, that in some nations it was made a capital crime to introduce legislation nullifying an existing law, however harmful the existing law may have been, and that even some who wished to be known as pillars of the State and patterns of virtue and wisdom resisted for a long time pleas for temperate language in writing and in speech, as though wholesome words were like rocks at sea or boxes of poison. On the fourth point, it was no child but rather a great cleric who said (in writing, even, for the remain to posterity) in passion peradventure, but yet he gave forth, That he had not seen any profit to come by any synod or meeting of the Clergy, but rather the contrary: And lastly, against Churchmaintenance and allowance, in such sort as the ambassadors and messengers of the great King of kings should be furnished, it is not unknown what a fiction or fable (so it is esteemed, and for no better by the reporter[6] himself, though superstitious) was devised: namely, That at such time as the professors and teachers of Christianity in the Church of Rome, then a true Church, were liberally endowed, a voice forsooth was heard from heaven, saying, Now is poison poured down into the Church, etc. Thus not only as oft as we speak, as one saith, but also as oft as we do any thing of note or consequence, we subject ourselves to every one's censure, and happy is he that is least tossed upon tongues; for utterly to escape the snatch of them it is impossible.

Resistance to Innovation Always Aimed at the Most Important People

If any man conceit, that this is the lot and portion of the meaner sort only, and that Princes are privileged by their high estate, he is deceived. As *the sword devoureth as well one as another,* as it is in Samuel;[7] nay, as the great commander charged his soldiers in a certain battle to strike at no part of the enemy, but at the face; and as the king of Syria commanded his chief captains[8] *to fight neither with small nor great, save only against the king of Israel:* so it is too true, that envy striketh most spitefully at the fairest, and the chiefest. David was a worthy prince, and no man to be compared to him for his first deeds; and yet for as worthy an act as ever he did, even for bringing back the ark of God in solemnity, he was scorned and scoffed at by his own wife.[9] Solomon was greater than David, though not in virtue, yet in power; and by his power and wisdom he built a temple to the Lord, such an one as was the glory of the land of Israel, and the wonder of the whole world. But was that his magnificence liked of by all? We doubt of it. Otherwise why do they lay it in his son's dish, and call unto him for easing[10] of the burden? *Make,* say they, *the grievous servitude of thy father, and his sore yoke, lighter.*[11] Belike he had charged them with some levies, and troubled them with some carriages: hereupon they raise up a tragedy, and wish in their heart the temple had never been built. So hard a thing it is to please all, even when we please God best, and do seek to approve ourselves to every one's conscience.

If we will descend to latter times, we shall find many the like examples of such kind, or rather unkind, acceptance. The first Roman Emperor[12] did never do a more pleasing deed to the learned, nor more profitable to posterity, for conserving the

benefit of future generations) that he had not seen any good to come from any ecclesiastical assembly, but rather the contrary. He said it in passion, perhaps, but he said it just the same. Finally, it is widely known what a myth was invented against adequate provision for the clergy. At the time when the professors and teachers of Christianity in the church of Rome (which was then a true church) received generous wages, a voice was purportedly heard from heaven, saying, "Now is poison poured down into the Church." That this is nothing more than a fable is admitted even by the one who originated it, superstitious as he was, but the point remains that even the virtue of generosity toward ministers of the church has aroused vigorous resentment. So not only whenever we speak, as someone said, but also whenever we do anything noteworthy or significant, we subject ourselves to everyone's censure. To be only lightly tortured by tongues is the best one can hope for; to completely escape their snapping is impossible.

Now if somebody imagines that this kind of thing happens only to unimportant people, and that kings are exempted by their high position, he is deceived. Just as "the sword devoureth as well one as another," as it says in Samuel, and, more to the point, as the great commander ordered his soldiers in a certain battle to strike at no part of the enemy except the face, and as the king of Syria commanded his chief captains to "fight neither with small nor great, save only with the king of Israel," so it is all too true, that envy strikes most spitefully at those of greatest beauty and at those of highest rank. David was an excellent king, whose early reign, at least, is peerless. Nevertheless one of the best things he ever did, bringing back the ark of God in dignity, earned him the scorn and scoffing of his own wife. Solomon was greater yet than David (in power though not in virtue), and by his power and wisdom he built for the Lord a temple so magnificent that it became not only Israel's glory but the wonder of the whole world. But did everyone appreciate his achievement? We doubt it. The contrary attitude manifests itself in the people's demand of his son: "Make the grievous servitude of thy father, and his sore yoke, lighter." Very likely he had burdened them with some taxes and tariffs, and the people had mounted a complaint and wished in their hearts that the temple had never been built. All this shows how difficult it is to please everyone, even when we please God most of all and seek to approve ourselves to everyone's conscience.

If we come down to later times, we will find many similar examples of this kind, or rather unkind, acceptance. The first Roman Emperor did nothing more pleasing to the scholars nor more beneficial to posterity, for maintaining historical records in proper record of times in true supputation, than when he corrected the Calendar, and ordered the year according to the course of the sun: and yet this was imputed to him for novelty and arrogancy, and procured to him great obloquy. So the first Christened Emperor[13] (at the least wise, that openly professed the faith himself, and allowed others to do the like,) for strengthening the empire at his great charges, and providing for the Church, as he did, got for his labour the name Pupillus, as who would say, a wasteful Prince, that had need of a guardian or overseer. So the best Christened Emperor,[14] for the love that he bare unto peace, thereby to enrich both himself and his subjects, and because he did not seek war, but find it, was judged to be no man at arms, (though indeed he excelled in feats of chivalry, and shewed so much when he was provoked,) and condemned for giving himself to his ease, and to his pleasure. To be short, the most learned Emperor of former times, (at the least, the greatest politician,)[15] what thanks had he for cutting off the superfluities of the laws, and digesting them into some order and method? This, that he hath been blotted by some to be an Epitomist, that is, one that extinguished worthy whole volumes, to bring his abridgements into request. This is the measure that hath been rendered to excellent Princes in former times, cum bene facerent, male audire, for their good deeds to be evil spoken of. Neither is there any likelihood that envy and malignity died and were buried with the ancient. No, no, the reproof of Moses taketh hold of most ages; Ye are risen up in your fathers' stead, an increase of sinful men.[16] What is that that hath been done? that which shall be done: and there is no new thing under the sun,[17] saith the wise man. And St. Stephen, As your fathers did, so do ye.[18]

chronology, than correcting the calendar and establishing the solar year. Yet this act brought him charges of novelty and arrogance, and he endured much abuse for it. Similarly the first Christian Emperor (first, at least, to profess the faith openly and allow others to do likewise), for strengthening the empire at great personal expense and for providing for the Church as he did, received as his thanks the epithet Pupillus, meaning a wasteful prince who needed a guardian to protect him from himself. Likewise the best of the Christian Emperors was viewed as a poor soldier and condemned for giving himself to ease and pleasure, all because he loved peace and went to war only when forced to do so. Those who viewed him so seemed ignorant that his aim was the prosperity not only of himself but also of his subjects and that he had proved himself quite formidable when provoked to combat. And what thanks did that most learned Emperor of former times (at least the greatest politician) receive for eliminating unnecessary laws and reducing the legal code to systematic order? His thanks was to be dubbed by some as an Epitomist, that is, one who destroyed whole volumes of excellent worth in order to create demand for his abridgments. This is the appreciation that has been rendered to excellent rulers in ages past, that their good deeds should be evil spoken of. Of course, neither envy nor hatefulness died and was buried with the ancient. No, no! Moses' reproof applies to nearly every generation: "Ye are risen up in your fathers' stead, an increase of sinful men." "What is it that hath been done? that which shall be done: and there is no new thing under the sun," the wise man says. Saint Stephen speaks likewise: "As your fathers did, so do ye."

King James's Firmness of Purpose

This, and more to this purpose, his Majesty that now reigneth[19] (and long, and long, may he reign, and his offspring forever,[20] *Himself, and children, and children's children always!*) knew full well, according to the singular wisdom given unto him by God, and the rare learning and experience that he hath attained unto; namely, That whosoever attempteth any thing for the publick, (especially if it pertain to religion, and to the opening and clearing of the word of God,) the same setteth himself upon a stage to be glouted upon by every evil eye; yea, he casteth himself headlong upon pikes, to be gored by every sharp tongue. For he that meddleth with men's religion in any part meddleth with their custom, nay, with their freehold; and though they find no content in that which they have, yet they cannot abide to hear of altering. Notwithstanding his royal heart was not daunted or discouraged for this or that colour, but stood resolute,[21] *as a statue immoveable, and an anvil not easily to be beaten into plates,* as one saith; he knew who had chosen him to be a soldier, or

All this and more is well known to his Majesty that now reigns (and long, and long, may he reign, and his descendants forever, "Himself and children, and children's children always!"). His God-given wisdom along with his own rare attainments in learning and experience have taught him that whoever attempts anything for the public (especially if it touches on religion and deals with interpreting and explaining the Word of God) exposes himself as an object of every ill intent; indeed, he throws himself headfirst into the swords and spears, to be gored by every sharp tongue. For he that in any way touches the people's religion touches their custom, indeed, their personal domain, and even though they are discontent with the religion they have, yet they cannot bear the thought of change. Nevertheless his royal heart was not daunted or discouraged because of one blustering argument or another, but he stood resolute, "as a statue immoveable, and an anvil not easily to be beaten into plates," as somebody said. He knew who had chosen him to be a rather a captain; and being assured that the course which he intended made much for the glory of God, and the building up of his Church, he would not suffer it to be broken off for whatsoever speeches or practices. It doth certainly belong unto kings, yea, it doth specially belong unto them, to have care of religion, yea, to know it aright, yea, to profess it zealously, yea, to promote it to the uttermost of their power. This is their glory before all nations which mean well, and this will bring unto them a far more excellent weight of glory in the day of the Lord Jesus. For the Scripture saith not in vain, *Them that honour me I will honour:*[22] neither was it a vain word that Eusebius[23] delivered long ago, That piety toward God was the weapon, and the only weapon, that both preserved Constantine's person, and avenged him of his enemies.

The Perfections of the Scriptures

But now what piety without truth? What truth, what saving truth, without the word of God? What word of God, whereof we may be sure, without the Scripture? The Scriptures we are commanded to search, *John* v. 39. *Isai.* viii. 20. They are commended that searched and studied them, *Acts* xvii. 11, and viii. 28, 29. They are reproved that were unskilful in them, or slow to believe them, *Matth.* xxii. 29. *Luke* xxiv. 25. They can make us wise unto salvation, *2 Tim.* iii. 15. If we be ignorant, they will instruct us; if out of the way, they will bring us home; if out of order, they will reform us; if in heaviness, comfort us; if dull, quicken us; if cold, inflame us. *Tolle, lege; tolle, lege;*[24] Take up and read, take up and read the Scriptures, (for unto them was the direction) it was said unto St. Augustine by a supernatural voice. *Whatsoever is in the Scriptures, believe me,* saith the same St. Augustine,[25] *is high and divine; there is verily truth, and a doctrine most fit for the refreshing and renewing of men's minds, and truly so tempered, that every one may draw from thence that which is sufficient for him, if he come to draw with a devout and pious mind, as true religion requireth.* Thus St. Augustine. And St. Hierome,[26] *Ama Scripturas, et amabit te sapientia,* etc. Love the Scriptures, and wisdom will love thee. And St. Cyrill[27] against Julian, *Even boys that are bred up in the Scriptures become most religious,* etc. But what mention we three or four uses of the Scripture, whereas whatsoever is to be believed, or practised, or hoped for, is contained in them? or three or four sentences of the Fathers, since whosoever is worthy the name of a Father, from Christ's time downward, hath likewise written not only of the riches, but also of the perfection of the Scripture? *I adore the fulness of the Scripture,* saith Tertullian[28] against Hermogenes. And again,[29] to Apelles an heretic of the like stamp he saith, *I do not admit that which thou bringest in* (or concludest) *of thine own* (head or store, *de tuo*) without Scripture. So St. Justin Martyr[30] before him; *We must know by all means* (saith he) *that it is not lawful* (or possible) *to learn*

soldier, or rather a captain, and being certain that what he intended to do would greatly glorify God and build up His Church, he would not allow those plans to be thwarted by any of the speeches and schemes raised up against him. It is certainly the responsibility of kings (in fact, it is especially their responsibility) to pay attention to religion: to know it rightly, profess it zealously, and to promote it to the fullest extent of their ability. This is their glory before all well-meaning nations, and this will bring unto them a far more excellent weight of glory in the day of the Lord Jesus. For the Scriptures say not in vain, "Them that honour me I will honour"; neither was it a vain statement that Eusebius made long ago, that piety toward God was the weapon, in fact the only weapon, that both preserved Constantine's life and avenged him of his enemies.

What piety is there, though, without truth? What truth, what saving truth is there without the Word of God? What Word of God is there, of which we may be certain, without the Bible? It is the Bible that we are commanded to search (John 5:39; Isa. 8:20). Those who searched and studied the Scriptures are commended (Acts 17:11; 8:28-29). Those who were unskillful in them, or slow to believe them, were rebuked (Matt. 22:29; Luke 24:25). The Scriptures can make us wise unto salvation (II Tim. 3:15). If we should be ignorant, they will instruct us; if lost, they will bring us home; if out of order, they will correct us; if sorrowful, comfort us; if sluggish, invigorate us; if cold, inflame us. *Tolle, lege; tolle, lege;* "Take up and read, take up and read" the Scriptures (for the command referred to the Bible), it was said unto Augustine by a supernatural voice. "Whatsoever is in the Scriptures, believe me," said the same Augustine, "is high and divine; there is verily truth, and a doctrine most fit for the refreshing and renewing of men's minds, and truly so tempered, that every one may draw from thence that which is sufficient for him, if he come to draw with a devout and pious mind, as true religion requireth." This is what Augustine said. And Jerome said, "Love the Scriptures, and wisdom will love thee." And Cyril said, against Julian, "Even boys that are bred up in the Scriptures become most religious. . . ." But why bother mentioning three or four uses of Scripture when they contain everything that we must believe, practice, and hope for? Or why quote three or four sentences from the Fathers, when everyone worthy of that title, from the time of Christ on, has written of both the riches and the perfection of the Scriptures? "I adore the fulness of the Scripture," said Tertullian against Hermogenes. And again, to Apelles, a heretic of the same sort, he said, "I do not admit that which thou bringest in" (or concludest) "of thine own" (thinking or learning) apart from Scripture. Justin Martyr, earlier than Tertullian, speaks the same way: "We must know by all means," he says, "that it is not lawful" (or possible) "to learn" (anything) "of God or (any thing) of *God or of right piety, save only out of the Prophets, who teach us by divine inspiration.* So St. Basil[31] after Tertullian, *It is a manifest falling away from the faith, and a fault of presumption, either to reject any of those things that are written, or to bring in* (upon the head of them, ἐπεισᾶγεῖν) any of those things that are not written. We omit to cite to the same effect St. Cyrill Bishop of Jerusalem in his 4. *Catech.* St. Hierome against Helvidius, St. Augustine in his third book against the letters of Petilian, and in very many other places of his works. Also we forbear to descend to later Fathers, because we will not weary the reader. The Scriptures then being acknowledged to be so full and so perfect, how can we excuse ourselves of negligence, if we do not study them? of curiosity, if we be not content with them? Men talk much of εἰρεσιώνη[32] how many sweet and goodly things it had hanging on it; of the Philosopher's stone, that it turneth copper into gold; of *Cornu-copia,* that it had all things necessary for food in it; of *Panaces* the herb, that it was good for all diseases; of *Catholicon* the drug, that it is instead of all purges; of Vulcan's armour, that it was an armour of proof against all thrusts and all blows, etc. Well, that which they falsely or vainly attributed to these things for bodily good, we may justly and with full measure ascribe unto the Scripture for spiritual. It is not only an armour, but also a whole armoury of weapons, both offensive and defensive; whereby we may save ourselves, and put the enemy to flight. It is not an herb, but a tree, or rather a whole paradise of trees of life, which bring forth fruit every month, and the fruit thereof is for meat, and the leaves for medicine. It is not a pot of *Manna,* or a cruse of oil, which were for memory only, or for a meal's meat or two, but, as it were, a shower of heavenly bread sufficient for a whole host, be it never so great, and, as it were, a whole cellar full of oil vessels; whereby all our necessities may be provided for, and our debts discharged. In a word, it is a panary of wholesome food against fenowed traditions; a physician's shop[33] (as St. Basil calls it) of preservatives against poisoned heresies; a pandect of profitable laws against rebellious spirits; a treasury of most costly jewels against beggarly rudiments; finally, a fountain of most pure water springing up unto everlasting life. And what marvel? the original thereof being from heaven, not from earth; the author being God, not man; the inditer, the Holy Spirit, not the wit of the Apostles or Prophets; the penmen, such as were sanctified from the womb, and endued with a principal portion of God's Spirit; the matter, verity, piety, purity, uprightness; the form, God's word, God's testimony, God's oracles, the word of truth, the word of salvation, etc.; the effects, light of understanding, stableness of persuasion, repentance from dead works, newness of life, holiness, peace, joy in the Holy Ghost; lastly, the end and reward of the study thereof, fellowship with the saints, participation of the heavenly nature, fruition of an inheritance immortal, undefiled, and that never shall fade away.

of right piety, save only out of the Prophets, who teach us by divine inspiration." And, after Tertullian, Basil also speaks the same way: "It is a manifest falling away from the faith, and a fault of presumption, either to reject any of those things that are written, or to bring in" (contrary to them) "any of those things that are" not written. We will refrain from citing to the same effect Cyril, Bishop of Jerusalem, in his fourth Catechism; Jerome against Helvidius; Augustine in his third book against the letters of Petilian and in numerous other places in his works. We will also refrain from descending to the later Fathers, in order not to weary the reader. Since the Scriptures are acknowledged to be so full and so perfect, how can we excuse our negligence if we do not study them, or our excessive curiosity if we are not content with them? Men exclaim about *Iresine,* how many sweet and pleasant things it had hanging on it; about the Philosopher's stone, that it turns copper into gold; about Cornucopia, that it contains all things necessary for food; about Panacea the herb, that it cures all diseases; about Catholicon the drug, that it purges the body of every harmful fluid; about Vulcan's armor, that it could not be penetrated by any thrust or blow, and so forth. Very well; what they falsely or vainly attributed to these things for physical good, we may properly and fully ascribe to the Scripture for spiritual good. It is not only an armor, but also a whole armory of weapons, both offensive and defensive, by which we may save ourselves and put the enemy to flight. It is not an herb, but a tree, indeed a whole paradise of trees of life, which bring forth fruit every month, whose fruit is good for food and whose leaves are good for medicine. It is not a pot of Manna or a jar of oil, which were good only for a remembrance (in the case of the Manna) or for a meal or two (in the case of the oil). Rather, the Scripture is, so to speak, a shower of heavenly bread sufficient for a whole multitude, no matter how great, and a whole cellar filled with barrels of oil by which all our needs may be met and, by selling some, our debts repaid. In a word, it is a pantry of wholesome food in exchange for moldy traditions, a pharmacy of antidotes to poisonous heresies, a compendium of sound legislation to restrain rebellious spirits, a treasury of most costly jewels rather than common rocks, and, finally, a fountain of purest water springing up unto eternal life. And should we be surprised? The Scriptures come from heaven, not from earth; the Author is God, not man; the composer is the Holy Spirit, not the intelligence of the apostles or prophets; the penmen had been set apart from the womb and filled with a special measure of God's Spirit; the subject matter is truth, piety, purity and uprightness; the form is God's Word, God's testimony, God's oracles, the word of truth, of salvation, and so forth. The Scripture grants enlightenment of mind, stability of conviction, repentance from dead works, newness of life, holiness, peace and joy in the Holy Spirit; and the goal and reward of studying it is fellowship with the saints, sharing in the

Happy is the man that delighteth in the Scripture, and thrice happy that meditateth in it day and night.

The Necessity of Bible Translations

But how shall men meditate in that which they cannot understand? How shall they understand that which is kept close in an unknown tongue? as it is written, *Except I know the power of the voice, I shall be to him that speaketh a barbarian, and he that speaketh shall be a barbarian to me.*[34] The apostle excepteth no tongue; not Hebrew the ancientest, not Greek the most copious, not Latin the finest. Nature taught a natural man to confess, that all of us in those tongues which we do not understand are plainly deaf; we may turn the deaf ear unto them.[35] The Scythian counted the Athenian, whom he did not understand, barbarous: so the Roman did the Syrian, and the Jew: (even St. Hierome[36] himself calleth the Hebrew tongue barbarous; belike, because it was strange to so many:) so the Emperor of Constantinople[37] calleth the Latin tongue barbarous, though Pope Nicolas[38] do storm at it: so the Jews long before Christ called all other nations *Lognasim,* which is little better than barbarous. Therefore as one[39] complaineth that always in the Senate of Rome there was one or other that called for an interpreter; so lest the Church be driven to the like exigent, it is necessary to have translations in a readiness. Translation it is that openeth the window, to let in the light; that breaketh the shell, that we may eat the kernel; that putteth aside the curtain, that we may look into the most holy place; that removeth the cover of the well, that we may come by the water; even as Jacob[40] rolled away the stone from the mouth of the well, by which means the flocks of Laban were watered. Indeed without translation into the vulgar tongue, the unlearned are but like children at Jacob's well[41] (which was deep) without a bucket or something to draw with: or as that person mentioned by Esay,[42] to whom when a sealed book was delivered with this motion, *Read this, I pray thee,* he was fain to make this answer, *I cannot, for it is sealed.*

The History of Bible Translations

Translations into Greek

While God would be known only in Jacob, and have his name great in Israel, and in none other place; while the dew lay on Gideon's fleece only, and all the earth besides was dry; then for one and the same people, which spake all of them the language of Canaan, that is, Hebrew, one and the same original in Hebrew was sufficient. But when the fulness of time drew near, that the Sun of righteousness, the Son of God, should come into the world, whom God ordained to be a reconciliation through faith in his blood, not of the Jew only, but also of the Greek, yea, of all them that were scattered abroad; then, lo, it pleased the Lord to stir up the spirit of a

divine nature, and the possession of "an inheritance immortal, undefiled, and that shall never fade away." Happy is the man that delights in the Scripture, and three times happy is the man who meditates in it day and night.

But how can men meditate on what they cannot understand? And how will they understand what is kept secret in a foreign language? As it is written, "Except I know the power of the voice, I shall be to him that speaketh a barbarian, and he that speaketh shall be a barbarian to me." The apostle makes no exceptions for any language; not for Hebrew, the most ancient, nor for Greek, with its vast vocabulary, nor for Latin, the most precise. Nature teaches a natural man to admit the obvious: in relation to languages which we do not know, we are deaf, and turning a deaf ear toward them is no fault. The Scythian thought the Athenian, whom he did not understand, a barbarian; the Roman thought the same of the Syrian and the Jew (even Jerome himself calls the Hebrew language barbarous, probably because it was foreign to so many); the Emperor of Constantinople took the same view toward the Latin tongue, despite the anger of Pope Nicholas at the insult. In the same way the Jews long before Christ called all other nations *Lognasim,* which is little better than barbarous. Therefore, just as someone complained that in the Senate of Rome somebody or another was always calling for an interpreter, so the Church, in order to avoid being driven to a similar extremity, must always have translations of the Bible readily available. Translation is the thing that opens the window to let in the light; it breaks the shell that we may eat the kernel; it draws aside the curtain that we may look into the most holy place; it uncovers the well and gives access to the water, just as Jacob rolled away the stone from the mouth of the well, enabling Laban's flocks to drink. In fact, in the absence of a translation into common language, the uneducated are no better off than children at Jacob's well (which was deep), having no bucket or anything with which to draw water. They are just the same as the one mentioned by Isaiah, who, when a sealed book was delivered to him with the request, "Read this, I pray thee," had to answer, "I cannot, for it is sealed."

When God wished to be known only in Jacob and to have his name great in Israel alone, while the dew lay only on Gideon's fleece and the rest of the ground was dry, then for a single people who all spoke the language of Canaan, that is, Hebrew, a single original in Hebrew was sufficient. But the time was coming when the Sun of righteousness, the Son of God, would come into the world, the one ordained by God to bring salvation by faith in his blood not to the Jews only, but also to the Greeks, and indeed to all who were scattered abroad. When this fulness of time drew near, behold, the Lord was pleased to stir up the spirit of a Greek prince (Greek by descent

Greek prince, (Greek for descent and language) even of Ptolemy Philadelph king of Egypt, to procure the translating of the book of God out of Hebrew into Greek. This is the translation of the Seventy interpreters, commonly so called, which prepared the way for our Saviour among the Gentiles by written preaching, as St. John Baptist did among the Jews by vocal. For the Grecians, being desirous of learning, were not wont to suffer books of worth to lie moulding in kings' libraries, but had many of their servants, ready scribes, to copy them out, and so they were dispersed and made common. Again, the Greek tongue was well known and made familiar to most inhabitants in Asia by reason of the conquests that there the Grecians had made, as also by the colonies which thither they had sent. For the same causes also it was well understood in many places of Europe, yea, and of Africk too. Therefore the word of God, being set forth in Greek, becometh hereby like a candle set upon a candlestick, which giveth light to all that are in the house; or like a proclamation sounded forth in the market-place, which most men presently take knowledge of; and therefore that language was fittest to contain the Scriptures, both for the first preachers of the gospel to appeal unto for witness, and for the learners also of those times to make search and trial by. It is certain, that that translation was not so sound and so perfect, but that it needed in many places correction; and who had been so sufficient for this work as the Apostles or apostolick men? Yet it seemed good to the Holy Ghost and to them to take that which they found, (the same being for the greatest part true and sufficient) rather than by making a new, in that new world and green age of the Church, to expose themselves to many exceptions and cavillations, as though they made a translation to serve their own turn; and therefore bearing witness to themselves, their witness not to be regarded. This may be supposed to be some cause, why the translation of the Seventy was allowed to pass for current. Notwithstanding, though it was commended generally, yet it did not fully content the learned, no not of the Jews. For not long after Christ, Aquila fell in hand with a new translation, and after him Theodotion, and after him Symmachus: yea, there was a fifth, and a sixth edition, the authors whereof were not known. These with the Seventy made up the Hexapla, and were worthily and to great purpose compiled together by Origen. Howbeit the edition of the Seventy went away with the credit, and therefore not only was placed in the midst by Origen, (for the worth and excellency thereof above the rest, as Epiphanius[43] gathereth) but also was used by the Greek Fathers for the ground and foundation of their commentaries. Yea, Epiphanius above-named doth attribute so much unto it, that he holdeth the authors thereof not only for interpreters, but also for prophets in some respect; and Justinian[44] the Emperor, injoining the Jews his subjects to use especially the translation of the Seventy, rendereth this reason thereof, Because

and language), Ptolemy Philadelph, king of Egypt, to have the book of God translated from Hebrew into Greek. This is the translation of the Seventy interpreters, commonly so called [known more widely today as the Septuagint, which is Latin for *seventy*], which prepared the way for our Savior among the Gentiles by written preaching, as John the Baptist did among the Jews with his voice. This happened because the Greeks, who esteemed education highly, were not content to allow valuable books to lie molding in kings' libraries. Rather, they put many of their servants, skilled scribes, to work at copying out such books in order to disseminate them widely. In addition, the Greek language was well known to most of the population of Asia as a result of the conquests made by the Greeks and the colonists they had sent abroad. For the same reasons Greek was also widely understood in much of Europe and even of Africa. So then the Word of God, translated into Greek, by that means becomes like a candle set on a candlestick, giving light to all that are in the house, or like a proclamation cried out in the marketplace, which most people immediately hear about. For this reason the Greek language was the best vehicle for the Scriptures, to provide a witness both for the first preachers of the gospel to appeal to and also for the first hearers to consult in order to verify what they heard and to learn yet more. It is certain that the Septuagint was in some respects an unsound and imperfect translation, needing correction in many places. Who would have been as qualified for this work as the apostles or their companions? Yet it seemed good to the Holy Spirit and to them to use the Bible commonly available (which was essentially true and sufficient) rather than to make a new translation, an act which, in that new world and in that tender age of the church, would have exposed them to much argument and opposition. To have made a new translation at that time would have appeared self-serving and, by putting the apostles in the position of bearing witness to themselves, would have discredited their testimony. We may suppose that such reasons prompted the apostles' choice to approve the Septuagint for regular use. Nevertheless, though it was generally accepted, it did not fully satisfy the theologians, not even the Jewish ones. Not long after Christ, Aquila produced a new translation, and after him Theodotion did the same, and after him Symmachus; indeed, there was a fifth and a sixth translation, the authors of which are unknown. All these together made up the Hexapla, a work skillfully and usefully compiled by Origen. Yet the Septuagint remained dominant and for that reason not only was given the central position in Origen's Hexapla (because it was the best, as Epiphanius understands it) but also was used by the Greek Fathers as the basis for their commentaries on Scripture. Indeed, the just-mentioned Epiphanius thought so highly of it that he viewed its authors not they were, as it were, enlightened with prophetical grace. Yet for all that, as the Egyptians are said of the Prophet to be men and not God, and their horses flesh and not spirit:[45] so it is evident (and St. Hierome[46] affirmeth as much) that the Seventy were interpreters, they were not prophets. They did many things well, as learned men; but yet as men they stumbled and fell, one while through oversight, another while through ignorance; yea, sometimes they may be noted to add to the original, and sometimes to take from it; which made the Apostles to leave them many times, when they left the Hebrew, and to deliver the sense thereof according to the truth of the word, as the Spirit gave them utterance. This may suffice touching the Greek translations of the Old Testament.

Translations into Latin

There were also within a few hundred years after Christ translations many into the *Latin* tongue; for this tongue also was very fit to convey the Law and the Gospel by, because in those times very many countries of the West, yea, of the South, East, and North, spake or understood Latin, being made provinces to the Romans. But now the Latin translations were too many to be all good; for they were infinite: (*Latini interpretes nullo modo numerari possunt,* saith St. Augustine.[47]) Again, they were not out of the *Hebrew* fountain, (we speak of the Latin translations of the Old Testament) but out of the Greek stream; therefore the Greek being not altogether clear, the Latin derived from it must needs be muddy. This moved St. Hierome, a most learned Father, and the best linguist without controversy of his age, or of any other that went before him, to undertake the translating of the Old Testament out of the very fountains themselves; which he performed with that evidence of great learning, judgment, industry, and faithfulness, that he hath for ever bound the Church unto him in a debt of special remembrance and thankfulness.

Translations into Native Languages of Many Nations

Now though the Church were thus furnished with Greek and Latin translations, even before the faith of Christ was generally embraced in the Empire: (for the learned know, that even in St. Hierome's[48] time the Consul of Rome and his wife were both Ethnicks, and about the same time the greatest part of the Senate also) yet for all that the godly learned were not content to have the Scriptures in the language which themselves understood, Greek and Latin, (as the good lepers were not content to fare well themselves, but acquainted their neighbours with the store that God had sent, that they also might provide for themselves,[49]) but also for the behoof and edifying of the unlearned, which hungered and thirsted after righteousness, and had

only as translators but also as prophets to some extent, and Justinian the Emperor, giving a reason for commanding his Jewish subjects to use the Septuagint above the other translations, says that the Seventy were, so to speak, enlightened with prophetic grace. Even so, just as the Egyptians are said by the Prophet to be men and not God, and their horses to be flesh and not spirit, even so it is evident (and Jerome affirms as much) that the Seventy were translators, not prophets. They did many things well, as scholarly men, but yet as men they stumbled and fell, here through oversight and there through ignorance. Sometimes they observably added to the original while other times they omitted things; for this reason the Apostles often abandoned the Septuagint, where it abandoned the Hebrew, and proclaimed the meaning of the original according to the truth of the word, as the Spirit enabled them. This is enough said about the Greek translations of the Old Testament.

Within a few centuries of the life of Christ, many Latin translations of the Bible were also made. This language was also well suited for disseminating the Law and the gospel, being understood throughout a great portion of the Roman Empire, especially in the West. The Latin translations, though, were very numerous (Augustine says there is no way to count them all), and not all of them were good. Furthermore, because the Latin Old Testament was translated from the Greek instead of the Hebrew (comparable to drinking from a stream instead of its fountain), any muddiness in the Greek taints the Latin as well. This situation prompted Jerome, a most learned Father, and without a doubt the best linguist who had ever lived, to undertake a translation of the Old Testament out of the original Hebrew. He accomplished this task with such a display of scholarship, discernment, diligence, and accuracy that the church of every succeeding generation owes him a debt of special remembrance and gratitude.

So it was that the church was supplied with Greek and Latin translations, even before the Christian faith was generally embraced in the Empire (for the educated know that, even in Jerome's time, the Consul of Rome and his wife were both pagans, as were the majority of the Senate). Nevertheless, educated Christians were not content to have the Scriptures in languages which they alone could understand, just as the good lepers were not content to enjoy a good meal themselves, but informed their neighbors about the abundance of food God had provided, that they might share the benefit. In the same way, educated Christians provided translations into native languages in order to benefit and edify their less educated souls to be saved as well as they, they provided translations into the vulgar for their countrymen, insomuch that most nations under heaven did shortly after their conversion hear Christ speaking unto them in their mother tongue, not by the voice of their minister only, but also by the written word translated. If any doubt hereof, he may be satisfied by examples enough, if enough will serve the turn. First, St. Hierome[50] saith, *Multarum gentium linguis Scriptura ante translata docet falsa esse quæ addita sunt*, etc., that is, *The Scripture being translated before in the languages of many nations doth shew that those things that were added* (by Lucian or Hesychius) *are false*. So St. Hierome in that place. The same Hierome[51] elsewhere affirmeth that he, the time was, had set forth the translation of the *Seventy, suæ linguæ hominibus;* that is, for his countrymen of Dalmatia. Which words not only Erasmus doth understand to purport, that St. Hierome translated the Scripture into the Dalmatian tongue; but also Sixtus Senensis,[52] and Alphonsus a Castro,[53] (that we speak of no more) men not to be excepted against by them of Rome, do ingenuously confess as much. So St. Chrysostome,[54] that lived in St. Hierome's time, giveth evidence with him: *The doctrine of St. John* (saith he) *did not in such sort* (as the Philosophers' did) *vanish away: but the Syrians, Egyptians, Indians, Persians, Ethiopians, and infinite other nations, being barbarous people, translated it into their (mother) tongue, and have learned to be (true) Philosophers*, he meaneth Christians. To this may be added *Theodoret*,[55] as next unto him both for antiquity, and for learning. His words be these, *Every country that is under the sun is full of these words,* (of the Apostles and Prophets;) *and the Hebrew tongue* (he meaneth the Scriptures in the *Hebrew* tongue) *is turned not only into the language of the Grecians, but also of the Romans, and Egyptians, and Persians, and Indians, and Armenians, and Scythians, and Sauromatians, and, briefly, into all the languages that any nation useth*. So he. In like manner Ulpilas is reported by Paulus Diaconus[56] and Isidore,[57] and before them by Sozomen,[58] to have translated the Scriptures into the *Gothick* tongue: John Bishop of Sevil, by Vasseus,[59] to have turned them into *Arabick* about the year of our Lord 717: Beda, by Cistertiensis, to have turned a great part of them into Saxon:[60] Efnard, by Trithemius, to have abridged the *French* Psalter (as Beda had done the *Hebrew*) about the year 800; King Alured, by the said Cistertiensis, to have turned the Psalter into *Saxon:* Methodius, by Aventinus,[61] (printed at Ingolstad) to have turned the Scriptures into *Sclavonian:*[62] Valdo Bishop of Frising, by Beatus Rhenanus,[63] to have caused about that time the Gospels to be translated into *Dutch* rhyme, yet extant in the library of Corbinian: Valdus, by divers, to have turned them himself, or to have gotten them turned into *French,* about the year 1160: Charles the Fifth of that name, surnamed *The wise,* to have caused them to be turned into *French* about 200

countrymen, who hungered and thirsted after righteousness and whose souls needed saving as much as those of the learned. As a result, most nations of the earth, shortly after their conversion, could hear Christ speaking to them in their native languages, not only by the voice of the preacher but also by the written word translated. If anyone doubts what we say, there are enough examples to satisfy him, if any number at all will do the job. First, Jerome says, "The Scripture being translated before in the languages of many nations shows that those things that were added [by the heretics Lucian or Hesychius] are false." This is Jerome's teaching in one passage. The same Jerome elsewhere affirms that, at one time, he had set forth the Septuagint "for the people of his own language," that is, for his countrymen of Dalmatia. That these words mean that Jerome translated the Scripture into the Dalmatian language was frankly admitted not only by Erasmus but also by Sixtus of Siena and by Alphonsus a Castro (to name but two), men with whom Catholics do not argue. Chrysostom, a contemporary of Jerome, gives further evidence, saying, "The doctrine of John did not in such sort [i.e., as the that of the philosophers did] vanish away, but the Syrians, Egyptians, Indians, Persians, Ethiopians, and infinite other nations, being barbarous people, translated it into their mother tongue and have learned to be true philosophers" (he means that they became Christians). To this we may add Theodoret, who comes just after Jerome both in time and in learning. These are his words: "Every country that is under the sun is full of these words [those of the apostles and prophets], and the Hebrew tongue [i.e., the Hebrew Scriptures] is turned not only into the language of the Greeks, but also of the Romans and Egyptians and Persians and Indians and Armenians and Scythians and Samaritans and, briefly, into all the languages that any nation uses." This is Theodoret's teaching. Similarly Ulfilas is reported by Paul the Deacon and Isidore, and before them by Sozomen, to have translated the Scriptures into Gothic; John, Bishop of Sevil, is said by Vasseus to have translated them into Arabic around A.D. 717; Bede is said by Cistertiensis to have translated much of them into Saxon. According to Trithemius, Efnard abridged the French Psalter (as Bede had done the Hebrew) about the year 800; King Alfred is said by the same Cistertiensis, to have translated the Psalter into Saxon; Methodius is said by Aventinus (printed at Ingolstadt) to have translated the Scriptures into Slavonic in about 900. Valdo, Bishop of Freising, is said by Beatus Rhenanus to have caused the Gospels to be translated into Dutch rhyme at about the same time; this work may yet be found in the library of Corbinian. Several witnesses testify that Peter Waldo either himself translated or prompted someone else to translate the Bible into French about the year 1160; Charles V, surnamed "The Wise," is said to have sponsored another French translation about 200 years later, of which many years after Valdus' time; of which translation there be many copies yet extant, as witnesseth Beroaldus.[64] Much about that time, even in our King Richard the Second's days, John Trevisa translated them into English, and many English Bibles in written hand are yet to be seen with divers; translated, as it is very probable, in that age. So the Syrian translation of the New Testament is in most learned men's libraries, of Widminstadius' setting forth; and the Psalter in Arabick is with many, of Augustinus Nebiensis' setting forth. So Postel affirmeth, that in his travel he saw the Gospels in the Ethiopian tongue: And Ambrose Thesius allegeth the Psalter of the Indians, which he testifieth to have been set forth by Potken in Syrian characters. So that to have the Scriptures in the mother tongue is not a quaint conceit lately taken up, either by the Lord Cromwell in England, or by the Lord Radevile in Polony, or by the Lord Ungnadius in the Emperor's dominion, but hath been thought upon, and put in practice of old, even from the first times of the conversion of any nation; no doubt, because it was esteemed most profitable to cause faith to grow in men's hearts the sooner, and to make them to be able to say with the words of the Psalm, *As we have heard, so we have seen.*[65]

Roman Catholic Resistance to Common-Language Translations

Now the church of Rome would seem at the length to bear a motherly affection toward her children, and to allow them the Scriptures in the mother tongue; but indeed it is a gift, not deserving to be called a gift,[66] an unprofitable gift: they must first get a licence in writing before they may use them; and to get that, they must approve themselves to their Confessor, that is, to be such as are, if not frozen in the dregs, yet sowered with the leaven of their superstition. Howbeit it seemed too much to Clement the Eighth, that there should be any licence granted to have them in the vulgar tongue, and therefore he overruleth and frustrateth the grant of Pius the Fourth.[67] So much are they afraid of the light of the Scripture, *(Lucifugæ Scripturarum,* as Tertullian[68] speaketh) that they will not trust the people with it, no not as it is set forth by their own sworn men, no not with the licence of their own Bishops and Inquisitors. Yea, so unwilling they are to communicate the Scriptures to the people's understanding in any sort, that they are not ashamed to confess, that we forced them to translate it into English against their wills. This seemeth to argue a bad cause, or a bad conscience, or both. Sure we are, that it is not he that hath good gold, that is afraid to bring it to the touchstone, but he that hath the counterfeit; neither is it the true man that shunneth the light, but the malefactor, lest his deeds should be reproved; neither is it the plain dealing merchant that is unwilling to have the weights, or the meteyard, brought in place, but he that useth deceit. But we will let them alone for this fault, and return to translation.

copies still exist, according to Beroalde. At just about that time, in the days of our King Richard II, John Trevisa translated the Scriptures into English, and many handwritten English Bibles are still in use here and there, very likely translated during that period. Also the Syriac translation of the New Testament, published by Widmanstadt, is in the libraries of most scholars, and the Psalter in Arabic, translated by Augustinus Nebiensis, is common. Postel affirms that in his travels he saw the Gospels in Ethiopian, and Ambrose Thesius claims that the Indians have the Psalter, set forth by Potken using the Syriac alphabet. We conclude, then, that having the Scriptures in the language of the people is not a strange notion recently conceived, either by Lord Cromwell in England or by Lord Radziwill in Poland, or by Lord Ungnadius in Germany. Rather, it has been carefully considered and carried out since long ago, since the earliest conversion of any nation. It has been done, no doubt, because it was viewed as most beneficial in order to speed the growth of faith in men's hearts and to bring them to the point where they could say with the Psalmist, "As we have heard, so we have seen."

Now the church of Rome gives the appearance of finally having come to show a motherly affection toward her children by allowing them the Scriptures in the mother tongue. But it is a gift undeserving to be called a gift, a worthless gift. Before a Catholic may use the Scriptures, he must first get permission in writing, and to get that permission, he must prove himself qualified to the priest who hears his confessions. And the only ones qualifed are those who, if not frozen in the dregs, are at least fermented by the leaven of Catholic superstition. Nevertheless Clement VIII was unwilling to grant any permission to have the Scriptures in common language, and therefore he overruled and nullified the permission of Pius IV. The Catholics are so afraid of the light of Scripture ("shunners of the light of the Scriptures," as Tertullian puts it) that they will not trust the people with it, not even as it is translated by their own sworn men, not even with the permission of their own bishops and inquisitors. In fact, they are so unwilling to communicate the Scriptures to people's understanding in any way that they shamelessly admit that we forced them to translate the Scriptures into English against their wills. This confession seems to indicate that they have either a bad case or a bad conscience, or both. We are sure that it is not the person with good gold who is afraid to bring it to the touchstone, but the one with the counterfeit; not the honorable man who shuns the light, but the criminal; not the honest merchant who is unwilling to have his weights and measures tested, but the deceitful. But we will leave them alone for this fault and return to the matter of translation.

The Present Translation Vindicated Against Objections to It

Objections Listed

Many men's mouths have been opened a good while (and yet are not stopped) with speeches about the translation so long in hand, or rather perusals of translations made before: and ask what may be the reason, what the necessity of the employment. Hath the church been deceived, say they, all this while? Hath her sweet bread been mingled with leaven, her silver with dross, her wine with water, her milk with lime? *(lacte gypsum male miscetur,* saith St. Irenee.[70]) We hoped that we had been in the right way, that we had had the oracles of God delivered unto us, and that though all the world had cause to be offended, and to complain, yet that we had none. Hath the nurse holden out the breast, and nothing but wind in it? Hath the bread been delivered by the Fathers of the Church, and the same proved to be *lapidosus,* as Seneca speaketh? What is it to handle the word of God deceitfully, if this be not? Thus certain brethren. Also the adversaries of Judah and Jerusalem, like Sanballat in Nehemiah, mock, as we hear, both at the work and workmen, saying, *What do these weak Jews, etc.? will they make the stones whole again out of the heaps of dust which are burnt? although they build, yet if a fox go up, he shall even break down their stony wall.*[71] Was their translation good before? Why do they now mend it? Was it not good? Why then was it obtruded to the people? Yea, why did the Catholicks (meaning Popish Romanists) always go in jeopardy for refusing to hear it? Nay, if it must be translated into English, Catholicks are fittest to do it. They have learning, and they know when a thing is well, they can *manum de tabula.*

Objections Answered

Objections of Protestants Answered

We will answer them both briefly: and the former, being brethren, thus with St. Hierome,[72] *Damnamus veteres? Minime, sed post priorum studia in domo Domini quod possumus laboramus. That is, Do we condemn the ancient? In no case: but after the endeavours of them that were before us, we take the best pains we can in the house of God.* As if he said, Being provoked by the example of the learned that lived before my time, I have thought it my duty to assay, whether my talent in the knowledge of the tongues may be profitable in any measure to God's Church, lest I should seem to have laboured in them in vain, and lest I should be thought to glory in men (although ancient) above that which was in them. Thus St. Hierome may be thought to speak.

And to the same effect say we, that we are so far off from condemning any of their labours that travelled before us in this kind, either in this land, or beyond sea, either in King Henry's time, or King

---

Many men have been talking for a long time (and have not yet been silenced), complaining about the translation (or rather the study of previous translations) so long in production. They ask why this is being done, why this work is necessary. "Has the church been deceived all this time?" they ask. "Has her sweet bread been mixed with leaven, her silver with dross, her wine with water, her milk with lime?" ("Lime mixes poorly with milk," said Irenaeus.) "We hoped that we were on the right road, that we had received the oracles of God, and that, though the rest of the world might have reason to be offended and to complain, we had none. Has the nursing mother offered her breast with nothing but wind in it? Have the Fathers of the Church given us bread that proves to be full of stones, as Seneca says? What does it mean to handle the Word of God deceitfully, if these men are not doing it?" This is how certain brethren are talking. We also hear some mocking, adversaries of God's work like Sanballat in Nehemiah, saying, "What do these weak Jews . . . ? Will they make the stones whole again out of the heaps of dust which are burnt? Although they build, yet if a fox go up, he shall even break down their stony wall." These mockers say, "Was their translation good before? Why are they now correcting it? Was it not good? Why then was it foisted upon the people? Indeed, why have the Roman Catholics always jeopardized their souls by refusing to hear it? Really, if it must be translated into English, the Catholics are best suited to do it. They are scholars; they know when something has been done well, and they know to leave well enough alone."

We will answer both these groups briefly. The first group, since they are our brethren, we will answer with the words of Jerome: "Do we condemn the ancient? Certainly not; but, with an eye to the efforts of those who were before us in the house of God, we labor to the fullest extent of our ability." It is as though he said, "Being provoked by the example of the scholars who lived before me, I have considered it my duty to try to make my linguistic skills at least somewhat useful to God's church, lest my work in the languages should seem to be in vain and lest I should appear to glory in men above what they deserve, ancient and venerable as they may be." This is Jerome's attitude.

To the same effect we maintain that we in no way condemn any of the labors of those who preceded us in this sort of work, either in this land, or beyond the sea, either in King Henry's time or King

Edward's, (if there were any translation, or correction of a translation, in his time) or Queen Elizabeth's of ever renowned memory, that we acknowledge them to have been raised up of God for the building and furnishing of his Church, and that they deserve to be had of us and of posterity in everlasting remembrance. The judgment of Aristotle[73] is worthy and well known: *If Timotheus had not been, we had not had much sweet musick: but if Phrynis* (Timotheus' master) *had not been, we had not had Timotheus.* Therefore blessed be they, and most honoured be their name, that break the ice, and give the onset upon that which helpeth forward to the saving of souls. Now what can be more available thereto, than to deliver God's book unto God's people in a tongue which they understand? Since of an hidden treasure, and of a fountain that is sealed, there is no profit, as Ptolemy Philadelph wrote to the Rabbins or masters of the Jews, as witnesseth Epiphanius:[74] and as St. Augustine[75] saith, *A man had rather be with his dog than with a stranger* (whose tongue is strange unto him). Yet for all that, as nothing is begun and perfected at the same time, and the latter thoughts are thought to be the wiser, so if we building upon their foundation that went before us, and being holpen by their labours, do endeavour to make that better which they left so good; no man, we are sure, hath cause to mislike us; they, we persuade ourselves, if they were alive, would thank us. The vintage of Abiezer, that strake the stroke: yet the gleaning of grapes of Ephraim was not to be despised. See Judges viii. 2. Joash the king of Israel did not satisfy himself till he had smitten the ground three times; and yet he offended the Prophet for giving over then.[76] Aquila, of whom we spake before, translated the Bible as carefully and as skilfully as he could; and yet he thought good to go over it again, and then it got the credit with the Jews, to be called κατ᾿ ἀκρίβειαν that is, accurately done, as St. Hierome[77] witnesseth. How many books of profane learning have been gone over again and again, by the same translators, by others? Of one and the same book of Aristotle's Ethicks there are extant not so few as six or seven several translations. Now if this cost may be bestowed upon the gourd, which affordeth us a little shade, and which to day flourisheth, but to morrow is cut down; what may we bestow, nay, what ought we not to bestow, upon the vine, the fruit whereof maketh glad the conscience of man, and the stem whereof abideth for ever? And this is the word of God, which we translate. *What is the chaff to the wheat? saith the Lord.*[78] *Tanti vitreum, quanti verum margaritum!* (saith Tertullian.[79]) If a toy of glass be of that reckoning with us, how ought we to value the true pearl! Therefore let no man's eye be evil, because his Majesty's is good; neither let any be grieved, that we have a Prince that seeketh the increase of the spiritual wealth of Israel: (let Sanballats and Tobiahs do so, which therefore do bear their just reproof;) but let us rather bless God from the ground of our heart for working this

Edward's (if there was any translation or revision in his time) or in the time of Queen Elizabeth of ever renowned memory. So far from condemning them, we in fact acknowledge that they were raised up by God to build and to provide for his church and that they deserve to be held always in remembrance by us and by our children. The declaration of Aristotle is well known and worth considering: "Without Timotheus we would not have had much sweet music, but without Phrynis (Timotheus's teacher) we would not have had Timotheus." Therefore, those who break the ice and put into motion things that yield progress toward the saving of souls deserve our blessing and honor. Now what can be more effective toward that goal than to deliver God's book to God's people in a language which they understand? After all, a hidden treasure or a sealed fountain has no value (as Ptolemy Philadelph wrote to the rabbis, or Jewish teachers, according to Epiphanius), and, as Augustine said, "A man would rather be with his dog than with someone who does not speak his language." We must also consider that nothing is begun and perfected at the same time and that later thoughts are thought to be wiser than earlier ones. So we are sure that nobody has any reason to disapprove of us for building upon the foundation laid by others and, with the help of their labors, improving upon what they did so well. Indeed, we feel sure that they, if they were still alive, would thank us. The vintage of Abiezer surpassed all rivals; nevertheless the gleaning of grapes of Ephraim was nothing to be despised (Judges 8:2). Joash the king of Israel was not satisfied until he had struck the ground three times; nevertheless he angered the prophet for stopping at that. Aquila, whom we mentioned earlier, translated the Bible as carefully and as skilfully as he could, yet he thought it good to go over it again; only then did the Jews sanction it as "accurately done," as Jerome witnesses. How many books of secular learning have been revised again and again, both by the same translators and by others? The single book of Aristotle's *Ethics* exists in no fewer than six or seven different translations. Now if this effort may be expended upon the gourd, which gives a little shade, flourishing today and being cut down tomorrow, what effort may we expend, indeed, what effort ought we not to expend upon the vine whose fruit makes man's conscience glad and whose stem abides forever? This vine, of course, is the Word of God, which we translate. "What is the chaff [worth in comparison] to the wheat? saith the Lord." "If glass is so precious, how much more so a genuine pearl!" said Tertullian. If a glass bauble is of such value to us, how ought we to value the true pearl! Therefore let no man resent his Majesty's generosity, and let no one be grieved that we have a king who seeks the increase of the spiritual wealth of Israel. Let Sanballats and Tobiahs do so, who therefore bear the rebuke they deserve, but let us rather thank God from the bottom of our heart for creating in our king this religious concern to have the translations of the religious care in him to have the translations of the Bible maturely considered of and examined. For by this means it cometh to pass, that whatsoever is sound already, (and all is sound for substance in one or other of our editions, and the worst of ours far better than their authentick vulgar) the same will shine as gold more brightly, being rubbed and polished; also, if any thing be halting, or superfluous, or not so agreeable to the original, the same may be corrected, and the truth set in place. And what can the King command to be done, that will bring him more true honour than this? And wherein could they that have been set a work approve their duty to the King, yea, their obedience to God, and love to his Saints, more, than by yielding their service, and all that is within them, for the furnishing of the work? But besides all this, they were the principal motives of it, and therefore ought least to quarrel it. For the very historical truth is, that upon the importunate petitions of the Puritanes at his Majesty's coming to this crown, the conference at Hampton-court having been appointed for hearing their complaints, when by force of reason they were put from all other grounds, they had recourse at the last to this shift, that they could not with good conscience subscribe to the communion book, since it maintained the Bible as it was there translated, which was, as they said, a most corrupted translation. And although this was judged to be but a very poor and empty shift, yet even hereupon did his Majesty begin to bethink himself of the good that might ensue by a new translation, and presently after gave order for this translation which is now presented unto thee. Thus much to satisfy our scrupulous brethren.

Objections of Roman Catholics Answered

No translation is unworthy to be called the Word of God.

Now to the latter we answer, That we do not deny, nay, we affirm and avow, that the very meanest translation of the Bible in English, set forth by men of our profession, (for we have seen none of their's of the whole Bible as yet) containeth the word of God, nay, is the word of God: as the King's speech which he uttered in Parliament, being translated into French, Dutch, Italian, and Latin, is still the King's speech, though it be not interpreted by every translator with the like grace, nor peradventure so fitly for phrase, nor so expressly for sense, every where. For it is confessed, that things are to take their denomination of the greater part; and a natural man could say, *Verum ubi multa nitent in carmine, non ego paucis offendar maculis, etc.*[80] A man may be counted a virtuous man, though he have made many slips in his life, (else there were none virtuous, for *in many things we offend all,*[81]) also a comely man and lovely, though he have some warts upon his hand; yea, not only freckles upon his face, but also scars. No cause therefore why the word translated should be denied to be the word, or forbidden to be current, notwithstanding that some imperfections

Bible reviewed and examined with full and careful deliberation. For by this means it comes about that whatever is already sound (and all is substantially sound in at least one of the Protestant editions, the worst of which is far better than the Romanists' authorized English version) will, like gold, shine more brightly because of the rubbing and polishing. And if anything should be found awkward or unwarranted or out of keeping with the original, it may be corrected, and truth may take the place of error. What can the king command to be done that will bring him more true honor than this? And how could those who have been appointed to the task better demonstrate their duty to the king, even more, their obedience to God and love for His saints, than by offering their service, with all that is in them, for the carrying out of the work? But besides all this, these complainers were the main promoters of the translation; therefore they ought least to oppose it. Consider the facts of history. When his Majesty came to the throne, a conference was appointed at Hampton Court to hear the grievances of the Puritans, who earnestly requested a new translation of the Bible. When forced by reason to abandon every other basis for this request, they finally contrived the claim that they could not with good conscience subscribe to the Book of Common Prayer, because it confirms and preserves the Bible translation it contains, which, according to them, is full of mistakes. Even though this argument was judged to be a very poor and empty one, still, at that point his Majesty began to consider the good that might result from a new translation, and soon he gave order for this translation, which is now presented to you. We can hope that these facts will satisfy our brethren whose consciences are troubled by our work.

To the second group, the mockers, we give this answer. We do not deny, in fact, we solemnly affirm that the very poorest translation of the Bible into English, set forth by men of Protestant conviction (for we have not yet seen a Catholic translation of the whole Bible) contains the Word of God; no, is the Word of God. This is just the same as the fact that a speech of the king in Parliament, when translated into French, Dutch, Italian, and Latin, is still the king's speech, even if it is not interpreted by each translator with equal refinement or perhaps with such stylistic beauty or such clarity of meaning in every passage. For it is commonly recognized that things are to be evaluated according to their overall character, and an ordinary man could say, as Horace has it, "Truly, when the splendors in a song are many, I will not complain about a few imperfections." A man may be considered virtuous in spite of having made many mistakes in his life (otherwise no one would be virtuous, for "in many things we offend all"), or he may be considered handsome and attractive in spite of having some warts on his hand or some freckles or even scars on his face. There is no and blemishes may be noted in the setting forth of it. For what ever was perfect under the sun, where Apostles or apostolick men, that is, men endued with an extraordinary measure of God's Spirit, and privileged with the privilege of infallibility, had not their hand? The Romanists therefore in refusing to hear, and daring to burn the word translated, did no less than despite the Spirit of grace, from whom originally it proceeded, and whose sense and meaning, as well as man's weakness would enable, it did express. Judge by an example or two.

Plutarch[82] writeth, that after that Rome had been burnt by the Gauls, they fell soon to build it again: but doing it in haste, they did not cast the streets, nor proportion the houses, in such comely fashion, as had been most sightly and convenient. Was Catiline therefore an honest man, or a good patriot, that sought to bring it to a combustion? or Nero a good Prince, that did indeed set it on fire? So by the story of Ezra[83] and the prophecy of Haggai it may be gathered, that the temple built by Zerubbabel after the return from Babylon was by no means to be compared to the former built by Solomon: for they that remembered the former wept when they considered the latter. Notwithstanding might this latter either have been abhorred and forsaken by the Jews, or profaned by the Greeks? The like we are to think of translations. The translation of the *Seventy* dissenteth from the Original in many places, neither doth it come near it for perspicuity, gravity, majesty. Yet which of the Apostles did condemn it? Condemn it? Nay, they used it, (as it is apparent, and as St. Hierome and most learned men do confess;) which they would not have done, nor by their example of using it so grace and commend it to the Church, if it had been unworthy the appellation and name of the word of God.

The value of a translation does not depend on the translator's theological convictions.

And whereas they urge for their second defence of their vilifying and abusing of the English Bibles, or some pieces thereof, which they meet with, for that hereticks forsooth were the authors of the translations: (hereticks they call us by the same right that they call themselves catholicks, both being wrong:) we marvel what divinity taught them so. We are sure Tertullian[84] was of another mind: *Ex personis probamus fidem, an ex fide personas?* Do we try men's faith by their persons? We should try their persons by their faith. Also St. Augustine[85] was of another mind: for he, lighting upon certain rules made by Tychonius a Donatist for the better understanding of the word, was not ashamed to make use of them, yea, to insert them into his own book, with giving commendation to them so far forth as they were worthy to be commended, as is to be seen in St.

reason, then, why a Scripture translation should be denied to be Scripture or be forbidden publication, even though some imperfections and blemishes may be apparent in the production of it. For what has ever been perfect under the sun, except where apostles or apostolic men (that is, men filled with an extraordinary measure of God's Spirit and privileged with infallibility) were involved? The Romanists, then, by refusing to hear and daring to burn translations of Scripture, did nothing less than insult the Spirit of grace, from whom the Scripture originally proceeded and whose sense and meaning, as well as human weakness would permit, the translations did express.

Consider an example or two. Plutarch writes that, after Rome had been burnt by the Gauls, they soon began to rebuild the city. But, in their haste, they did not lay out the streets or proportion the houses in the most attractive and convenient possible manner. Was Catiline then demonstrating honesty or patriotism when he tried to set the city on fire? Or was Nero a good prince for succeeding in burning it down? In the same way, we may gather from the story of Ezra and the prophecy of Haggai, that the temple built by Zerubbabel after the return from Babylon was not at all comparable to the former one, built by Solomon, for those who remembered the former temple wept when they looked upon the latter. Should Zerubbabel's temple then have been either forsaken by the Jews or profaned by the Greeks? We should take the same view toward translations. The Septuagint differs from the original Hebrew in many places, and it comes nowhere near it with respect to clarity, dignity, and majesty. Yet which of the apostles condemned it? Condemn it? No, indeed! They used it (as is obvious, and as Jerome and most Bible scholars agree), something they would not have done, nor would they have set an example that honored it and commended it to the church, if it had been unworthy to be called the Word of God.

Now the Catholics' second defense for vilifying and abusing the English translations of the Bible (or of some portion of it) that they encounter is that the translators were, of all things, heretics (they call us heretics for the same reason that they call themselves Catholics, and they are wrong on both counts). This claim astonishes us, and we wonder what kind of theology taught them to think like this! We are sure that Tertullian thought otherwise: "Do we approve men's beliefs based on their place in the world, or do we approve their place in the world based on their beliefs?" Certainly we should do the latter. Augustine thought otherwise as well, for when he came across a helpful set of rules for interpreting the Bible, rules authored by a Donatist named Tychonius, he was not ashamed to make use of them. In fact, he put them into his own book,

Augustine's third book *De Doctr. Christ.* To be short, Origen, and the whole Church of God for certain hundred years, were of another mind: for they were so far from treading under foot (much more from burning) the translation of Aquila a proselyte, that is, one that had turned Jew, of Symmachus, and Theodotion both Ebionites, that is, most vile hereticks, that they joined them together with the Hebrew original, and the translation of the *Seventy* (as hath been before signified out of Epiphanius) and set them forth openly to be considered of and perused by all. But we weary the unlearned, who need not know so much; and trouble the learned, who know it already.

Roman Catholics revise their translations no less than Protestants.

Yet before we end, we must answer a third cavil and objection of their's against us, for altering and amending our translations so oft; wherein truly they deal hardly and strangely with us. For to whom ever was it imputed for a fault (by such as were wise,) to go over that which he had done, and to amend it where he saw cause? St. Augustine[86] was not afraid to exhort St. Hierome to a *Palinodia* or recantation. The same St. Augustine[87] was not ashamed to retractate, we might say, revoke, many things that had passed him, and doth even glory that he seeth his infirmities.[88] If we will be sons of the truth, we must consider what it speaketh, and trample upon our own credit, yea, and upon other men's too, if either be any way an hinderance to it. This to the cause. Then to the persons we say, that of all men they ought to be most silent in this case. For what varieties have they, and what alterations have they made, not only of their service books, portesses, and breviaries, but also of their Latin translation? The service book supposed to be made by St. Ambrose, *(Officium Ambrosianum)* was a great while in special use and request:[89] but Pope Adrian, calling a council with the aid of Charles the Emperor, abolished it, yea, burnt it, and commanded the service book of St. Gregory universally to be used. Well, *Officium Gregorianum* gets by this means to be in credit; but doth it continue without change or altering? No, the very Roman service was of two fashions; the new fashion, and the old, the one used in one Church, and the other in another; as is to be seen in Pamelius a Romanist, his preface before *Micrologus.* The same Pamelius reporteth out of Radulphus de Rivo, that about the year of our Lord 1277 Pope Nicolas the Third removed out of the churches of Rome the more ancient books (of service,) and brought into use the missals of the Friers Minorites, and commanded them to be observed there; insomuch that about an hundred years after, when the above named Radulphus happened to be at Rome, he found all the books to be new, of the new stamp. Neither was there this chopping and changing in the more ancient times only, but also of late. Pius Quintus himself confesseth, that every bishoprick almost had a

commending them to the extent that they deserved commendation; they are in his third book *Of the Teachings of Christ.* To keep things brief, Origen and the whole Church of God for several hundred years thought otherwise, for consider how they treated the Greek translation of Aquila, a proselyte to Judaism, and those of Symmachus and Theodotion, both of whom were Ebionites, adherents to a vile heresy. Far from treading these translations under foot, let alone from burning them, they put them together with the original Hebrew and the Septuagint (as the earlier mention of Epiphanius suggested) and published them openly to be examined and studied by everyone. But we are wearing out the unlearned, who do not need to know so much, and annoying the learned, who know it already.

Nevertheless, before we stop we must answer a third complaint and objection of the Catholics against us, that we revise and correct our translations so often. In this matter they treat us harshly and strangely indeed. For who was ever charged with a fault (by the wise, that is) for going over what he had done and correcting it where he saw good reason to do so? Augustine was not afraid to exhort Jerome to a *palinodia*, that is, a recantation. The same Augustine was not ashamed to retract, or perhaps more accurately, to revoke, many things that he had earlier approved, and he even takes pride in the fact that he can recognize his faults. If we wish to be sons of the truth, we must give heed to what the truth says, and we must trample upon our own reputation, and even upon that of other men, if either should in any way present a hindrance to the truth. This is our answer to the complaint itself. But to the persons we say, that, of all men, they ought to be most silent in this case. For what differences do they have, and what changes have they made, not only in their service books, hymnals, and breviaries, but also in their Latin translation? The service book reputed to have been produced by Ambrose (*Officium Ambrosianum*) was widely used and especially popular for a long time. But Pope Adrian, calling a council with the aid of Charles the Emperor, abolished it. In fact, he burned it, and he commanded the service book of Gregory to be used exclusively. Very well; *Officium Gregorianum* then becomes the standard, but does it continue without change or revision? No; the Roman service itself was of two kinds, the new and the old, and some churches used one while others used the other. Pamelius, a Catholic, reflects this situation in his preface to *Micrologus.* The same Pamelius reports that in about A.D. 1277, according to Radulphus de Rivo, Pope Nicholas III removed the more ancient service books from the churches of Rome and brought into use the missals [liturgical books] of the Friars Minorites, commanding them to be used in that city. This change was so thorough that, when the above-named Radulphus happened to be at Rome about a hundred years later, he found peculiar kind of service, most unlike to that which others had; which moved him to abolish all other breviaries, though never so ancient, and privileged and published by Bishops in their Dioceses, and to establish and ratify that only which was of his own setting forth in the year 1568. Now when the Father of their Church, who gladly would heal the sore of the daughter of his people softly and slightly, and make the best of it, findeth so great fault with them for their odds, and jarring; we hope the children have no great cause to vaunt of their uniformity. But the difference that appeareth between our translations, and our often correcting of them, is the thing that we are specially charged with; let us see therefore whether they themselves be without fault this way, (if it be to be counted a fault, to correct) and whether they be fit men to throw stones at us: *O tandem major parcas insane minori:* They that are less sound themselves ought not to object infirmities to others. If we should tell them, that Valla, Stapulensis, Erasmus, and Vives, found fault with their vulgar translation, and consequently wished the same to be mended, or a new one to be made; they would answer peradventure, that we produced their enemies for witnesses against them; albeit they were in no other sort enemies, than as St. Paul was to the Galatians, for telling them the truth;[90] and it were to be wished, that they had dared to tell it them plainlier and oftner. But what will they say to this, That Pope Leo[91] the Tenth allowed Erasmus' translation of the New Testament, so much different from the vulgar, by his apostolic letter and bull? That the same Leo exhorted Pagnine to translate the whole Bible, and bare whatsoever charges was necessary for the work? Surely, as the apostle reasoneth to the Hebrews,[92] that *if the former Law and Testament had been sufficient, there had been no need of the latter:* so we may say, that if the old vulgar had been at all points allowable, to small purpose had labour and charges been undergone about framing of a new. If they say, it was one Pope's private opinion, and that he consulted only himself; then we are able to go further with them, and to aver, that more of their chief men of all sorts, even their own Trent champions, Paiva and Vega, and their own inquisitor Hieronymus ab Oleastro, and their own Bishop Isidorus Clarius, and their own Cardinal Thomas a vio Cajetan, do either make new translations themselves, or follow new ones of other men's making, or note the vulgar interpreter for halting, none of them fear to dissent from him, nor yet to except against him. And call they this an uniform tenor of text and judgment about the text, so many of their worthies disclaiming the new received conceit? Nay, we will yet come nearer the quick. Doth not their Paris edition differ from the Lovain, and Hentenius's from them both, and yet all of them allowed by authority? Nay, doth not Sixtus Quintus[93] confess, that certain Catholicks (he meaneth certain of his own side) were in such an humour of translating the Scriptures into Latin, that Satan taking occasion by them,

all the service books to be of the new type. But do not suppose that this chopping and changing took place only in earlier ages; it has also happened recently. Pius V himself admits that nearly every diocese had a unique kind of service, quite different from the service of others. This situation prompted him to establish and authorize the breviary that he produced himself in 1568, abolishing all others with no regard to their antiquity or to the fact that they enjoyed official sanction and publication. Now when the father of their church, who would gladly heal the sore of the daughter of his people softly and slightly, and make the best of it, finds so much fault with the children for their differences and conflicts, we suspect that the children have no great reason to brag about their uniformity. But their particular charge against us is not that we have changed at all, but rather that the changes are substantial and that we make them so often. Let us see, then, whether our accusers themselves are faultless in this respect (if correcting may be considered a fault) and whether they are fit to throw stones at us. Somebody wrote, "O greater madman, may you come, at last, to spare a less," which is to say that those who are less sound themselves ought not to make accusations about the infirmities of others. If we should tell them that Valla, Stapulensis, Erasmus, and Vives found fault with the Latin Vulgate and consequently wanted it to be either revised or replaced with a new translation, they would answer, perhaps, that we have called their enemies as witnesses against them. (We observe, though, that they were enemies only in the sense in which Paul was the Galatians' enemy, for telling them the truth; they would have done well to tell it to them more clearly and more often!) But what will they say to the fact that Pope Leo X, by his apostolic letter and bull, approved Erasmus' translation of the New Testament, even though it was so much different from the Vulgate? What will they say to the fact that the same Leo exhorted Pagnine to translate the whole Bible and bore all the expenses necessary for the work? Surely, just as the apostle argues to the Hebrews, that "If the former Law and Testament had been sufficient, there had been no need of the latter," so we may point out that if the Vulgate had been acceptable at every point, there would have been little reason to go to the work and expense of producing a new Latin Bible. Perhaps the Catholics would respond that this was simply the private opinion of one pope, who consulted no one else on the matter. But we can go further and maintain that many of their most important men, of all sorts (including their champions at Trent, Paiva, and Vega, their inquisitor Hieronymus ab Oleastro, their Bishop Isidorus Clarius, and their Cardinal Thomas a vio Cajetan), either make new translations themselves, or use new translations made by others, or point out the Vulgate's awkwardness. None of them fear to disagree with it or to contradict it. Do they call this a consistent state of the text itself and of opinion about the text, when so many of their leaders reject the though they thought of no such matter, did strive what he could, out of so uncertain and manifold a variety of translations, so to mingle all things, that nothing might seem to be left certain and firm in them, etc.? Nay further, did not the same Sixtus ordain by an inviolable decree, and that with the counsel and consent of his Cardinals, that the Latin edition of the Old and New Testament, which the council of Trent would have to be authentick, is the same without controversy which he then set forth, being diligently corrected and printed in the printing-house of Vatican? Thus Sixtus in his preface before his Bible. And yet Clement the Eighth, his immediate successor to account of, publisheth another edition of the Bible, containing in it infinite differences from that of Sixtus, and many of them weighty and material; and yet this must be authentick by all means. What is to have the faith of our glorious Lord Jesus Christ with yea and nay, if this be not? Again, what is sweet harmony and consent, if this be? Therefore, as Demaratus of Corinth advised a great King, before he talked of the dissensions among the Grecians, to compose his domestick broils; (for at that time his queen and his son and heir were at deadly feud with him) so all the while that our adversaries do make so many and so various editions themselves, and do jar so much about the worth and authority of them, they can with no shew of equity challenge us for changing and correcting.

Purposes and Procedures Underlying the Present Translation

But it is high time to leave them, and to shew in brief what we proposed to ourselves, and what course we held, in this our perusal and survey of the Bible. Truly, good Christian Reader, we never thought from the beginning that we should need to make a new translation, nor yet to make of a bad one a good one; (for then the imputation of Sixtus had been true in some sort, that our people had been fed with gall of dragons instead of wine, with wheal instead of milk;) but to make a good one better, or out of many good ones one principal good one, not justly to be excepted against; that hath been our endeavour, that our mark. To that purpose there were many chosen, that were greater in other men's eyes than in their own, and that sought the truth rather than their own praise. Again, they came, or were thought to come, to the work, not *exercendi causa*, (as one saith) but *exercitati*, that is, learned, not to learn; for the chief overseer and ἐργοδιώκτης under his Majesty, to whom not only we, but also our whole Church was much bound, knew by his wisdom, which thing also Nazianzen[94] taught so long ago, that it is a preposterous order to teach first, and

currently popular notion? But, indeed, we will probe yet closer to the nerve. Does not their Paris edition differ from the Lovain, and that of Hentenius from both of those, and yet all of them have official approval? Indeed, does not Sixtus V maintain that certain Catholics (he means those on his own side) were so taken with the idea of translating the Scriptures into Latin that, although they had no such intent, Satan took advantage of them and did what he could to create such confusion out of so great a variety of translations that nothing in the Bible seemed to be left firm and certain? Yet further, did not the same Sixtus establish by an inviolable decree, supported by the advice and consent of his cardinals, that the Latin version of the Old and New Testament which the council of Trent determined should be official is undeniably the one which he published at that time, carefully corrected and printed in the Vatican press? This is what Sixtus writes in the preface to his Bible. And yet Clement VIII, the very next pope of any importance, publishes another version of the Bible, containing innumerable differences from that of Sixtus, many of which are weighty and substantial, and yet this must be the official version at any cost. What does it mean to "have the faith of our glorious Lord Jesus Christ with yea and nay," if this is not it? And what good is "sweet harmony and consent" if this is it? Therefore, as Demaratus of Corinth advised a great king to resolve his domestic quarrels before addressing the strife among the Greeks (for at that time his queen and his son were his mortal enemies), even so, until our enemies themselves stop making so many versions of the Bible with such great differences between them, and stop quarreling so much about the value and authority of these versions, they cannot fairly challenge us for revising and correcting.

But it is high time to change the subject from our enemies to a brief discussion of our own plans and procedures for examining and surveying the Bible. In all honesty, good Christian Reader, we have never intended, from the beginning, to make a new translation, or even to turn a bad one into a good one (for then the accusation of Sixtus would have been true to some degree, that our people had been fed with the bile of dragons instead of wine, with pus instead of milk). Rather, our intent has been to make a good translation better, or to combine many good ones into one foremost good one, a translation against which no one could object with any fairness; this has been the goal toward which we have labored. To that end there were many chosen who were greater in other men's esteem than in their own and who sought the truth rather than their own praise. Furthermore, they came to the work, not as men seeking to gain skill in the field, but as men highly skilled, or at least thought to be so. For the head overseer and supervisor under his Majesty, to whom not only we but also our whole church was much indebted, knew in his wisdom what Nazianzen also to learn after; that τὸ ἐν πίθῳ κεραμίαν μανθάνειν,[95] to learn and practise together, is neither commendable for the workman, nor safe for the work. Therefore such were thought upon, as could say modestly with St. Hierome, *Et Hebræum sermonem ex parte didicimus, et in Latino pene ab ipsis incunabilis, etc. detriti sumus; Both we have learned the Hebrew tongue in part, and in the Latin we have been exercised almost from our very cradle.* St. Hierome maketh no mention of the Greek tongue, wherein yet he did excel; because he translated not the Old Testament out of Greek, but out of Hebrew. And in what sort did these assemble? In the trust of their own knowledge, or of their sharpness of wit, or deepness of judgment, as it were in an arm of flesh? At no hand. They trusted in Him that hath the key of David, opening, and no man shutting; they prayed to the Lord, the Father of our Lord, to the effect that St. Augustine[96] did; *O let thy Scriptures be my pure delight; let me not be deceived in them, neither let me deceive by them.* In this confidence, and with this devotion, did they assemble together; not too many, lest one should trouble another; and yet many, lest many things haply might escape them. If you ask what they had before them; truly it was the Hebrew text of the Old Testament, the Greek of the New. These are the two golden pipes, or rather conduits, wherethrough the olive branches empty themselves into the gold. St. Augustine[97] calleth them precedent, or original, tongues; St. Hierome,[98] fountains. The same St. Hierome[99] affirmeth, and Gratian hath not spared to put it into his decree, That *as the credit of the old books* (he meaneth of the Old Testament) *is to be tried by the Hebrew volumes; so of the new by the Greek tongue,* he meaneth by the original Greek. If truth be to be tried by these tongues, then whence should a translation be made, but out of them? These tongues therefore, (the Scriptures, we say, in those tongues) we set before us to translate, being the tongues wherein God was pleased to speak to his Church by his Prophets and Apostles. Neither did we run over the work with that posting haste that the *Septuagint* did,[100] if that be true which is reported of them, that they finished it in seventy two days; neither were we barred or hindered from going over it again, having once done it, like St. Hierome,[101] if that be true which himself reporteth, that he could no sooner write any thing, but presently it was caught from him, and published, and he could not have leave to mend it: neither, to be short, were we the first that fell in hand[102] with translating the Scripture into English, and consequently destitute of former helps, as it is written of Origen, that he was the first in a manner, that put his hand to write commentaries upon the Scriptures, and therefore no marvel if he overshot himself many times. None of these things: The work hath not been huddled up in seventy two days, but hath cost the workmen, as light as it seemeth, the pains of twice seven times seventy two days, and more. Matters of such weight and consequence are to be speeded with maturity:[103] for in a

taught so long ago, that to teach first and to learn later is to turn things backward, and that "to learn pottery by making a wine jar," that is, to build skill by undertaking a task requiring professional expertise, is neither commendable for the workman nor safe for the work. Therefore men were sought out who could say modestly with Jerome, "We have learned Hebrew in part, and we have also been exercised in the Latin language almost from our very cradle." (Jerome makes no mention of the Greek language, in which he also excelled, because he did not translate the Old Testament from the Greek but from the Hebrew.) And with what attitude did these men come together? With confidence in their own knowledge or in the exactness of their reasoning or in the depth of their understanding? In other words, did they trust in the arm of flesh? They certainly did not. They trusted in Him who has the key of David, who opens and no man shuts; they prayed to the Lord, the Father of our Lord, just like Augustine did: "O let thy Scriptures be my pure delight; let me not be deceived in them, neither let me deceive by them." With this confidence and in this devotion they assembled together. There were not too many of them, to minimize inconvenience and conflict, yet there were many, to insure adequate attention to detail. Regarding the texts they had in front of them, they had the Hebrew text of the Old Testament and the Greek of the New. These are the two golden pipes, or rather channels, through which the olive branches empty themselves into the golden candlestick. Augustine calls them precedent, or original languages; Jerome calls them fountains. The same Jerome affirms, and Gratian did not refrain from putting it into his decree, that "As the credit of the old books [he means the books of the Old Testament] is to be tried by the Hebrew volumes, so of the new by the Greek tongue [he means by the original Greek]." If truth is to be tested by these languages, then from what other languages should a translation be made? Therefore these are the Scripture texts we set before us from which to translate, since they are the languages in which God was pleased to speak to his Church by his Prophets and Apostles. We have not run through our task with the wild haste that characterized the Septuagint translators, if the tradition that they finished their work in seventy-two days is true. Neither were we forbidden or hindered from revising our first draft, in contrast to Jerome, assuming that what he says is true, that as soon as he wrote anything it was immediately snatched from him and published, without his having a chance to revise it. Neither, to be short, were we the first ones to undertake a translation of the Bible into English and therefore destitute of previous examples, in contrast to Origen, of whom it is written that he was in a sense the first one to attempt the writing of commentaries on the Bible, and therefore it is no surprise if he made many mistakes. But none of these things characterized our work. The translation was not thrown together in seventy-two days; rather it business of moment a man feareth not the blame of convenient slackness. Neither did we think much to consult the translators or commentators, Chaldee, Hebrew, Syrian, Greek, or Latin; no, nor the Spanish, French, Italian, or Dutch; neither did we disdain to revise that which we had done, and to bring back to the anvil that which we had hammered: but having and using as great helps as were needful, and fearing no reproach for slowness, or coveting praise for expedition, we have at length, through the good hand of the Lord upon us, brought the work to that pass that you see.

Some peradventure would have no variety of senses to be set in the margin, lest the authority of the Scriptures for deciding of controversies by that shew of uncertainty should somewhat be shaken. But we hold their judgment not to be so sound in this point. For though, *whatsoever things are necessary are manifest,*[104] as St. Chrysostome saith; and, as St. Augustine,[105] *in those things that are plainly set down in the Scriptures all such matters are found, that concern faith, hope, and charity:* Yet for all that it cannot be dissembled, that partly to exercise and whet our wits, partly to wean the curious from lothing of them for their every where plainness, partly also to stir up our devotion to crave the assistance of God's Spirit by prayer, and lastly, that we might be forward to seek aid of our brethren by conference, and never scorn those that be not in all respects so complete as they should be, being to seek in many things ourselves, it hath pleased God in his Divine Providence here and there to scatter words and sentences of that difficulty and doubtfulness, not in doctrinal points that concern salvation, (for in such it hath been vouched that the Scriptures are plain,) but in matters of less moment, that fearfulness would better beseem us than confidence, and if we will resolve, to resolve upon modesty with St. Augustine,[106] (though not in this same case altogether, yet upon the same ground) *Melius est dubitare de occultis, quam litigare de incertis:* It is better to make doubt of those things which are secret, than to strive about those things that are uncertain. There be many words in the Scriptures, which be never found there but once,[107] (having neither brother nor neighbor, as the Hebrews speak) so that we cannot be holpen by conference of places. Again, there be many rare names of certain birds, beasts, and precious stones, etc., concerning which the Hebrews themselves are so divided among themselves for judgment, that they may seem to have defined this or that, rather because they would say something, than because they were sure of that which they said, as St. Hierome[108] somewhere saith of the *Septuagint.* Now, in such a case, doth not a margin do well to admonish the Reader to

has cost the laborers (as light as the labor seemed) the trouble of twice seven times seventy-two days, and more. Maturity is better than speed in carrying out matters of such importance and consequence, for a man engaged in a weighty project does not fear being blamed for taking an appropriate amount of time. We did not hesitate to consult other translations or commentaries, whether in Aramaic, Hebrew, Syriac, Greek, or Latin, or in the modern languages: Spanish, French, Italian, or Dutch. Neither did we think our work too good to revise, so we brought back to the anvil that which we had already hammered. So, availing ourselves of every help that we needed, and neither fearing reproach for slowness nor coveting praise for speed, we have finally, through the good hand of the Lord upon us, brought the work to the result that you see.

Some people perhaps wish to have no marginal notes giving alternate readings, fearing that such a display of uncertainty might to some extent shake the authority of the Scriptures for settling controversies. But we think their judgment is not entirely sound on this point. For, although "whatsoever things are necessary are manifest," as Chrysostom says, and, according to Augustine, "in those things that are plainly set down in the Scriptures all such matters are found, that concern faith, hope, and charity," nevertheless it cannot be denied that God has been pleased, in his divine providence, to scatter here and there words and sentences of such difficulty and uncertainty that we do better to respond to them with fearfulness than with confidence. Of course, we need not fear that such uncertainties affect doctrinal points concerning salvation, for we have already quoted authorities maintaining that the Scriptures are clear on these things; nevertheless in less important matters there are difficulties regarding which, if we wish to decide anything, we do best to decide to be moderate along with Augustine, who said (though not regarding exactly the same situation, yet using the same reasoning), "It is better to make doubt of those things which are secret than to strive about those things that are uncertain." It seems that God has put these uncertainties into the Scripture, partly to exercise and to sharpen our minds, partly to teach inquisitive people not to look down upon the Scripture as being so clear on every point that it contains no challenge, partly also to arouse our devotion to plead for the assistance of God's Spirit by prayer, and finally, that we might be eager to seek help from our brethren by conferring with them, and that we might never scorn those who in some areas do not fully measure up to what they should be, since we ourselves are deficient in many respects. There are many words in the Bible that appear only once (having neither brother nor neighbor, as the Hebrews say) so that we can get no help with their meaning by comparing contexts. Similarly, there are many rare names of certain birds, beasts, precious stones, and other things concerning which seek further, and not to conclude or dogmatize upon this or that peremptorily? For as it is a fault of incredulity, to doubt of those things that are evident; so to determine of such things as the Spirit of God hath left (even in the judgment of the judicious) questionable, can be no less than presumption. Therefore, as St. Augustine[109] saith, that variety of translations is profitable for the finding out of the sense of the Scriptures: so diversity of signification and sense in the margin, where the text is not so clear, must needs do good; yea, is necessary, as we are persuaded. We know that Sixtus Quintus[110] expressly forbiddeth that any variety of readings of their vulgar edition should be put in the margin; (which though it be not altogether the same thing to that we have in hand, yet it looketh that way;) but we think he hath not all of his own side his favourers for this conceit. They that are wise had rather have their judgments at liberty in differences of readings, than to be captivated to the one, when it may be the other. If they were sure that their high priest had all laws shut up in his breast, as Paul the Second bragged,[111] and that he were as free from error by special privilege, as the dictators of Rome were made by law inviolable, it were another matter; then his word were an oracle, his opinion a decision. But the eyes of the world are now open, God be thanked, and have been a great while; they find that he is subject to the same affections[112] and infirmities that others be, that his skin is penetrable;[113] and therefore so much as he proveth, not as much as he claimeth, they grant and embrace.

Another thing we think good to admonish thee of, gentle Reader, that we have not tied ourselves to an uniformity of phrasing, or to an identity of words, as some peradventure would wish that we had done, because they observe, that some learned men somewhere have been as exact as they could that way. Truly, that we might not vary from the sense of that which we had translated before, if the word signified the same thing in both places, (for there be some words that be not of the same sense every where,[114]) we were especially careful, and made a conscience, according to our duty. But that we should express the same notion in the same particular word; as for example, if we translate the Hebrew or Greek word once by *purpose,* never to call it *intent;* if one where *journeying,* never *travelling;* if one where *think,* never *suppose;* if one where *pain,* never *ache;* if one where *joy,* never *gladness,* &c. Thus to mince the matter, we thought to savour more of curiosity than wisdom, and that rather it would breed scorn in the atheist, than bring profit to the godly reader. For is

the opinion of the Hebrews themselves is so divided that they seem to have defined this or that more because they wished to say something than because they were sure of what they said, as Jerome somewhere says regarding the Septuagint. Now, in a case like that, is it not a good thing for a marginal note to warn the reader that further study is necessary and that he should not conclude or dogmatize closemindedly on this or that? For just as the doubting of things that are evident is the fault called unbelief, in the same way to claim certainty about things which the Spirit of God has left questionable, even in the judgment of competent judges, can be nothing less than presumption. Therefore, as Augustine says that a variety of translations helps one to discover the meaning of the Scriptures, just the same, marginal notations of various possibilities of significance and meaning must do good. Indeed, we are persuaded, they are necessary. We know that Sixtus V explicitly forbids any alternate readings from the Vulgate to be put in the margin (which, though it does not match our case exactly, yet it tends in the same direction), but we suspect that he does not have all the Catholics behind him regarding this position. Those who are wise would rather have freedom to decide among alternative readings than to be captive to one, when the other may be correct. If they were sure that their high priest had all laws under lock in his own breast, as Paul II bragged, and that his special privilege rendered his reliability as absolute as Roman law rendered a dictator's authority, it would be a different matter. In that case, his word would be a divine utterance, his opinion a decision. But the eyes of the world are now open, thank the Lord, and have been for a long time. People have discovered that he is subject to the same passions and infirmities that others are and that his skin is not impenetrable; therefore, they acknowledge and embrace what he can prove, not what he merely claims.

Another thing we think you need to know, gentle reader, is that we have not tied ourselves to a uniformity of phrasing or to a consistent equivalence of words, as some perhaps may wish we had done, observing that some scholarly men somewhere have been as exact as they could in that matter. Now in fact, in order to avoid varying from the sense of what we had translated earlier, if a word before us signified the same thing as in the earlier passage (for there are some words that do not mean the same thing in every context) we fulfilled our duty by being especially careful and conscientious. But we did not follow the notion that we should always express the same idea with the same particular word, as, for example, that once we translated a Hebrew or Greek word by "purpose" we should never call it "intent"; once we used "journeying" never "travelling"; once we used "think" never "suppose"; once we used "pain," never "ache"; once we used "gladness," never "joy," and so on. We thought that to reduce the matter of word choice to such a mechanical exercise the kingdom of God become words or syllables? Why should we be in bondage to them, if we may be free? use one precisely, when we may use another no less fit as commodiously? A godly Father, in the primitive time, shewed himself greatly moved, that one of newfangledness called κράββάτονε σκίμπουςε though the difference be little or none; and another reporteth, that he was much abused for turning *cucurbita* (to which reading the people had been used) into *hedera*.[115] Now, if this happen in better times, and upon so small occasions, we might justly fear hard censure, if generally we should make verbal and unnecessary changings. We might also be charged (by scoffers) with some unequal dealing towards a great number of good English words. For, as it is written of a certain great Philosopher, that he should say, that those logs were happy that were made images to be worshipped; for their fellows, as good as they, lay for blocks behind the fire: so if we should say, as it were, unto certain words, Stand up higher, have a place in the Bible always; and to others of like quality, Get you hence, be banished for ever; we might be taxed peradventure with St. James's words, namely, *To be partial in ourselves, and judges of evil thoughts.* Add hereunto that niceness in words was always counted the next step to trifling;[116] and so was to be curious about names too; also that we cannot follow a better pattern for elocution than God himself; therefore he using divers words in his holy writ, and indifferently for one thing in nature: we, if we will not be superstitious, may use the same liberty in our English versions out of the Hebrew and Greek, for that copy or store that he hath given us. Lastly, we have on the one side avoided the scrupulosity of the Puritanes, who leave the old Ecclesiastical words, and betake them to other, as when they put *washing* for *baptism*, and *congregation* instead of *Church:* as also on the other side, we have shunned the obscurity of the Papists, in their *azymes, tunike, rational, holocausts, prepuce, pasche,* and a number of such like, whereof their late translation is full, and that of purpose to darken the sense, that since they must needs translate the Bible, yet, by the language thereof, it may be kept from being understood. But we desire that the Scripture may speak like itself, as in the language of Canaan, that it may be understood even of the very vulgar.

Conclusion

Many other things we might give thee warning of, gentle Reader, if we had not exceeded the measure of a preface already. It remaineth that we commend thee to God, and to the Spirit of his grace, which is able to build further than we can ask or

would smack more of fastidiousness than wisdom and that it would do more to breed scorn in the atheist than to bring profit to the godly reader. After all, has the kingdom of God become words and syllables? Why should we be in bondage to them if we may be free? Why should we rigidly restrict ourselves to one word when we may profitably use another one that is no less fitting? A godly father, in the early days of the church, became very angry that an innovator called a *krabbaton* [the Greek word for a cot-like bed] a *skimpous*, though there is little or no difference, and another reports that he was greatly abused for changing *cucurbita* (the reading to which the people had been accustomed) to *hedera* [Latin plant names]. Now, if this happened in better times than ours, and over such small issues, we might justly fear severe rebuke if we were to make a large number of unnecessary changes in wording. We might also be charged (by scoffers) with treating a great number of good English words unfairly. For, as it is written about a certain great philosopher, that, in his opinion the logs fashioned into images for worship were better off than their neighbors who, though equally good, lay as blocks behind the fire, even so if we should say, as it were, to certain words, "Stand up higher; we will use you regularly in the Bible," and to others of equal quality, "Get out of here; be banished forever," we might perhaps be labeled with the words of James, "to be partial in ourselves, and judges of evil thoughts." Consider further that to quibble about words has always been seen as just a step away from deception, and it is the same with fussiness over names. And there is no better example for us to follow in our literary style than God Himself. Since in his holy Scriptures he freely uses a variety of words to stand for one idea, we, if we will not be over-scrupulous, may take the same liberty in our English translations from Hebrew and Greek, in view of the abundant supply that He has given us. Finally, we have on the one hand avoided the distrustfulness of the Puritans, who repudiate the old ecclesiastical words in favor of others, as when they use "washing" in place of "baptism" and "congregation" in place of "church," and on the other hand we have shunned the obscurity of the Catholics with their "azumes," "tunike," "rational," "holocausts," "prepuce," "pasche," and many similar things, of which their recent translation is full. The Catholics have done this intentionally, in order to obscure the meaning so that, even though they are forced to translate the Bible, yet, by the language they use, they may keep it from being understood. But we desire that the Scripture may speak like itself, as in the language of Canaan, so that it may be understood even by the most common people.

We might give you warning of many other things, gentle reader, if we had not already exceeded the limits of a preface. It remains only for us to commend you to God, and to the Spirit of His

think. He removeth the scales from our eyes, the vail from our hearts, opening our wits that we may understand his word, enlarging our hearts, yea, correcting our affections, that we may love it above gold and silver, yea, that we may love it to the end. Ye are brought unto fountains of living water which ye digged not;[117] do not cast earth into them, with the Philistines, neither prefer broken pits before them, with the wicked Jews.[118] Others have laboured, and you may enter into their labours. O receive not so great things in vain: O despise not so great salvation. Be not like swine to tread under foot so precious things, neither yet like dogs to tear and abuse holy things. Say not to our Saviour with the Gergesites,[119] Depart out of our coasts; neither yet with Esau[120] sell your birthright for a mess of pottage. If light be come into the world, love not darkness more than light: if food, if clothing, be offered, go not naked, starve not yourselves. Remember the advice of Nazianzene,[121] *It is a grievous thing* (or dangerous) *to neglect a great fair, and to seek to make markets afterwards:* also the encouragement of St. Chrysostome,[122] *It is altogether impossible, that he that is sober* (and watchful) *should at any time be neglected:* lastly, the admonition and menacing of St. Augustine,[123] *They that despise God's will inviting them, shall feel God's will taking vengeance of them.* It is a fearful thing to fall into the hands of the living God;[124] but a blessed thing it is, and will bring us to everlasting blessedness in the end, when God speaketh unto us, to hearken; when he setteth his word before us, to read it; when he stretcheth out his hand and calleth, to answer, here am I, here are we to do thy will, O God. The Lord work a care and conscience in us to know him and serve him, that we may be acknowledged of him at the appearing of our Lord JESUS CHRIST, to whom with the Holy Ghost be all praise and thanksgiving. Amen.

grace, which is able to build beyond what we can ask or think. He removes the scales from our eyes and the veil from our hearts, opening our minds that we may understand His word, enlarging our hearts and even correcting our emotions that we may love it more than gold and silver, and that we may love it to the end. You are brought to fountains that you did not have to dig; do not dump dirt into them, with the Philistines, and do not prefer broken pits over them, with the wicked Jews. Others have labored, and you may benefit from their labors. Oh, do not receive such great things in vain; oh, do not despise so great salvation! Do not be like pigs, treading under foot such precious things; neither be like dogs, tearing and abusing what is holy. Do not say to our Savior with the Gergesites, "Depart out of our coasts," and do not, with Esau, sell your birthright for a mess of pottage. If light has come into the world, do not love darkness more than light; if you are offered food and clothing, do not go naked and starve yourselves. Remember the advice of Nazianzene: "It is a grievous thing (or dangerous) to neglect a great fair, and to seek to make markets afterwards" and the encouragement of Chrysostom: "It is altogether impossible that he that is sober (and watchful) should at any time be neglected." Finally, heed the warning and threat of Augustine: "They that despise God's will inviting them shall feel God's will taking vengeance of them." It is a fearful thing to fall into the hands of the living God, but it is a blessed thing, and it will bring us to everlasting blessedness in the end, to listen when God speaks to us, to read His word when He sets it before us, and, when He stretches out His hand and calls, to answer, "Here am I, here are we to do thy will, O God." May the Lord create within us a concern and a conscience to know Him and serve Him, that we may be acknowledged by Him at the appearing of our Lord JESUS CHRIST, to whom, with the Holy Spirit, may all praise and thanks be given. Amen.

Notes

[1]An account of these learned and judicious translators will be found in the Introduction to the Work; one of whom, Dr. Smith, afterwards Bishop of Glocester, wrote this excellent Preface.

[2]ἔξζω βέλους. [3]*Anacharsis, with others.*

[4]*In Athens: witness Libanius in Olynth. Demosth., Cato the elder.*

[5]*Gregory the Divine.* [6]*Nauclerus.* [7]*2 Sam. 11. 25.*

[8]1 Kin. 22. 31. [9]*2 Sam. 6. 16.* [10]σεισάχθειαν.

[11]1 Kin. 12. 4. [12]*C. Cæsar. Plutarch.* [13]*Constantine.*

[14]*Aurl. Vict. Theodosius. Zosimus.* [15]*Justinian.*

[16]Num. 32. 14. [17]Eccles. 1. 9. [18]Acts 7. 51.

[19]King James I. [20]Αὐτὸς, καὶ παῖδες, καὶ παίδων πάντοτε παῖδες.

[21]Ὥσπερ τις ἀνδριὰς ἀπερίτρεπτος καὶ ἄκμων ἀνήλατος, *Suidas.* [22]1 Sam. 2. 30.

[23]Θεοσέβεια, *Eusebius, lib.* 10, *cap.* 8. [24]*St. August. Confess. lib.* 8., *cap.* 12.

[25]*St. August. De utilit. credendi, cap.* 6. [26]*St. Hieron. ad Demetriad.*

[27]*St. Cyrill 7, contra Julian.* [28]*Tertull. advers. Herm.* [29]*Tertull. De carn. Christ.*

[30]Οἱόν τε, *Justin.* προτρεπτ. πρὸς Ἕλλην.

[31]Ὑπερηφανίας κατηγορία, *St. Basil.* περὶ πίστεως.

[32]Εἰρεσιώνη σῦκα φέρει, καὶ πίονας ἄρτους, καὶ μέλι ἐν κοτύλῃ, καὶ ἔλαιον. κ. τ. λ. An olive bough wrapped about with wool, whereupon did hang figs and bread, and honey in a pot, and oil.

[33]Κοινὸν ἰατρεῖον, *St. Basil in Psal. primum.* [34]1 Cor. 14. 11.

[35]*Clem. Alex. 1. Strom.* [36]*St. Hieronym. Damaso.* [37]*Michael, Theophili fil.*

[38]2 *Tom. Concil. ex edit. Petri Crab.* [39]*Cicero 5. De Finibus.*

[40]Gen. 29. 10. [41]John 4. 11. [42]Isai. 29. 11.

[43]*Epipahn. De mensuris et ponderib. St. August. 2. De. doctrin. Christian. c. 15.*

[44]*Novel. diatax.* 146. Προφητικῆς ὥσπερ χάριτος περιλαμψάσης αὐτούς.

[45]Isai. 31. 3. [46]*St. Hieron. de optimo genere interpret.*

[47]*St. August. de doctrin. Christ. lib. 2, cap. 11.* [48]*St. Hieron. Marcell. Zosim.*

[49]2 Kin. 7. 9. [50]*St. Hieron. Præf. in 4 Evangel.*

[51]*St. Hieron. Sophronio.* [52]*Six. Sen. lib. 4.* [53]*Alphon. a Castro, lib. 1, cap. 23.*

[54]*St. Chrysost. in Joann. cap. 1, hom. 1.* [55]*Theodor. 5. Therapeut.*

[56]*P. Diacon. lib. 12.* [57]*Isid. in Chron. Goth.* [58]*Sozom. lib. 6, cap. 57.*

[59]*Vasseus in Chro. Hisp.* [60]*Polydor. virg. 5., hist. Anglorum testatur idem de Aluredo nostro.*

[61]*Aventin. lib. 4.* [62]*Circa annum 900.* [63]*B. Rhenan. rerum German. lib. 2.*

[64]*Beroald. Thuan.* [65]Psal. 48. 8. [66]Δῶρον ἄδωρόν κ᾽οὐκ ὀνήσιμον. *Sophocl.*

[67]See the observation (set forth by Clement's authority) upon the 4th rule of Pius the 4th's making in the *Index lib. prohib.* page 15, *ver.* 5.

[68]*Tertull. de resur. carnis.* [69]John 3. 20. [70]*St. Iren. lib. 3, cap. 19.*

[71]Neh. 4. 2, 3.   [72]*St. Hieron. Apolog. advers. Ruffin.*

[73]*Arist. 2. Metaphys. cap.* 1.   [74]*St. Epiphan. loco ante citato.*

[75]*St. August. lib.* 19, *De civit. Dei, cap.* 7.   [76]2 Kin. 13. 18, 19.

[77]*St. Hieron. in Ezech. cap.* 3.   [78]Jer. 23. 28.

[79]*Tertull. ad Martyr. Si tanti vilissimum vitrum, quanti preciosissimum margaritum! Hier. ad Salvin.*

[80]*Horace*   [81]Jam. 3. 2.   [82]*Plutarch in Camillo.*

[83]Ezra 3. 12.   [84]*Tertull. de præscript. contra hæeses.*

[85]*St. August.* 3, *de doct. Christ. cap.* 30.

[86]*St. August. Epist.* 9.   [87]*St. August. lib. Retract.*   [88]*Video interdum vitia mea. St. August. Epist.* 8.

[89]*Durand. lib.* 5, cap. 2.   [90]Gal. 4. 16.   [91]*Sixtus Senens.*

[92]Heb. 7. 11, & 8. 7.   [93]*Sixtus* 5, *Præf. fixa bibliis.*   [94]*Nazianz.* εἰς ρν. ἐπισκ. παρουσ.

[95]*Idem in Apologet.*   [96]*St. August. lib.* 11, *Confess. cap.* 2.

[97]*St. August.* 3. *De doctr.* 3. *etc.*   [98]*St. Hieron. ad Suniam et Fretel.*

[99]*St. Hieron. ad Lucinium, Dist.* 9. *Ut veterum.*   [100]*Joseph. Antiq. lib.* 12.

[101]*St. Hieron. ad Pammach. pro lib. advers. Jovinian.*   [102]πρωτόπειροι.

[103]Φιλεῖ γὰρ ὀκνεῖν πραγμ᾿ ἀνὴρ πράσσων μέγα. *Sophocl. in Elect.*

[104]πάντα τὰ ἀναγκαῖα δῆλα. *St. Chrysost. in* 2 *Thess. cap.* 2.

[105]*St. August.* 2 *De doctr. Christ. cap.* 9.   [106]*St. August. lib.* 8. *De Gen. ad liter. cap.* 5.

[107]ἅπαξ λεγόμενα.   [108]*Hier. in Ezek. cap.* 3.   [109]*St. Aug.* 2. *De doctr. Christ.*

[110]*Sixtus* 5. *Præf. Bibl.*   [111]*Plat. in Paulo secundo.*   [112]ὁμοιοπαθὴς.

[113]Τρωτός γ᾿ οἱ χρώς ἐστί.   [114]πολύσημα.

[115]Abed. *Niceph. Calist. lib.* 8, *cap.* 42. *St. Hieron. in* 4. *Jonæ. See St. Aug. Epist.* 10.

[116]λεπτολογία. ἀδολεσχία. τὸ σπουδάζειν ἐπὶ ὀνόμασι. *See Euseb.* προπαρασκ. *lib.* 2, *ex Plat.*

[117]Gen. 26. 15.   [118]Jer. 2. 13.   [119]Mat. 8. 34.

[120]Heb. 12. 16.

[121]*Nazianz.* περὶ ἀγ. βαπτ. Δεινὸν πανήγυριν παρελθεῖν καὶ τηνικαῦτα πραγματείαν ἐπιζητεῖν

[122]*St. Chrysost. in Epist. ad Rom. c.* 14, *orat.* 26, *in* ἠθικ. Ἀμήχανον, σφόδρα ἀμήχανον.

[123]*St. August. ad artic. sibi falso object. Art.* 16.   [124]Heb. 10. 31.